Gladiator Farm

Mason Origins Book Two

by

REX HOLLOWAY

Contents

1

The Duke of Hell

July 1983

Texas Department of Corrections, Jim Ferguson Unit, Midway, Texas, USA

The sun ruled mercilessly over the prison fields. Morning dew soaked the grass, clinging to the inmates' boots as they worked. Hundreds of male prisoners, each dressed in white cotton uniforms with black leather boots and white caps on their heads, toiled in the dirt. Most of the men were Black, and the bleached cotton of their uniforms contrasted starkly with their dark skin. They were from tough inner-city neighborhoods like Fifth Ward in Houston, Oak Cliff in Dallas, or Stop Six in Fort Worth. They stood shoulder-to-shoulder, like a Civil War picket line, but instead of muskets they heaved aggies: long wooden gardening hoes topped with heavy steel blades. In perfect synchrony, they lifted their aggies high overhead, then crashed the blades into the dust with a resounding thump. As a unit, they chopped the grass four times with their aggies before taking a single step forward.

Thump, thump, thump, thump, step.

The convicts repeated the rhythmic chopping and stepping over and over, cutting the tough grass down to the dirt beneath. "Flat weeding" or "four stepping," it was called—a primitive lawn-mowing practice employed by the prison as a monotonous and grueling form of redemptive labor. At the front of the picket line, a single man looked back at the other inmates while he called cadence.

"One and uh two and uh three and uh fo' step!" he bellowed in a deep voice.

"One and uh two and uh three and uh fo' step!" the men called back in chorus as they beat the ground.

Thump, thump, thump, thump, step.

"I used to drive a Cadillac, now I eat a Johnny sack. One and uh two and uh three and uh fo' step," he yelled.

"I used to drive a Cadillac, now I eat a Johnny sack. One and uh two and uh three and uh fo' step," they yelled back.

Thump, thump, thump, thump, step.

The aggies rose and fell, rose and fell, as the lead row called count. Sweat beaded and ran down their faces, and dust swirled around their boots. Giant horse flies buzzed, and they chopped right through fire ant mounds, the angry creatures clinging to the dusty cuffs of their prison-issued trousers. Heat waves rippled along the ground in the distance, and mirages conjured memories of beaches and lakes not seen by sorrowful eyes in many years.

Fifty feet away, sitting astride a sorrel horse, a hulking White man in a gray uniform with a stainless steel revolver on his hip watched intently. A straw cowboy hat sat on his head, and spurs clinked on his boots. The field boss kept a close eye on the prisoners through dark aviator sunglasses. Another guard riding a dappled mare shadowed the hoe squad from a hundred yards away. He was called the high rider, and a scoped 30-30 rifle rested on his hip.

"Johnson!" shouted the field boss through his handlebar mustache. "Get that aggie up!"

A tall, young, black inmate with a single gold tooth looked up from his furrowed, sweaty brow and glared at the field boss. His hat was cocked at a jaunty angle. He cursed under his breath, but, nevertheless, raised his aggie higher for a few beats.

"Judge said I did the crime, now I gotta do the time. One and uh two and uh three and uh fo' step," the lead row yelled.

"Judge said I did the crime, now I gotta do the time. One and uh two and uh three and uh fo' step," the hoe squad yelled back.

Thump, thump, thump, thump, step.

"Johnson!" the field boss barked again through his droopy mustache. "Get that aggie up. Don't make me tell you again."

Johnson grumbled something under his breath.

"Duke! Ay, lead row!" the field boss yelled.

The lead row, Duke, stopped calling the four count and looked up. He was in his late 20s, dark-skinned, over six feet tall, and his arms rippled with muscle. He was both darker from the sun and older than most of the other inmates, many of whom were teenagers.

"Yes, boss?" Duke called out.

"What kind of squad are you runnin'?" the field boss asked. "Six Hoe must want to stay out late today. Captain wants somebody to clean out behind the pig pens. Maybe Johnson can be Six Hoe's new lead row, and y'all can go play with the warden's pigs until sunset. How does that sound?"

Duke glared at Johnson.

"No, thank you, boss. Six Hoe ain't tryin' to play with no pigs. Shit, I don't even eat pork," Duke called back.

"Well, seems to me like you better get your squad in order," the field boss replied. He spit tobacco on the ground and leaned forward onto the saddle's pommel, the leather creaking.

"Yessuh, boss," the lead row said, "I'ma get it in order alright, boss. Can I handle my business?"

"Handle your business, lead row," the field boss drawled, then spit again and looked away.

"Aggies down!" Duke called out.

Work stopped, and the inmates let their aggies drop to the dirt, all except for Johnson, who let his aggie's head fall but didn't release the handle. He chuckled, his lone gold tooth sparkling in the sunlight. A fly buzzed and landed on his hat.

"Oh, yeah," Johnson said. "So, what? Now we supposed to fight because this White man said so? Is that how it's goin' down, brotha'?"

"Oh, it ain't gonna be much of a fight," Duke said as he peeled off his sweaty shirt. Tattooed muscles rippled across his torso. Years of weightlifting and field labor had turned Duke into stone. His torso displayed several puffy knife scars. Johnson chuckled, dropped his aggie handle, and peeled off his own shirt. Unlike the older lead row, his body appeared soft.

In a blur of black skin and white pants, Johnson and Duke circled each other in the dust. The other inmates stood back and watched as the field boss walked his horse a little closer, his hand resting on the butt of his revolver in case anyone tried to jump in or swing and aggie. Duke came in with his shoulders up and his chin tucked, elbows pressed tight to his ribs. His right fist protected his chin while his left fist lashed out in a blurred double jab. The young and agile Johnson managed to slip both punches and fired back with a looping overhand right. Duke weaved the punch easily and took a pendulum step back.

"Oh, you think you got a little somethin', huh, youngsta'?" Duke said.

"You about to see," Johnson said back, as the men circled each other. "I'm from Acres Homes. You better ask somebody. Acres Shakers, baby. I can do this all day."

The men's feet shuffled in the dust, and their heads bobbed up and down and side to side as each man searched for an opening. While Johnson stood tall with his head back, Duke tucked his chin and pressed the attack. He threw fast, vicious combos: jab-jab-cross-hook and jab-cross-uppercut. Johnson weaved and parried most of the punches and countered with rattlesnake-fast counter strikes of his own. Duke parried and weaved, changed levels, dropped low, and delivered a vicious left hook to Johnson's liver. Johnson dropped his guard, and Duke delivered a left hook and a right cross directly to his jaw, the last punch decimating his lips. Johnson sat down hard on his butt and covered his mouth. He spit blood into his hands, then looked in his palm. His gold tooth, broken off at the gumline, glittered in the sunlight.

Duke walked over, then bent low at the waist so he was face-to-face with the defeated younger man.

"Too bad, youngsta, because I'm from the Dirty Nickel, and all we do is collect gold teeth all day. Now, listen, wet-behind-the-ears ass boy, while I school you real fast. I hate that cracka' mother fucka' on that horse more than you could ever know. But you just got here, while me, I've been here twelve motha' fuckin' years, and I ain't cleanin' no motha' fuckin' pig pens over yo' young ass, ya' dig? You may not have minded nobody in the free world, but yo' ass is gonna mind somebody in here."

Duke shoved Johnson's head with his index finger as he stood up.

"Boss, inmate Johnson said he understands now, and he said he won't buck no mo'."

The field boss leaned over and spit another stream of tobacco.

"That better be right," he said, glaring through his sunglasses. "Now, get my hoe squad back to work, lead row."

"Aggies up!" Duke yelled. "Aggies up and fall in."

Duke picked up his hat and swatted it against his leg to shake the dust. He leaned down and picked up Johnson's shirt, wadded it up, and threw it in his face.

"Get up, lil' boy," he said. "Yo' mamma ain't here to wipe yo' tears."

Glaring back through swollen eyes, his lips split and trembling, Johnson stood up. Slowly, he walked to his aggie, picked it up, and took his place in line with the other inmates. Blood leaked from his mouth and stained the front of his shirt. Duke donned his shirt and took position at the front of the line as if nothing had happened.

"Fo' step, on me!" he yelled, raising his aggie high overhead. "Aggies up!"

The men all raised their hoes in the air and waited for the count.

"And uh one and uh two and uh three and uh fo' step!" Duke began.

"One and uh two and uh three and uh fo' step!" the prisoners called back, beating the dirt as the field boss chewed, the grasshoppers buzzed, and the high rider kept silent watch like an angel of death in the distance.

"Aggies up!" the field boss shouted once the day's work was complete.

The men shouldered their aggies and lined up two-by-two. When the mounted field boss gave the order, the filthy, exhausted prisoners marched along the dusty road back towards the Jim Ferguson Unit, known in the Texas prison system as the "Gladiator Farm." The hulking red brick structure stretched out in either direction, looming over them like the red cliffs of

West Texas Comanche country. They marched past the corrugated metal tractor barns where gray-haired trustees leaned on shovels, to the back gate of the prison where the field bosses waited to search them. The field workers stripped naked and stood in line, holding their filthy boots and uniforms. Hundreds of naked men shuffled forward one-by-one to spin and dance for the guards before passing through the chain link and razor wire gate. From there, they were funneled into the shower room, where they had two minutes to rinse off under shared faucets, quickly scrubbing with broken pieces of blue, state-issued soap which they discarded into a coffee can as they exited the shower and dressed in clean white uniforms.

Once the men of Six Hoe were dressed, a female correctional officer wearing a blue smock over her gray uniform opened a steel door with a set of oversized brass rings. The inmates filed through the door and into the main corridor of the prison. The roar of men's voices and clanging steel echoed down the hall like rolling thunder. As they passed a cellblock, a group of staff support inmates, or SSI's, leaning on brooms gave Duke respectful nods.

"What's up, Duke?" one said, a bald, medium-complected man with teardrops tattooed under his left eye. "How many did you knock out today?"

Duke grinned, "Oh, you know, blood. I just be doin' my thang."

"That brotha' got some cold hands," the tear-dropped SSI said to another man as the line of inmates continued down the hall.

The men arrived at the chow hall where they ate beef stew, greens, pinto beans, and cornbread on metal trays before returning to their cell block. There, some prisoners congregated in the day room, while others went to their cell doors and waited for the guards to call "in and out." The dayroom TV sat on a stand high on the wall. NBC News played while the inmates spread to steel benches and tables, with each ethnic group—Black, White, and Mexican—separating to their own areas.

Duke strolled onto the cell block and immediately stopped at a set of bars behind which stood the officer in charge of operating, or "rolling", the cell doors. The picket officer that shift was a middle-aged woman with brown skin, short hair, and arched eyebrows. Her curvy lower half stretched the seams of her uniform pants. Duke smiled coyly, leaning against the picket bars.

"Damn, Ms. Williams, is that you smellin' like a flower in the sunshine? You know, I haven't smelled something so sweet in over twelve years."

"Ha!" she said, frowning. "Boy, get off my bars."

"Ah, come on now, Ms. Williams," he continued. "You know I'm getting out in two months, right?"

"Oh, yeah?" she said, cutting her eyes at him quickly. "Where you goin'?"

"Shit," he drawled, "back to 'the H'."

"You from Houston? I thought you was a South Dallas brotha," she replied.

"Me? Hell, nah! What made you think that?" he said. "Can't no Dallas sucka' do it like me."

"Do what like you?" she asked, a touch of gold glinting in the corner of her mouth. Her eyeshadow was carefully applied to elongate and tilt her eyes, and her lips shimmered with fresh lipstick.

"Shit," Duke said more quietly, looking around, "you know what I mean. Houston ain't too far from here either. Where do you stay at? Midway? Madisonville?"

"Boy," she snapped, looking him up and down, "don't you worry where I stay at. Now get the hell where you supposed to be."

Sensing their game was over for the day, Duke sucked his teeth.

"A'ight, Ms. Williams. You have a blessed day now," Duke said, and with a wink and a sly grin, he sauntered into the dayroom.

Inmates were gathered in groups of their own kind. Blacks sat with Blacks, Mexicans sat with Mexicans, and Whites sat with Whites. Duke strolled to the table where his partners from the north side of Houston played dominoes.

"What's up, Duke?" one man said as he studied the dominoes in his hand. He had an afro pick with a handle shaped like the African continent shoved into the back of his curly hair.

"Same shit, Mario," he said. "I got next on the bones."

"Word," Mario said. Suddenly, he slammed a domino on the steel table, rattling the other pieces.

"Give me ten!" he shouted.

Another man marked him ten points on a piece of paper.

Slam! Another player banged a domino onto the table.

He shouted, and the scorekeeper marked him down for fifteen points.

Duke glanced around the dayroom. The Texas Department of Corrections had integrated under federal court order just a few years before, and it was still strange to see black, white, and brown faces in the same dayroom. Just past the Mexican table, at the benches by the TV, Duke saw Johnson sitting quietly, leaning on his elbows, hands clinched before him, his foot bouncing rapidly. Every so often, he touched his gums where his tooth had broken off. The corners of Duke's eyes tightened a little, but he went back to watching the domino game.

At the top of the hour, the male prison guard on the block yelled, "In and out!"

The cell block had three tiers of cells covered in steel bars. Inmates walked down the runs to stand in front of their cells.

"Roll one row!" the male guard yelled, and Ms. Williams in the control picket spun the wheel to open all the cell doors on the first floor so those inmates who wished to return to their cells could do so.

"Let me run up here and check on this boy right quick," Duke said to Mario.

"Alright, blood. Go check on those Zoo Zoos and Wham Whams," Mario said with a big smile.

"Shit, you already know," Duke said back.

The two men bumped fists, then Duke turned and walked out of the dayroom toward the steel staircase leading up to his cell on the highest tier. He climbed the steps with several other inmates to the very top, then turned left and began the long walk down the row of barred cells. He lived in 23 cell, but that wasn't his first destination. Instead, he stopped in front of the open door to 16 cell. Placing both hands on the door frame, he leaned inside. The cell was tiny, only five feet wide and 9 feet long. It had a porcelain toilet in the back, and a matching sink in the corner. Two bunks were attached to the wall, each with a flimsy mattress and a grey blanket, and there were two shelves over the door.

Siting on the bottom bunk was a young man, resting his elbows on his knees and staring at the wall. He had pale skin, a thin frame, and wore glasses. His cheeks were smooth, like he didn't need to shave yet. He was wearing the white uniform and black boots of a prisoner, and his brown hair was combed to the side. As soon as Duke's shadow darkened his cell, he jumped up from the bunk and backed away towards the toilet.

Duke chuckled. He rubbed his hair down with his palm, then took a step into the cell, staring the younger, smaller boy in the eyes. He never blinked, and his wide shoulders filled the space from the top bunk to the wall, blocking the doorway completely.

"What's up, Chris?" he asked.

"Nothing much, Duke. Just hanging out," the boy said softly.

Duke smirked.

"Just hangin' out, huh? Hangin' out, doin' what?"

"Nothin'. Nothin'," the boy stammered. "Just waiting for you to get back."

"Well, did you go to the sto'?" Duke asked.

"Yeah," Chris said softly.

"Huh?" Duke said loudly, taking another step into the cell. "Speak up. I can't hear you."

"Ye-Yes," Chris stammered, instinctively leaning back, but he was already jammed against the toilet with nowhere else to go.

"Good," Duke said more calmly. Then, after a brief pause, he said, "Well? You gonna' make me ask for it, or you gonna' show me what you owe me?"

"I got it," Chris said. "Here!"

With that, Chris reached onto the floor in the back corner of the cell and lifted a large white bag filled with contents. He offered it to Duke, who snatched it out of his hands with a frown.

He stared at Chris for a moment longer, and the boy looked down at his feet.

"They were out of a few things. Summer sausage an-an-and coffee, I think," said Chris.

"What!" Duke yelled. "They ain't had no coffee?"

Duke untied the string holding the bag closed and began rummaging through it. Inside was a collection of commissary items: cookies, Ramen noodles, jars of peanut butter, hair grease, and tubes of toothpaste. Duke rustled around for a moment, then pulled the drawstring closed and looked up.

"I know you got some coffee though," Duke said.

"I mean, I have half a jar, but that's it," Chris said.

"Gimme that," Duke growled.

Quickly, Chris squeezed past Duke and reached up to his locker. It was nearly empty, with only a Bible, a cup, a plastic spoon, and an empty peanut butter jar half-filled with instant coffee. He took it down, then pulled down his cup. He set the cup on the top bunk, opened the peanut butter jar, and started to scoop a spoonful of coffee out to put in the cup.

"I just need a cup for in the morning..." he started to say, but his words were cut short.

With a resounding *smack*, Duke slapped Chris hard across the face. The younger boy dropped the cup and the spoon, scattering coffee grounds as he stumbled. The force of the blow was so powerful Chris had to catch his balance on the toilet. He scurried to the back corner of the cell by the sink, grabbing to adjust his glasses, his eyes wide, a red handprint forming on his cheek.

"Boy, I didn't say give me *some* of your coffee. I said give me yo' motha' fuckin' coffee," Duke roared.

He held his hand up and lunged at Chris as if to slap him again. Chris threw his hands up to protect himself.

"OK, Duke, OK!" he said quickly. "There, take it!"

Duke relaxed. He stared at the weaker man in contempt, then turned to the top bunk, screwed the lid onto the jar of coffee, and dropped it into the bag.

"I need the rest of that list by next week," Duke said.

Chris didn't say a word. His eyes were starting to water and he was shaking.

"Did you hear me?" Duke yelled.

"Y-yes," Chris said quickly. "I'll get it. I'll get the rest of it."

"Good," Duke replied, then he walked out of the cell with the bag of goods.

He strolled down a few more cells to his own and walked in just as the guards closed the doors. He set the bag of commissary down on the floor, then looked around. While Chris's cell had been stark and empty, Duke's cell was filled with everything from radios to cooking pots. A variety of tennis shoes were lined up next to his bunk. His sheets were crisp and white, and his walls freshly painted and covered in photos of beautiful women and fancy cars torn from magazines or drawn by prison artists. Even his floor shined with a fresh coat of wax. His shelves were packed to the ceiling with snacks and toiletry items. He had a moment where he wasn't sure where to put the full bag of groceries he had just extorted from the new boy. He looked under the bottom bunk, but it was already filled with cases of Ramen noodles and cans of chili and beef stew. He had more stock than he knew what to do with, so he set the bag on his bunk and stood at the mirror over his sink brushing waves into his hair as he waited for the doors to roll again. When they opened, he returned to the dayroom where he informed Mario that he needed him to hold a bag of groceries in his cell, which Mario agreed to do for a fee. Duke spent the rest of the evening laughing and slamming dominoes.

The next morning, after a quick breakfast in the chow hall of scrambled eggs, sausage, and biscuits, the hoe squads turned out for work at 4:00 am. They filed out through the back gate, retrieved their aggies from the tool wagon, and lined up for another day of hard labor. They spent the morning chopping weeds from between endless rows of green beans and okra, then finished off clearing overgrown weeds out of a drainage ditch after lunch. By the end of the day, the men were all exhausted and covered in mud. Back inside the prison fence, they showered, ate dinner, and returned to the cellblock.

Mario and the other men from North Houston gathered around their table for their evening games. Duke joined them at the domino table, making sure to keep his back to the wall. He made it a habit to always keep an eye on the various men who might have a reason to get revenge. He had noticed that Johnson, the boy whose gold tooth he had knocked out, still looked angry about the fight. When they called the first in-and-out, Duke stayed in the dayroom while Johnson stood and walked to his cell.

"Gimme ten, and that's domino," shouted a light-skinned man named G Dog. He stood up as he slammed his final domino on the table.

The other men all dropped their last game pieces and grunted.

"Man," groaned Mario, "bring some money, and let's shoot for it."

"Shit, you ain't said nothin'," G Dog said loudly. "Who got some dice?"

"Melvin's got some," Duke said. "That sucka' still in his cell?"

"Shit, probably," Mario said.

"Let me go see," said G Dog, and he walked away.

"Say, man, you better watch out for that youngsta' you handled in the field yesterday. That boy looks off to me," Mario said to Duke as he shuffled the dominos.

"Shit," Duke said, grinning and puffing his chest out, "I ain't worried about that sucka'. I'll take the rest of his baby teeth if he fucks around."

"Who wants to lose some money?" G Dog asked as he returned shaking a pair of homemade dice.

"Man, you don't want none," Mario said, snatching up the dice and walking towards the back corner of the dayroom.

"What about you, Duke? You wanna test yo' luck?" G Dog grinned.

"Nah, man, I'm gonna keep my little groceries today. I will watch Mario take yo' shit though," Duke replied.

"Shit," G Dog frowned, "that sucka couldn't get money if they was givin' it away for free."

"Let's see then, ol' Lionel-Richie-on-crack lookin' ass sucka'," Mario snapped back.

At the back of the dayroom, Mario, G Dog, and several others squatted with their backs to the picket and took turns shooting dice against the brick wall, wagering cigarettes, coffee, stamps, and other commissary items.

Duke stood back, spectating. He noticed when Johnson re-entered the dayroom looking sullen. The younger boy didn't so much as glance towards the dice players but instead walked to a corner of the dayroom where a wheeled metal bucket sat with a wooden mop handle leaning against the brick wall. He watched as Johnson grabbed the mop handle and rolled the bucket out of the dayroom and towards the cells.

The evening passed quickly, and soon it was time for the prisoners to rack up for the night.

"In for the night," called a male officer. "Let's go!"

The inmates all stood from their tables and benches and made their way out of the dayroom towards their cells. Duke's cell was on the top row, so he clapped G Dog's hand goodnight and climbed the metal staircase. Mario was also housed on three row, just two cells down from Duke, so they walked together, laughing and joking along the way. At the third tier landing, as they turned left to walk toward their cells, Duke noticed the utility closet door to his right was open. Dismissing it, he continued walking towards his cell with Mario just in front of him.

Mario was looking back, talking loudly over his shoulder about the dice game, when suddenly he was startled and shouted, "Watch out!"

Duke had just turned his head and saw movement from behind when a shower of liquid splattered over him. Instantly, a flash of intense pain washed over his back and shoulder. A mop bucket clattered to the floor, still steaming from the scalding water someone had thrown on him.

Duke yelled in agony and grabbed the railing as he turned. Sure enough, Johnson was there. He'd been hiding behind the closet door while using an electric stinger to boil the water. Holding the broken mop stick like a spear, he jabbed it into Duke's side, the splintered wood piercing under his ribs. Duke grunted as the force knocked the wind from him.

Mario lunged around Duke toward Johnson, grabbed the broken mop stick, and yanked it from him. Johnson released the stick, reached into his waistband, and, in a flash, pulled out a steel shank. He had broken the mop head and hastily sharpened a piece of the metal rod into an ice pick. Mario slipped in the water as Johnson lunged, landing on his back, dazed. Standing over the downed man, Johnson stabbed Mario repeatedly in the face and neck. Blood spurted onto the tier, mixing with the steaming water running over the edge and splashing twenty feet below as Johnson plunged the knife into Mario's neck repeatedly.

Mario gasped on the ground, desperately gripping his punctured throat. Johnson's eyes locked on Duke. Animal rage covered his face as he lifted the shank to strike again. In that moment, all of Duke's pain vanished. With a primordial roar, he leapt over Mario and attacked the shank-wielding boy with a blizzard of punches. Grabbing his knife arm by the wrist, Duke punched

Johnson over and over again in the face, his fist a blur, the thuds and smacks of knuckles against flesh echoing down the block. Johnson, caught off guard by the lightning-fast attack, flailed about, trying to free his arm and protect his face at the same time, but it was futile. Enraged, Duke grabbed Johnson around the waist and heaved the boy over the third floor railing, his body cartwheeling down and smacking heavily on the concrete floor below.

The block erupted with shouting men as Duke screamed a savage war cry and sprinted toward the stairs, blood soaking down his white uniform pants. On the ground floor, inmates gathered around Johnson in shock. The fall had broken the boy but not killed him. Duke could see him choking and coughing up blood, convulsing, reaching here and there, searching for help. Guards shouted and keys jangled loudly from the hall as back-up came running.

Duke peeled off his still-steaming shirt, the skin from his back peeling with it, revealing blistered white meat beneath. He kicked Johnson in the face, then kneeled on his chest, pinning him. Methodically, Duke beat the boy until his face came apart, and he choked to death on his own teeth and blood. Duke screamed into the dead boy's destroyed face, drowning out the guards surrounding him, pleading for him to stop.

2

Go InZane

April 2023

South Central, Los Angeles, California, USA

"Get up, Zane!" a rough man with face tattoos shouted. He was white with a shaved head, daggers tattooed as sideburns, and cauliflower ears. His thick neck bulged with muscle as he yelled into the makeshift octagon and beat his fist on the wooden barrier. The back of his black t-shirt read, "Team #InZane".

People were gathered around the clapped-together ring shouting advice and encouragement. Inside, locked in combat like cobras, two grapplers struggled on the dirty, worn astroturf. One fighter, a white kid with brown hair, had the other fighter in an arm lock.

The scene took place in a walled backyard in South Central Los Angeles. The sun beamed brightly, providing the perfect lighting for the cameras live streaming the amateur brawl to subscribers worldwide. The show's producer, a thin man with dreadlocks, wore a black-and-white striped referee's shirt. From inside the ring, he watched the fighters closely. The crowd began to countdown from ten as the round neared its end. The fighters grunted and struggled, but the buzzer sounded, and the referee broke the fighters apart.

The combatants stood, and the crowd cheered, their cellphones held high in the air.

"Go, Zane!" a young woman screamed.

One of the fighters grinned at the excited fan. Zane had just turned 21. He had sun-bleached, curly blond hair despite his medium tan complexion, giving him an exotic Caribbean look. He was of average height and lean but broad-shouldered, and his body rippled with muscle. He was inked here and there with colorful tattoos, including a Jamaican flag on his chest and a large portrait of Bob Marley on his side. He wore green, black, and gold trunks, and his waistband read, "Go InZane".

Zane sat on the stool in his corner. His trainer, the big man with the dagger tattoos on his face, poured water over Zane's head. He leaned into the younger man's face and growled in a thick Cockney accent, "You're letting him take the fight to the bloody Penny A Pound, and that's his game. You need to start playing your game. What did we Captain Kirk the bloody mitts for just for you to Rattle and Hum out here and roll around in the muck? You're a striker. Now get out there and run the bloody combinations we practiced. Don't let that Berkeley Hunt get you to the blood mat, again. Are you reading me?"

The trainer squirted water into Zane's mouth. The younger man spit it out, then nodded in agreement.

A ding sounded, and the fighters stepped from their corners to the center of the ring where the referee waited.

"Fighters, are you ready?" he asked.

Zane's opponent, a 19-year-old from Oklahoma named Stetson Willis, nodded. He had a mullet and was covered in freckles and bluish, homemade tattoos.

The referee looked to Zane, who brought his gloves up, and nodded.

"Fight!" the referee shouted, and the fight recommenced.

Taking a tall stance, Zane leaned back slightly, extending his left hand, and gauging the distance. Stetson, who had been a state wrestling champion, feinted and searched for an opening. Zane stepped in, luring Stetson in with soft jabs. Stetson took the bait, dropped low, and shot in for the double-leg takedown. Zane side-stepped, pivoted, and clocked Stetson in the temple with a check hook. Rocked but determined, the Oklahoman hung onto one of Zane's legs. Zane cross-faced him with his boney forearm and sprawled, then spun and took Stetson's back. He wrapped his arm around the wrestler's throat before he had a chance to stop it. Zane cranked the choke hold, and the two fighters tipped over and floundered, legs kicking wildly as Stetson tried to pry himself free. After grunting and straining, Stetson escaped. He tried to reverse and tie up Zane, but the taller boy fended him off and leapt back to his feet. The crowd cheered as the fighters squared off again.

"Holy...!" a young man shouted into a microphone as he livestreamed to his fans. "Zane almost choked out Stetson. It's crazy to see a fight of this caliber going down on Backyard Brawls. Both of these guys are on the verge of going pro, and here they are beating the shit out of each other in somebody's backyard. This is totally insane! Or, should I say, 'InZane?' Zane's millions of social media followers know he is capable of any stunt at any time, and this is exactly the kind of everything-on-the-line action they have come to expect from the influencer-turned fighter."

Zane watched calmly as Stetson stalked him around the ring. But now, having taken a powerful blow to the face, the Oklahoman was cautious. Having a shorter reach than Zane, the only way Stetson could hope to take him out was to get under his guard. But Zane was clearly onto the plan, because anytime Stetson lunged in, Zane used quick footwork and punishing fists to escape.

The backyard rocked with the energy of a hundred spectators, all eyes glued to the two fighters in the center. Zane's knuckles connected with his opponent's jaw, sending a sickening crunch through the air. The crowd roared in a symphony of cheers and groans.

A flurry of punches and kicks followed as the fighters exchanged blows. Empowered with the taste of blood, Zane felt unstoppable. He weaved and ducked, evading punches, waiting for the perfect moment to strike. Stetson, discouraged by his failed plan to submit Zane, swung a left hook then a right at Zane's head. In a blur, Zane slipped right, loaded up a devastating uppercut, and released it like a coiled spring, connecting with Stetson's chin and sending him crashing to the ground. The referee counted to ten as Stetson sat dazed. With a showman's flourish, the referee declared the fight over, and the crowd erupted in a deafening roar.

Zane stood tall, chest heaving, and yelled into the sky. He walked over and extended a hand to his downed opponent. Stetson took it, a bloody grin splitting his swollen face. "Nice hit, man," he grunted.

"Good fight," Zane replied, his own voice gruff from exertion. The young men embraced, and the crowd cheered for Zane—along with all 14.7 million of his social media fans.

The 2023 Dodge Challenger SRT Demon 170 makes 1,000 horsepower and can hit 60 miles per hour in under 1.7 seconds. Chrysler, newly merged into Stellantis N.V., only made 3,300 of the ferocious muscle cars—and Zane had one. He also had a McLaren, a Porche 911, and a Brabus 800. Painted a glossy Burgundy red with black wheels, the SRT Demon looked like it was drenched in blood. The slightest tap on the accelerator sent the supercharged HEMI into a screaming fit of torque and fury. Zane handled the monstrous machine like a master, mashing the gas and sending the car's tail sliding with a shriek of smoldering tires. He grinned ear-to-ear, the sweet smell of burned rubber pouring through the open windows.

He was in his element. Master of the "sideshow", as the impromptu—and illegal—car meets were called. Organized through social media, car-loving youngsters from all over L.A. had converged on an intersection for the sole purpose of performing high-octane stunts for the cameras. The crowd of onlookers was large enough to block traffic, with hundreds of excited teens lining the curbs, phones in the air, recording the action. Engines revved up and screaming, muscle cars spun around the intersection performing "donuts", black smoke filling the air as fearless passengers hung out the windows. Camera men raced about, risking their lives for the perfect shot. Girls jumped and screamed while fireworks sparkled and flashed. Here and there, gang members flashed hand signs and fist fights broke out.

Zane cut the steering wheel sharply, the tires of his Dodge Challenger screeching as the car whipped into another tight turn. Smoke billowed from under the car. The crowd roared in excitement, their camera phones capturing every second. Zane grinned, adrenaline pumping through his veins as the rear tires screamed louder, carving black circles into the pavement.

Just as he prepared to drift out of the circle and light up the street for another stunt, a flash of motion caught his eye, but too late.

Crunch!

The sickening sound of metal on metal rang through the chaos as Zane's car slammed into the side of a red Ford Mustang that had foolishly nosed into the intersection. The Challenger lurched to a stop, and the crowd's roared in shock.

Zane's heart raced. He gripped the wheel, scanning himself for injuries, but he was fine.

He flung the door open and climbed out, stepping into the lingering smoke. The Challenger's front bumper was crushed in, a headlight smashed, but it wasn't as bad as it could've been. The Mustang's front quarter panel, on the other hand, was crumpled like a soda can, its driver-side door barely hanging on its hinges.

A chorus of cell phones flashed in his face as Zane inspected the wreck, his heart pounding in his ears. The driver of the Mustang threw open his door and stumbled out, unhurt but furious.

He was a big Latino, broad shouldered and covered in tattoos, his eyes wild with anger as he approached Zane. The crowd parted around them as the man stormed towards Zane.

"You fucking idiot," the man shouted, pointing at Zane. "You can't fuckin' drive!"

Zane held up a hand, trying to keep his cool, though his blood was boiling. "Hey, man. You pulled in front of me. You didn't see what was going on?"

The guy, taller and built like a tank, puffed out his chest. "I pulled out in front of *you*? You were the one doing your little circus shit in the middle of the street, pendejo. You fucked up my ride."

Zane looked him up and down, sizing him up. The guy's jaw and fists were clenched.

"Look, nobody's hurt," Zane said, his voice low and steady. "We can figure this out like grown men."

The man shoved Zane in the chest hard enough to make him stumble back. "Yeah, homie, we're figuring this out right here, right now. You wanna act tough in front of the cameras? Let's see what you got, pussy."

The crowd buzzed in excitement, their phones held high. Zane raised his hands to reason with the man, but also to be ready in case he threw a punch. His adrenaline was spiked.

The Mustang driver took a step forward, raising his fists. "You think you're 'InZane', homie? Let's run this shit."

Zane stood his ground, staring into the other driver's furious eyes. He was big, sure, but Zane had been in enough fights to know size didn't always matter. But still, he didn't want this to turn into a brawl. Not here. Not now.

With a deep breath, he shook his head and turned to walk away. "Not worth it, man," he muttered, his voice calm, as the crowd shifted, murmuring with disappointment.

"Yeah, that's right!" the driver shouted at Zane's back. "Walk away, tough guy. Go run home to your little bitch girlfriend."

Zane froze. His muscles tensed as he turned slowly back toward the man. His girlfriend, Hannah, was standing near the edge of the crowd, her eyes locked on him, her face flushing with anger.

Zane's heart thudded in his chest.

"What did you say?" his voice was low, dangerous now. He turned back around, eyes locked on the man.

The guy smirked, taking the bait. "You heard me, pussy. That bitch of yours? She's just as fake as you. She ain't nothin' but an internet slut. Ain't nothin' real about either of you lames."

"Bro, I'll stomp your ass right here in front of everybody," Zane replied.

Before Zane could say another word, the man swung. His fist flew toward Zane's face, a wild haymaker.

Zane's training took over instantly.

With lightning-fast reflexes, he ducked under the punch, feeling the air ruffle his hair. In one fluid motion, he pivoted and delivered a punishing kick to the man's lead leg, his shin connecting with the outside of his knee. The impact made a loud crack, and the driver grunted in pain and staggered, losing his balance.

Zane didn't wait. He stepped in, closing the distance. The crowd erupted, cameras raised as they realized they were about to witness something epic. Phones were already live-streaming the action.

The driver swung wildly at Zane again, but he weaved the punches like a seasoned pro, dodging each attack with precision. He slipped under a hook and countered with a crisp uppercut to the man's jaw. The crowd gasped as the man's head snapped back.

Dazed, the bigger man tried to tackle Zane, but Zane sprawled with ease and clocked him twice in the face. The larger man stumbled forward and fell to the sidewalk. The crowd surged forward, shouting and filming, the glow of their phones illuminating the fight.

The guy lay on the ground, gasping for air. Zane backed up, breathing heavily but still in control. He glanced at his girlfriend, Hannah, who was cheering him loudly.

"Stay down," Zane said to the driver coldly, then turned to the crowd, which erupted in cheers, phones flashing like crazy.

The whole fight was on camera. Every punch, every dodge, every second of Zane putting the guy in his place. Zane dusted his hands off and walked away, the roar of the crowd following him as the man lay on the ground, utterly defeated.

Later that night, Zane posted a video on his social media, still buzzing from the fight. "What's up, InZane family?" he said, his voice energetic. "You saw what happened today. Just another reminder: don't mess with my crew. But seriously, keep your head on a swivel, and always be ready to throw down if you have to!"

That night, he and Hannah soaked in his marble jacuzzi tub. She played with his curly hair while the hot water loosened his aching muscles. Her blonde hair was pinned up on top of her head, a few loose strands framing her doll-like face. With pouty lips, dazzling eyes, and an hourglass figure, she was one of the most-followed models on social media with high-paying sponsorships from some of the top cosmetic and clothing companies.

"Do you think that shit today will come back on me?" Zane asked.

"Come back how, baby?" she purred, running her fingers along his chest.

"Like, with sponsors or whatever. Or like the media," he responded.

She laughed. "How many followers did you gain today?" she asked. "After the fight?"

"Shit," he mumbled. "Like 500k so far."

She laughed. "I think you'll be ok. You gave the people what they want. It's what every one of them dreams of doing themselves. Knocking out bullies in the street, riding off in sports cars with a beautiful girl. They all wish they were you, baby."

Zane thought for a moment.

"Yeah," he said. "I guess you're right."

Then he slipped his head under the soapy water, blocking out the spotlight for just a moment.

The next day, clips of the fight spread like wildfire across all platforms, and hashtags like #InZaneVsTheWorld and #StreetFightChampion trended within hours. Memes surfaced featuring Zane's punch landing squarely on the driver's jaw, captioned with phrases like, "When the bully gets bullied." Others praised his skills, calling him an "influencer-turned-fighter" who had proved he could hold his own outside the ring. Fans loved his authenticity. Comments flooded in, asking for more content—fights, training tips, and a behind-the-scenes look at his life as a social media star.

As the fight videos spread like wildfire, they quickly transcended the usual social media circles. Within hours, major news outlets and sports commentators picked up the story. Headlines read: "Street Brawl Star 'InZane' Goes Viral After Defeating Aggressive Driver in Self-Defense!" Clips from the fight played on morning talk shows and sports segments, accompanied by pundits discussing Zane's raw talent and MMA skills.

"Have you seen this kid, Zane? He's got serious potential," one sports analyst said during a televised broadcast. "The way he handled that situation—not just with brute force, but with technical precision—that's not something you see every day in a street fight. This guy could have a real career in professional MMA if he wanted to."

Other analysts chimed in, praising his ability to stay composed under pressure. Some fighters, including current and former UFC professionals, shared the video, commenting on Zane's striking ability and quick thinking during the altercation. One well-known fighter even tweeted, "This kid has a real future in the cage!"

Zane's social media exploded. His follower count shot up by millions, and his direct messages were flooded with fans, sponsors, and fight promoters trying to get him on their cards. The hashtag #InZaneFighter was trending for days, with people from all walks of life chiming in on whether Zane had what it took to go pro. Some fans compared him to up-and-coming fighters already in the UFC, saying he could give them a run for their money.

Within days, morning talk shows were hosting MMA coaches and analysts to discuss his prospects. "Look, we all know young Zane from his prank videos and social media antics. I mean, the kid has been online since he was like 14. But let's be real. Little annoying Zane is grown up now. He's been training with some of the best coaches in the game, and it shows. He's got a winning record, too, albeit an untraditional one, but maybe that adds something to his mystique. He's got the physicality, he's got the fanbase—if he gets the right opportunity, I don't see why he couldn't make it to the top," one famous retired fighter said during an interview.

Zane watched it all unfold from his plush couch, unable to believe how quickly his life was changing. He'd been fighting for recognition for years, and now, after one chaotic moment, it seemed like the world was finally paying attention. Hannah cozied next to him, scrolling through the countless news clips and tweets, giggling, and sharing photos of them together.

"You see all this?" she asked, nudging him with a grin, her honey-colored hair spilling around her angelic face. "They're talking about you like you're already the champ."

Zane shook his head, still in disbelief. "Yeah, it's wild. I mean, it was just one fight, right?"

"One fight the internet and TV can't stop talking about," she said. "What are you gonna do? You think you could really go pro?"

Zane leaned back, his mind racing. This could be his shot—the opportunity to go from backyard brawls and viral videos to real fights and real belts. But there was no denying it: stepping into that world would mean committing to something far bigger than he'd ever imagined.

"I don't know yet," Zane replied, though a fire was already building inside him.

3

A Hero's Welcome

Mason stood at the edge of the stage, his eyes scanning the room packed with eager attendees. Rows upon rows of faces, from amateur gun enthusiasts to seasoned military veterans, stared back at him with rapt attention. The Caesar's Palace conference hall buzzed with energy. Before him sprawled a sea of tactical gear, military patches, and custom weapons. It was the largest gun show in the country, and Mason was the headlining speaker—a man whose story had captured the attention of every professional and hobbyist alike.

He shifted his weight, the scars on his body pulling tight under his shirt as he raised the microphone to his lips.

"I'm not here to tell war stories or impress you with some high-speed, low-drag bull," Mason began, his voice gravelly but clear. "I'm here to talk about survival—about engaging threats at any distance, with whatever you have on hand. And I'm here to tell you that you're only as good as your ability to adapt. Adaptation is survival."

The projector behind him flickered to life, showing a photograph of a street scene. Two blue Chevrolet Suburbans sat smoldering in the middle of a city street. Bullet holes punctured nearly every inch of their steel bodies, and there windows were shattered spiderwebs. Smoke drifted from the wreckage, making the photos hazy. The audience murmured as they recognized the ambush scene that had turned Mason from a quiet war-veteran-turned-security-guard into a living legend.

Mason paced the stage as the slideshow continued. His brown hair was pulled into a ponytail, and his beard was trimmed shorter than in the photos playing behind him. He wore tan cargo pants and a fresh green Polo with "Green Zone Defense" embroidered on the left breast and "Mason, Chief Training Officer" on the right. He was tall and lean, and moved with silent, soft steps, like a big cat pacing its cage.

The room went silent, anticipation thick in the air.

More photos of the destroyed Suburbans flashed by followed by close-ups of piles of empty rifle shells on the asphalt, dried blood puddles on the sidewalk, police and EMTs with stretchers, a broken quadcopter drone, a body on a roof behind a sniper rifle, and a single combat boot, blown off some unlucky bastard's foot, laying amongst a slew of red shotgun shells behind a dumpster.

"We were caught by surprise, outgunned, and pinned down. But you don't think about that in the moment. What you think about is survival—how to fight and keep fighting. How to eliminate threats, whether they're right in front of you or half a mile away." He paused, letting the words sink in. "In that shootout, I used everything at my disposal: a knife for up-close engagements, a pistol when I ran dry on rifle rounds, a sniper system for long-range suppression, and even hand-to-hand when it came down to it. You've got to have tools for every range."

Mason pulled out a sleek combat knife from his belt sheath and held it up for the audience to see. "This isn't just for show. When you run out of bullets—and trust me, it can happen—this becomes your best friend. You need to know how to handle it as well as how to shoot."

He sheathed the knife and held up an AR-15 that was laying on a table. "Mid-range engagements? That's where your carbine comes in. You can run a suppressor, low-magnification optics, whatever you need, but you need to know your distances and your engagement times."

The crowd nodded along as he spoke, many taking notes or recording the presentation with their phones. Mason shifted the slide to a picture of the .50-caliber rifle the biker gang had used during the shootout, the massive weapon dwarfing the police officer in the photo holding it up like a trophy fish.

"Long-range threats? This right here is what you want when someone's over a thousand yards away, trying to take your head off. And trust me, I almost lost mine. He only missed by an inch. I felt the air cut beside my ear. But I stayed calm. Why? Because I knew I had my own sniper system that could handle the job."

A photo of Mason peering through the scope on an MK14 Mod 0 EBR sniper rifle flashed on the screen. He was leaning on the hood of the Suburban, scanning for targets. The photo had been snapped by a pedestrian and used on the cover of Time magazine.

He took a step back, letting the enormity of his words linger. The room was still, the only sound the quiet hum of the projector.

"I almost didn't make it. Between the bullets, the IEDs, and God knows what else, the worst injury I walked away with..." Mason paused for effect, letting the audience lean in slightly, "...was from a tomahawk."

The crowd erupted in a mix of gasps and laughter, unable to believe what they had just heard.

"You heard me right. A tomahawk. Out of everything we faced that day, it was an ancient, edged weapon that nearly ended me. Took a chunk out of my arm, severing muscle to the bone, and I almost bled out."

"That's the point I'm making. You never know what's coming, or how close it's going to get. That's why I say you need close-range, mid-range, and long-range weapons in your arsenal. Because when it's your life on the line, and the lives of your friends, you have to be prepared for anything."

Mason looked around the room, locking eyes with a few attendees. "I didn't survive that firefight because I was lucky. I survived because I was prepared. And if there's one thing I want you to take away from this, it's that preparation isn't just about having the gear—it's about knowing how to use it when the time comes. Thank you."

The room filled with applause as Mason lowered the mic.

As the crowd filed out, several attendees gathered around, eager to shake his hand, take a photo, or to ask more about his methods. Mason, now sober and focused, gave each one his full attention.

He stepped down from the stage, the crowd's applause still ringing in his ears. As he walked toward the back of the huge conference room, he spotted Caleb standing by the Green Zone Defense (GZD) booth, grinning like a proud brother.

Caleb, in his early 30s now, waved Mason over. He was leaner than Mason, with short-cropped black hair, sharp features, and the calm confidence of a man who had seen the worst but never let it break him.

"You killed it up there," Caleb said, clapping Mason on the back. "The crowd couldn't get enough."

Mason smirked. "Everybody loves the tomahawk story. Gotta keep 'em entertained, right? But seriously, it's good to see this many people interested in what we're doing. The industry's changing."

Caleb nodded, gesturing to the GZD booth set up behind him. The display was impressive: tactical gear, training courses, and sleek branding showcasing what GZD had become. The company had evolved from an armored car service into a state-of-the-art training facility, specializing in close-quarters combat, firearms, and survival techniques for law enforcement, military personnel, and civilians alike.

"I never thought we'd get this far," Caleb said, looking around the massive hall filled with booths and eager attendees. "But here we are, and GZD is making a real impact. I've been locking down contracts left and right all weekend."

Mason crossed his arms, glancing at the booth with pride. After years of chaos and recovery, GZD had given him a purpose again. As the lead instructor, he spent his days training people in everything from weapons systems to survival tactics, passing on hard-learned lessons from his combat days. It wasn't just about shooting or fighting—it was about teaching people how to think under pressure, how to adapt, and how to stay alive.

"It's crazy how far we've come," Mason said, turning to Caleb. "You and Frazier took GZD to another level."

Caleb grinned. "Couldn't have done it without you, brother. You're the reason half these people are here, man. The story—what we went through—that's what sells it. People want to learn from someone who's been in the shit."

Mason let the words sink in, appreciating the recognition. He had come a long way since his darkest days—fighting his demons, battling sobriety, and finding a new path through work. Caleb had been there through it all, helping build something bigger than any of them could have imagined.

"By the way," Caleb said, his tone shifting slightly, "I've got some big news. It looks like I finally landed a contract with LAPD. Their new commissioner want us to train their tactical units. Full access to everything we've got."

Mason's eyebrows raised. "That's huge. When does it start?"

"Next month," Caleb said. "They're sending their first group of SWAT officers for advanced hand-to-hand and mid-range weapons training."

Mason nodded, a sense of excitement building in his chest. "Outstanding, Caleb. Great work, buddy."

As they spoke, a few attendees approached the GZD booth, curious about what the company offered. Caleb immediately launched into a smooth pitch, explaining their training programs and the innovative techniques they specialized in.

Mason stepped aside, letting Caleb handle the crowd while he took a moment to soak in the atmosphere. Caesar's Palace was buzzing with energy, the hall packed with gun enthusiasts, military personnel, and companies eager to make their mark in the industry.

Caleb finished with the group, then turned back to Mason, a look of satisfaction on his face. "We're on the map, brother. GZD is on the way up!"

Mason clapped Caleb on the shoulder. "The Colonel would be proud."

As their plane leveled out above the clouds, Mason stared out the window, lost in thought. Below them, the vast desert landscape of Nevada gave way to endless skies as the plane carried them back to Denver and the GZD Training Center. Caleb, seated next to him, was flicking through the news on his tablet, the faint glow of the screen casting shadows on his face.

"Man, Ukraine is wild. They've been using drones in ways we never would've thought of a decade ago," Caleb said, breaking the silence. He tilted the screen so Mason could see the headline: "Ukraine's New Drone Arsenal: Changing the Face of Modern Warfare."

Mason nodded, pulling his gaze away from the window. "It's not the same battlefield I trained for. When we were in the thick of it, we had boots on the ground, eyes on targets. Now, you've got guys controlling drones from miles away, dropping payloads with pinpoint accuracy. It's changing everything."

Caleb swiped through the article, showing images of compact drones being loaded with explosives, hovering silently over enemy positions before delivering precise strikes. "Hell, it's not even just about drones for recon anymore. They're using them for combat. Small enough to avoid detection, lethal enough to end a fight in seconds."

Mason crossed his arms, thinking about the implications. "That's the thing. The battlefield is moving away from direct engagement. You can't just prepare for close-quarters combat anymore. You have to anticipate threats coming from every direction, from the sky, from the shadows."

Caleb nodded, his brow furrowed. "Makes you think. How do we prepare people for that? We train them for hand-to-hand, for small arms engagements, but what happens when a drone can take you out without you even seeing it?"

Mason leaned back in his seat. "That's the challenge. We can teach them awareness, train them for anything, but it's the changing technology that'll test them. People are still needed on the ground, but they have to be smarter, faster, more adaptable. We have to evolve with it. One day, even traditional sniping will become as outdated as spears and slings."

For the rest of the flight, they discussed strategies and ways to incorporate drone warfare into their training at GZD. Caleb tossed around the idea of partnering with tech companies to get access to the latest FPV drone models, to teach their students how to spot, track, and avoid being targeted by these unmanned threats.

As the plane descended into Denver, Mason looked out the window again. The Rocky Mountains loomed in the distance, and the city's skyline appeared small from this height but growing larger as they approached. Finally, the roar of the engines filled the cabin, and the plane lurched as the wheels touched down.

After grabbing their bags, Mason and Caleb made their way out of the terminal. The clean Colorado air hit them as they stepped outside, the mountains standing tall in the background.

Waiting for them at the curb was a shiny new blue Chevrolet Suburban— fully armored, as all GZD vehicles were now. Captain Doug Frazier leaned against the hood, arms crossed, sunglasses perched on his face, a gray felt cowboy hat tilted back on his head. Standing next to him, tail wagging furiously, was Mason's Dalmatian, Bud.

Mason's face lit up as Bud barked in excitement, his black-and-white-spotted coat gleaming under the afternoon sun. The dog bounded over, jumping up to greet Mason, who knelt down to scratch behind his ears.

"Hey, buddy! Did you miss me?" Mason laughed as Bud licked his face, tail wagging even harder.

Frazier walked up, giving both men a firm handshake. "Welcome back. Figured I'd bring the newest ride to pick you guys up in style."

Mason stood patting Bud's side as he opened the back door of the Suburban. "Let's get back to the center. Got a lot to unpack from the gun show."

As they piled into the SUV, Bud hopped into the back seat, settling down as Frazier pulled away from the curb. The road stretched ahead of them, leading back to the training center, where work never ceased.

4

The Prince and the Falcon

Zane's house, Los Angeles, California, USA

Zane reclined on the plush couch in his modern hillside home, overlooking the sprawling city of Los Angeles. The sunlight poured in through the floor-to-ceiling windows, casting long shadows on the sleek furniture. His phone buzzed constantly with notifications—followers, sponsors, and fight promoters. After his viral street fight, it seemed like the world couldn't get enough of him.

Hannah, his girlfriend, sat across the room, tapping away on her laptop. Her long, sun-kissed hair draped over her shoulders as she glanced up at him, blue eyes twinkling with mischief.

"Baby, we've got a visitor," she called out as she glanced through the window, noticing a black luxury sedan pulling up outside.

Zane's brows furrowed. He wasn't expecting anyone, but curiosity piqued, he stood and made his way to the door. A sharply dressed man with dark hair and a trim beard stepped out of the sedan, holding a white envelope embossed with gold script. The man approached Zane's front door, offering the envelope with a bow and a crisp, practiced smile.

"Mr. Zane?" the man asked.

Zane nodded. "Yeah, that's me."

"My name is Nasir al-Amri. I am here on behalf of His Royal Highness Prince Omar bin Talal al-Mansour," he said, handing the envelope over. "He extends an invitation for a private meeting."

Zane blinked, taking the envelope. "A prince?"

"Yes, sir. The Prince has the honor of serving as Minister of Sports and Recreation for the Kingdom of Saudi Arabia," the man replied, nodding respectfully before stepping back. "The details are inside. His Royal Highness hopes for your response soon."

Before Zane could respond, the man was already on his way back to the sedan. Zane stood in the doorway, staring at the opulent envelope, the gold letters shimmering in the California sun.

Hannah appeared at his side, eyes wide. "What's that?"

"An invitation for a meeting with an Arab prince," Zane said, holding it up.

Hannah's eyes bulged. "What's an Arab prince want?"

"I don't know," Zane replied, walking back inside.

He tore open the envelope, revealing a handwritten letter, adorned with the Prince's official seal. The note was brief but impressive, inviting Zane to a private meeting in Los Angeles to discuss "a mutually beneficial opportunity." It included contact details and instructions for the meeting.

"Prince Omar bin Talal al-Mansour," Zane repeated, rolling the name over in his head. "Never heard of him."

Hannah sat down beside him, picked up her laptop, and tapped quickly. "Let's look him up."

Within seconds, Hannah found a series of articles and profiles. "Okay, check this out. He's legit—he's part of the Al-Mansour royal family in Saudi Arabia. This says he's one of the wealthiest, youngest members. His father is a high-ranking minister, and Omar is known for investing in tech, sports, and entertainment. He's involved with international fight promotions, too."

Zane's eyes widened as he listened. "No kidding..."

Hannah smirked. "Well, you *have* been trending non-stop for the past three weeks. Maybe he wants to sponsor you or get you into a big fight."

Zane leaned back, thinking it over. He wasn't usually one to get starstruck, but the idea of meeting a royal—especially one who had a foot in the fight world—had his adrenaline pumping. "Could be big," he said slowly, excitement creeping into his voice. "Real big."

Hannah grabbed his arm tightly. "I mean, this could take you global, baby. You could be fighting on a whole different level."

He nodded slowly, imagining the possibilities. "You're right. And with his kind of backing, who knows what doors that could open?"

Hannah grinned. "So, what do you say? Do we meet the Prince?"

Zane shot her a smile. "Yeah. Let's do it."

With renewed energy, Zane grabbed his phone and dialed the number provided on the invitation. As the line rang, he felt his stomach swirl.

Zane and Hannah pulled up to the Prince's Beverly Hills mansion in his black McLaren, the sleek curves of the car reflecting the towering palm trees and opulent gardens surrounding the estate. When he announced himself at the intercom, the gate slid open with silent precision, revealing a long driveway lined with perfectly manicured hedges. At the end of the path stood a fountain, and then the mansion—a sprawling, modern palace of glass and stone glimmering in the late afternoon sun.

Hannah glanced at Zane, excitement and nervousness flickering across her face. "You ready for this?"

Zane grinned, gripping the steering wheel. "Ready as I'll ever be. This feels surreal though."

They parked in front of the mansion, where two sharply dressed attendants stood waiting. One of them stepped forward to open Hannah's door, while the other greeted Zane with a respectful bow. "Mr. Zane, His Royal Highness is expecting you. Please follow me."

They were led through the grand entrance of the mansion, down gleaming marble halls into a massive living room that opened up to a breathtaking garden. The scent of incense and polished wood filled the air as they entered a space adorned with priceless art and modern furniture.

There, seated on a luxurious sofa, was Prince Omar bin Talal al-Mansour. He was younger than Zane expected, in his thirties, with a smooth, polished appearance. Dressed in a tailored suit, the Prince exuded confidence and authority. His dark hair was combed back perfectly, and his piercing eyes locked onto Zane and Hannah as they approached. A subtle smile played on his lips.

"Mr. Zane, Miss Hannah," Prince Omar greeted them, standing up to shake Zane's hand. "It is an honor to meet you both. Please, sit. We have much to discuss."

Zane nodded, feeling the weight of the moment, and they took their seats across from the Prince. Hannah sat beside him, her eyes darting around the room, taking in the lavish surroundings.

"I've followed your rise with great interest, Zane," Prince Omar began, leaning back. "You've captured the attention of millions, not just with your fighting ability but with your presence. It's clear you have the potential to transcend the world of social media and underground fighting."

Zane leaned forward slightly, intrigued. "I appreciate that, Your Highness. I'm curious—what's this opportunity you wanted to talk about?"

Servants appeared with trays of drinks. Zane chose a class of water, while Hannah took a glass of mango juice.

Prince Omar's smile widened. "I won't waste your time. I want to offer you the chance to participate in an exhibition boxing match that will surely make history. A global event, broadcast to millions, with the largest purse in boxing history—$450 million dollars."

Zane blinked, stunned by the number. Hannah gasped and spilled a little juice on her lap.

"$450 million? That's... insane," Zane muttered, trying to wrap his head around the figure.

The Prince nodded. "Indeed. The match will be a spectacle like no other. You'll be facing a former European champion—someone who has dominated the sport for years. But with your talent and your growing fanbase, you're the perfect candidate to make this event a global phenomenon."

Zane's heart raced. This was bigger than anything he could've imagined. "$450 million," he repeated under his breath, trying to keep his cool. "This would be the biggest fight ever."

"And the most lucrative," Prince Omar added smoothly. "I believe in your potential, Zane. You've built a persona that captivates people, and now you have the chance to solidify your legacy. This match will elevate you to heights you've never dreamed of."

Zane leaned in. "This is incredible. What's the catch?"

Prince Omar chuckled softly, his eyes gleaming. "No catch. But you'll need to dedicate yourself entirely to training. The world will be watching. We're talking about months of preparation, and you'll need the best trainers, facilities, and security around the clock."

As if on cue, a tall, imposing figure stepped into the room. Dressed in a tailored black suit with a medium length beard and thick wavy hair, the man exuded strength and control. His dark eyes scanned the room like a falcon, assessing everyone and everything with calm precision. His presence alone sent a ripple of tension through the air.

"This is Karim al Rashid," Prince Omar said, gesturing to the man. "He is the head of my personal security team, and if you agree to the fight, Karim will oversee your security from now until the day of the match. He has protected royals, dignitaries, and some of the most powerful figures in the world."

Karim stepped forward, his deep voice cutting through the room. "Mr. Zane, Miss Hannah, it's an honor. My team and I will ensure your safety throughout the training and the event. You will have nothing to worry about but your fight preparation."

Zane sized Karim up. The man was built like a fortress—tall, muscular, with a battle-hardened face. He was clearly more than just muscle. His eyes were sharp, calculating.

"Sounds like you've got everything covered."

"I assure you, I take my job very seriously," Karim replied.

Prince Omar smiled, pleased with the interaction. "So, Zane, what do you think? Are you ready to take this opportunity? To cement your legacy in the world of combat sports and become a true legend?"

Zane exchanged a glance with Hannah. She was practically glowing with excitement, her hand squeezing his arm in encouragement. This was everything he'd ever dreamed of.

Zane turned back to the Prince, his mind made up. "Yes. I'm in. Let's make history."

Prince Omar's smile widened. "Excellent. I knew you were the right man for this." He reached across to shake Zane's hand firmly. "The world will be watching, and we will make sure this is an event no one will ever forget."

Hannah, still holding Zane's arm, could barely contain her excitement. "Oh my god! Babe, this is huge!"

Prince Omar leaned back, looking pleased with himself. "You'll be facing none other than Mickie Donovan. I'm sure you've heard of him."

Zane's eyes narrowed. "Mickie Donovan?" The name struck him like a bolt. He'd followed Donovan's career for years—a brawler from Dublin, Ireland, known for his brutal knockout power and iron chin. Donovan had been a lightweight world champion for years.

"He's no joke," Zane muttered, thinking back to some of Donovan's most famous fights. The man was a beast, a hardened veteran of the ring who had knocked out some of the best fighters in the world. But Zane wasn't backing down. In fact, the challenge only fueled his excitement. "He's one of the toughest guys in boxing."

Prince Omar nodded, his gaze steady. "Indeed. Donovan is a fighter through and through. Some say he's past his prime. I think he's still dangerous. But perhaps this is your time, Zane. You're younger, faster, and you've got the heart of a lion with something to prove."

"And the fight?" Zane asked. "Where's it happening?"

"In Houston, Texas," Prince Omar replied. "At the Toyota Center. It's the perfect venue for a fight of this magnitude. We expect a packed house and millions tuning in worldwide."

Hannah's eyes lit up even more. "Houston! I've heard it's fun there."

The Prince stood, gesturing for Zane and Hannah to do the same. "I'll have my team handle all the logistics—training facilities, accommodations, media appearances. Karim and his security detail will ensure your safety and privacy. You focus on preparing for the fight."

Zane shook the Prince's hand again. "Thank you for this opportunity. I won't let you down."

"I'm certain you won't," Prince Omar replied smoothly. "Prepare yourself,

Zane. You're about to step onto the biggest stage in combat sports."

As they left the mansion and slid into the McLaren, Hannah squealed with excitement. "Can you believe this? You're going to fight Mickie Donovan. This is crazy!"

Zane grinned, revving the engine as they rolled down the driveway. "Yeah, it's surreal. But this is what I've been preparing for. It's time to show the world what I can do."

The entire drive back, they couldn't stop talking about the fight. Back home, they stared at their phones, reading article after article about Mickie Donovan's career, watching highlight reels of his brutal knockouts, and talking about the trip to Texas. Zane felt a rush of anticipation. He knew the road ahead was going to be grueling, but he was ready for the challenge.

"Houston," Zane said. "I've never been there. I wonder what it's like?"

"I can't wait to find out," Hannah sang as she bounced on the couch in excitement.

5

The Farm

The Duke's mansion, River Oaks, Houston, Texas, USA

The vast bedroom was lit by the soft, golden glow of morning sun filtering through floor-length curtains. It was a place of opulence—vastly different from the brutal fields and cellblocks of the Ferguson Unit all those years ago. The Duke stood before a mirror buttoning up a silk shirt as smooth as water, the deep crimson fabric gleaming against his dark skin.

His back bore grotesque scars, the tissue twisted and contorted in swirling patterns like the boiling water that had created them forty years ago. Through the opening of the unbuttoned shirt, a tattoo on his chest stood stark against his black skin. It was an afro pick, the handle shaped like the continent of Africa. Below it, in black ink, were the words "Mario, RIP, July 12, 1983."

In the plush bed behind him, half-covered by luxurious satin sheets, lay a stunning young woman. Her skin was like mahogany, smooth and flawless, her long, braided hair spilling over the pillows like a waterfall. She stirred, lazily letting the sheet fall away from her breasts as she propped herself up.

"Baby, come back to bed," she purred, her voice sultry and inviting. Her eyes followed the Duke's every move, lingering on his muscled frame, as he adjusted his collar in the mirror.

The Duke, now in his sixties, didn't look at her. Instead, he focused on his reflection, on the image of power he had cultivated over the decades. His face was now lined with age, and his short hair showed gray at the temples, but his eyes were just as intense as they had been. His movements were slower, more deliberate, but there was no mistaking the dangerous edge he still carried.

"Girl, I got shit to do," he said gruffly, his voice a low rumble. "I ain't got time to lay around all day."

The woman pouted playfully but didn't push further. She sank back into the pillows, her eyes half-lidded as she watched him finish dressing.

The Duke walked over to a table by the window where a sleek Rolex watch lay beside a money clip bulging with cash. He slipped the watch onto his wrist, its weight familiar. He strode toward the door, leaving the woman to rest in the luxurious bed. As he stepped into the hallway, his bodyguard—a massive, bearded Black man wearing a blue suit with a bundle of long dreadlocks down his back—fell into step behind him without a word.

As they stepped outside onto the veranda that overlooked his River Oaks estate, the hot Texas sun beat down on them. The Duke settled into his patio chair, the soft creak of wicker and leather barely audible above the faint sound of water trickling from a nearby marble fountain. His estate stretched out around him, perfectly manicured lawns and gardens framed by palm trees that swayed gently in the warm breeze. He sat at the head of a long, polished Teak table, a freshly lit cigar dangling from the corner of his mouth, its thick smoke curling lazily into the air.

Across the table, a spread of fine cuisine was laid out—steaming platters of grilled meats, scrambled eggs, homemade enchiladas, sautéed vegetables, and freshly baked bread. His servants moved with practiced efficiency, quietly serving the dishes without making eye contact. The Duke took a deep puff of his cigar, then set it in a crystal ashtray as one of the servants placed a glass of expensive bourbon and a cup of Rwandan coffee next to his plate.

His bodyguard's, Bishop's, hulking figure approached from the doorway, moving with surprising grace for someone his size.

"Boss," Bishop said in his deep, gravelly voice as he walked toward the patio. "Got somethin' you might want to look at."

The Duke sliced into a piece of steak, chewing slowly as his eyes flicked up to his bodyguard. "What is it?"

Bishop paused beside him, his hands resting casually in front of him, though his posture was anything but relaxed. "This kid from L.A.," he began, "Zane. He's blowin' up all over the place. Used to do prank videos and shit. Then he started doing underground fights and got real famous online. Now, he's about to fight Mickie Donovan. Some people are sayin' he could be the next big thing."

The Duke raised an eyebrow, lifting a fork filled with scrambled eggs. He chewed thoughtfully before speaking. "Who did you say he was?"

Bishop pulled out his phone, tapping on the screen as he continued. "Zane. He's got millions of Instagram followers. And dig this: the fight with Donovan is set to be the biggest payout in boxing history: $450 million. Could be a real money-maker. And best of all: the fight is right here in 'The H.'"

The Duke leaned on his elbows and chewed his brunch. His diamond cufflinks sparkled. "Sounds like another fly-by-night joker," he muttered. "How the fuck he land a fight like that?"

Bishop's expression remained serious as he held out the phone, showing the Duke a video of one of Zane's recent fights. With a frown, the Duke sat back in his chair, took his time wiping his mouth and hands on a white cloth napkin, then took the phone. The screen lit up with footage of Zane in action. He was quick, precise, and powerful. The crowd around him screamed in excitement as Zane knocked his opponent down with a clean uppercut, the punch landing with a brutal thud.

The Duke watched, his eyes narrowing as the clip continued. Zane moved with a kind of raw, untamed energy—different from the seasoned fighters he had managed in the past. This kid had something dangerous about him, something unpredictable.

"You see?" Bishop said. "That right there? That's the kind of talent that gets people talkin'. He's young, fast, and hungry. The fans love him. You know what that means—money. Big money."

The Duke watched the next video. The young fighter had the crowd wrapped around his finger, every punch drawing gasps and cheers.

"Hmm," the Duke grunted, puffing on his cigar. He handed the phone back. "He might have some potential. Maybe."

Bishop put the phone away and folded his hands, his expression serious. "Prince Omar's putting on the fight in Houston. That kind of money, that kind of attention—could be an opportunity."

The Duke smirked, tapping ash off the end of his cigar. "An opportunity, huh? Yeah, maybe." He picked up his bourbon, swirling the glass before taking a sip. "If he's thinkin' about comin' here, we'll need to make sure he's down with the program."

Bishop nodded, a knowing glint in his eye. "Houston's your turf, boss. Nobody makes moves here without goin' through you."

"Mmmmm," the Duke agreed, placing the bourbon glass back down on the table.

"Keep eyes on him," the Duke said, turning his attention back to his meal. "I want to know everything about this Zane—where he's stayin', who he's talkin' to, what his plans are."

Bishop smiled, his dreads shifting slightly as he nodded. "Already on it, boss."

The Duke took another slow drag of his cigar, a sly smile curling at the corners of his lips. Zane might be the rising star, but in Houston, no one rose higher than the Duke.

"Good. Now, take me to see Mama Heloise."

After brunch, the Duke adjusted his gold-rimmed sunglasses as he stepped out of the mansion and approached the sleek, black Rolls Royce Phantom parked in the circular driveway. The vehicle looked more like a silent predator than a luxury car. Bishop, his ever-watchful bodyguard, stood by the rear door, ready to escort him on their journey to his private sanctuary—his ranch in a neighboring county.

The Duke slid into the backseat, inhaling the familiar scent of leather and luxury, as Bishop climbed into the driver's seat. The Rolls Royce purred to life with barely a sound, and they glided smoothly out of the gated estate inside the posh River Oaks district. As they moved through Houston's busy streets, the Duke's mind was already at the ranch, at the place where his fighters bled and sweat, and where darker things took place far away from prying eyes.

The Rolls Royce hit I-10 heading west, cutting through the landscape like an obsidian blade, eventually pulling up to the ranch's entrance. The huge iron gates read "The Reserve," the 4,000 acre estate's official name, but nobody called it that. Within the Duke's organization, it was known by another name: "Gladiator Farm". They passed through the automatic gates and followed the smooth concrete drive toward the main ranch house.

The property was vast, the outer stretches covered in hay fields and pastures filled with fat Angus cattle. As they passed the massive gymnasium where world champion boxers trained, the Duke watched a group of young fighters exercise in the yard as their trainers barked orders.

"Strong group of youngsters comin' up," Bishop commented from the front seat.

The Duke grunted in acknowledgment, his mind elsewhere. They soon approached a multi-car garage where a small fleet of Range Rovers sat waiting. Bishop parked the Rolls and the two men prepared to switch to one of the glossy black SUVs.

Looking around the garage, the Duke spotted what he needed.

"Load that case in the back," the Duke said, pointing towards a wooden crate sitting on the garage floor.

Bishop picked up the box. Bottles clinked inside as he loaded it into the back of the SUV. The two set off driving again, this time taking a dirt road heading away from the house.

They drove deeper into the ranch, past the manicured lawns and painted barns, into the forgotten, overgrown parts of the property where the trees closed in and the air grew thick with the smell of stagnant water and wild animals. It was here, in the back corner of Gladiator Farm, that Mama Heloise lived.

Deep in the backwoods, she lived in the property's original, decrepit homestead. The house was barely standing, a dilapidated shack made of rotting wood and rusted tin, half-consumed by the wilderness around it.

Vines climbed the walls, and the roof sagged like an old horse.

As the Range Rover rolled to a stop in front of the shack, the Duke exhaled loudly. He wasn't easily rattled, but Mama Heloise's world always made his skin crawl. Bishop followed close behind, his eyes scanning the tree line for any threats, though they both knew no one was foolish enough to venture this far into the Duke's domain.

As they got out, cicadas buzzed in the distance and sweat beaded on Bishop's forehead.

"Grab those bottles and come on," Duke instructed.

Bishop retrieved the box from the back of the Rover, and they started walking toward the house.

Looking around with an irritated frown, the Duke muttered, "Where's this crazy ol' Creole bitch at?"

A low, eerie cackle came from the side of the shack, where a group of large hogs snorted and rooted around in a mud pit behind wooden pickets. Near the hog pens, another enclosure held a muddy pond filled with alligators, their rough, scaly hides blending with the mossy water. But it was another pen that caught the Duke's attention.

As they passed the low, chicken wire construction, the stench grew stronger. The sweet, sickening smell of decay and slime and animal shit filled the air. Inside, behind the wire mesh, a filthy black buzzard picked at a skeleton, its beak scraping against bone as it tore at the remaining scraps of cloth and flesh. The skeleton was human. Its hands and feet were bound to steel rings set in concrete blocks, its body stretched flat on the ground. Other buzzards huddled in the corner, preening after their meal.

"You come to see Mama, huh?" a raspy voice called from the shadowy porch of the shack.

Mama Heloise stepped out, her hunched form wrapped in layers of old fabric that had once been a dress. Her skin was leathery from years under the brutal Louisiana sun, her white hair a wild tangle that framed her deeply lined face. She shuffled toward them with a slow, deliberate gait, her eyes sharp and knowing despite her frail appearance. She held an old tobacco pipe in her hand, and a necklace of finger bones and bright beads hung about her neck.

The Duke gave her a nod. "Mama Heloise."

She grinned, revealing yellowed, uneven teeth, her bony fingers reaching out to him. "What you bring me today, Duke?"

"Rum. Cuban. A whole case," he replied gruffly, watching as she eyed him like a predator sizing up its prey.

Mama Heloise laughed softly, a sound that sent shivers through even the most hardened men. "Mmmmm, you always keep Mama busy." She gestured toward the buzzard pen with a bony finger. "Buzzards get hungry, Duke. Jus' like de gators. Jus' like de hogs."

The Duke glanced at the skeleton in the pen, the buzzard tearing at the remains. "You'll have more soon enough," he said, his voice cold. "Business is never slow. What that sucka' say before he died?"

"He said, 'Ahhhhh! Ahhhhh!'" she croaked, then laughed a feverish, high pitched squeal. "De buzzards like to eat de face and de tongue first, you know. Soft, tender meat. Den dey take de manhood, den de asshole..."

"Yeah, yeah," the Duke cut her off. "They some real connoisseurs. Damn, dumb ass boy should have just paid."

Mama Heloise smiled, a thin, sinister expression. "Mmmmm. But I tell you somethin', Duke—when de fight comes, dey'll be plenty food fo' my pets."

The Duke's brow furrowed. "What fight?"

"Big one, comin' soon. Dat boy, Zane," she said, her eyes gleaming with something almost supernatural. "He bring a storm wit' 'im. Lots of money, lots of blood."

Bishop stood silently, his face impassive as he watched the buzzard do its ghastly work.

The Duke narrowed his eyes at Mama Heloise. "Zane? What you know about him?"

Mama Heloise chuckled again, shaking her head. "Oh, I know many things, Duke. But you'll see soon enough. You'll want his blood. You'll come back to Mama."

The Duke stared at her for a long moment, then turned back to the Range

Rover. "I'll be in touch, Mama. Enjoy the rum."

As he climbed back into the vehicle, the sounds of the swamp and the low rumblings of the animals surrounded him. He lit another cigar, inhaling deeply as Bishop drove them back toward the main grounds, letting the smoke wash the smell and thought of Mama Heloise from his nostrils.

Later that night, the heavy bass of a nightclub thumped through the walls, the sound vibrating beneath the soles of the Duke's Italian leather shoes as he made his way through the dimly lit entrance. The club was packed, bodies swaying under flashing lights, while VIP sections spilled over with celebrities, athletes, and influencers sipping champagne and flashing diamond-studded watches. It was one of Houston's hottest spots.

The Duke moved smoothly through the crowd, his presence undeniable. Dressed in an expertly tailored suit, a cigar perched between his fingers, he looked out of place among the younger patrons. Yet everyone knew who he was. The moment he entered, people parted to let him through and whispers followed in his wake.

At the far end of the club, in the most plush VIP section, his son Michael sat surrounded by beautiful women and young men who wanted nothing more than to bask in his glow. He was everything the Duke had groomed him to be—suave, powerful, and commanding. Michael was dressed in the latest designer fashion: a fitted black Dolce and Gabbana blazer with gold accents, handmade leather shoes, and a custom diamond chain that glinted under the neon lights. His hair was perfectly faded, his face sharp and confident, exuding charm with every gesture.

As the Duke approached, Michael caught sight of him and raised a glass in acknowledgment. The crowd parted for the Duke, allowing him to slide into the VIP booth beside his son. The women beside Michael exchanged nervous glances but smiled politely.

"Pop," Michael said smoothly. "Didn't expect to see you here tonight."

The Duke took a long pull from his cigar, the smoke curling lazily above his head. "I'm here for business, not pleasure, boy."

Michael leaned back, nodding to one of his friends to refill his drink. He knew when his father came calling, it wasn't for small talk. "What's up, Pop?"

The Duke scanned the room before focusing on Michael. "You've heard about Zane? The fight? All that?"

Michael's grin widened. "Who hasn't? The kid's blowin' up. That fight with Mickie Donovan? People are callin' it the biggest event in fight history."

The Duke nodded, his expression hard. "Exactly. And we need to make sure we've got our hands in it. That kid is comin' into our city, about to make millions. But he doesn't know how things work around here. Not yet. You're gonna meet with him, make sure he understands that no one operates in H-Town without my say."

Michael's brow arched slightly, amused by the challenge. "And what's our angle?"

"Simple," the Duke said, leaning closer. "You're gonna convince him to sign a management contract with us. He needs to know that if he wants to stay safe and keep makin' that kind of money, he's gonna need protection. And we're the only ones who can give it to him."

Michael chuckled, sipping his champagne. "So, you want me to go play diplomat? Butter him up, show him the ropes, and get him to sign over a cut."

"Exactly," the Duke replied. "He's young, probably cocky, but you know how to talk to these kids. He's flashy, like you. That'll work in your favor."

Michael's eyes sparkled with interest. He thought for a moment, then said, "I've got this, Pop. Zane won't know what hit him. He'll be signed up before he even realizes it."

The Duke gave an approving nod. "Good. But keep it tight. He's a fighter, and if he doesn't play ball, we might have to remind him who runs shit."

Michael nodded, his demeanor shifting slightly, the casual arrogance replaced by something more serious. "Don't worry, I'll handle it. Zane's just another kid in over his head. He'll come around."

The Duke stood. "Make sure he does. This fight is worth too much for us to lose."

Michael raised his glass in acknowledgment. "You'll get what you want,

Pop. As usual."

The Duke nodded and turned to leave, making his way through the crowd with the same authority as when he'd arrived. Michael leaned back in his seat, watching his father and bodyguard disappear into the sea of bodies. He finished his drink in silence, then smiled at the two models sitting next to him.

"Change of plans. How about the three of us take a flight tonight instead? I know a great brunch spot in Marina del Rey."

The next evening, Michael sat comfortably in a velvet booth in one of L.A.'s most exclusive rooftop clubs, his drink barely touched as he leaned back, flashing a grin at Zane across the table.

"I appreciate you meeting me in such short notice," he began. "I figured you'd never see my DM, but then I was watching your latest Backyard Brawl video and I saw Charlie's crazy British ass in your corner. Nobody can miss that ugly mug. You know he worked at our training center for years, right? Great trainer. I'm glad he was able to connect us. Does he still talk all that crazy Cockney shit? "Keep yer old mugs up. Move yer plates. Remember to heave!"

Zane laughed. "Yeah, Charlie's the best. I have no idea what he's saying most of the time, but I'm sure he'll kill me if I don't figure it out, so it motivates the hell out of me."

"Well, clearly its working," Michael replied. "So, let's talk about you. You're already rich from your prank videos. You pick up fighting— for what? For fun? And now you find yourself with the opportunity of a lifetime, right?"

Zane sipped his mojito and nodded. "Something like that."

"I mean, you've been killing it though. I knew who you were from like four years ago. Your pranks always had me rolling. I know money and fame are nothing new to you, but this is on a whole other level. Can we agree?"

Zane nodded again. The rooftop lounge was moderately busy, and groups of patrons who recognized him stopped to snap pictures from a distance.

Michael sipped his drink. "I'm curious, my man, tell me: where are you from originally?"

"I'm from L.A.," he said. "My mom is from here, but my dad was from Jamaica."

"Oh yeah?" Michael chuckled. "You're hella light skinned, but I thought I detected some brotha in there."

"Yeah. My mom is this like blonde-blonde, you know? And my dad was pretty light skinned, too."

"Ay, you're good with me. I love Jamaica. We have a spot in Belize you should check out. It's an incredible place. You'd love it."

Zane nodded.

"So, have you thought about your team yet? Where you're going to train? Who's going to handle your diet and conditioning? Cut man? Mitt man? Merchandising? Have you got all that covered?"

"Nah," Zane said. "I mean, not yet. Really, it's all just been coming at me so fast. I can't hardly answer all the calls. Honestly, I really came to meet with you just to clear my head for a minute."

Michael smiled.

"Well, unfortunately, this is just the beginning, and it's only going to get worse, especially when it comes time to start training. You're going to need someone to take the load off of you, get you organized, and build you a plan for success. You can't do it all *and* train. You need to focus on the fight and only the fight. That's where we come in. Did you know we have eighteen world title belts in our camp? Plus, we're the highest earning boxing promotion and management company on earth. My dad has basically run boxing for the last twenty years."

"Yeah, I did know that," Zane agreed. "But Prince Omar said he would handle all the management stuff."

Michael smiled patiently.

"Look, 'Prince O' is good at writing checks. But what does he know about boxing? Who is he going to pick as your coach, and based on what criteria? How can a man who never boxed know what a boxer needs? Don't forget, I was two time welterweight champion of the world myself."

"And you won the gold medal in London in 2012. I know. Charlie told me all about you," Zane said.

"So, you already know then. My family lives, breathes, and eats boxing. We are the whole thing, from the promotion to the cat who holds your spit bucket. We do it all. We treat our boxers as brothers. A failure of one of our brothers is a failure for us all. You take an "L," we all take an "L", and none of us like to lose. In fact, we can't stand to lose. So, we go the extra mile to prepare. You understand what I'm sayin'?"

Zane sipped his drink and nodded. He was glancing around, looking a little uneasy, so Michael eased back in his seat and changed the subject.

"Say, I saw you pull up to valet in that McLaren. Have you ever taken it through the hills?" Michael asked, his tone casual, though his eyes gleamed with a challenge.

Zane's eyebrow arched. He knew a dare when he heard one. "Yeah, sure. The F1 handles those roads pretty well. Why?"

Michael laughed, leaning forward. "I've got a place out here, too. Got a few cars stashed there. Nothing too crazy, just some toys I keep around. But if you're down, we could see what's up."

Zane smirked. "OK. Let's do it."

Michael's grin widened. "Perfect. I'll drop you a pin. Meet me in an hour."

Zane left the club, excitement buzzing through him. He wasn't sure what kind of car Michael was hiding, but he had confidence in his McLaren F1. It was one of the fastest, rarest cars in the world, and he was confident that nothing Michael pulled out could beat the F1's reputation on the open road.

By the time Zane rolled up to the meeting point in the black supercar, the Santa Monica Mountains just north of Malibu were quiet. He revved the engine, the car purring like a beast ready to strike. He was idling on the side of the road checking his phone when the sound of another engine roared up from behind. Zane turned, expecting something fast but not up to par with his F1. Instead, a low-slung, aggressive machine glided into view—Michael's Pagani Huayra BC, the body glistening under the night sky like a lethal weapon. The sleek, matte finish and bold lines of the Pagani made it look like something out of a dream. Zane's jaw clenched, but he couldn't hide the impressed look on his face.

Michael stepped out of the car with a cocky smile. "Told you. Nothing too serious."

Zane whistled, taking in the sight of the Pagani. "Damn, you downplayed that one. That's no ordinary 'toy,' man."

Michael shrugged, flashing a devilish grin. "Figured I'd keep it a surprise. What's the fun in showing all your cards upfront?"

Zane smirked, the adrenaline already kicking in. "Alright, let's see what it can do."

The two men hopped into their respective machines, engines rumbling as they revved them to life.

They pulled up side-by-side, the curves of the winding roads ahead stretching out into the darkness. The moonlight glinted off the hoods of their cars, the McLaren's classic black sheen contrasting with the futuristic curves of the Pagani.

Michael looked over at Zane and shouted, "Ready?"

Zane nodded, gripping the wheel tightly. "Let's run it."

With a roar, the two cars shot forward, tires screeching against the pavement as they blasted down the winding road, weaving in and out of sharp turns with precision. Zane's McLaren tore through the hills, its low-weight-to-high-power combination making it a dream to handle on the tight curves. But Michael's Pagani was no slouch. The Huayra BC was a different kind of beast—hyper-responsive and agile. The twin-turbo V12 growled like a lion as Michael expertly maneuvered through the sharp bends, keeping pace with Zane every step of the way.

The two cars flew past the cliffs, the wind whipping through open windows. Each man pushed his machine to the limit, laughing as they tore through the winding roads, adrenaline coursing through their veins.

For a while, the race was neck and neck—each curve, each straightaway a battle of wills between the two men. Zane's McLaren had the edge on handling, cutting through corners like a scalpel, but Michael's Pagani responded with raw power, its engine roaring as it pulled ahead on the straights.

They pushed their cars harder, taunting each other over the roar of the engines. As they reached the final stretch, Zane gave it everything, the McLaren's engine screaming as it fought to edge out Michael's Pagani on the last straightaway. But Michael wasn't holding back either, the Huayra BC surging forward with blistering speed, the two cars tearing toward the finish line side-by-side.

In the end, the Pagani won by a nose. They both skidded to a stop, their cars settling into a low, satisfied growl.

The gullwing doors opened, and Michael stepped out of his car, walking over to Zane's McLaren, his eyes twinkling. "You've got some serious skills, Zane. But if you're running with me, there's always room for more."

Zane slid out of his car, feeling the rush still pulsing through his veins. "We'll see, man. But this was fun."

Michael clapped him on the back, his tone shifting slightly, more serious now. "We're just gettin' started. Imagine the moves we could make if we teamed up. You think this race was wild? Wait 'til you see what we can do together in the ring."

Zane couldn't stop smiling as he looked out over the ocean to Los Angeles, the city below sparkling as brightly as his future.

6

New Home

Zane sat at a sleek glass table in his home. The management contract lay in front of him, printed on expensive paper, embossed with Michael's signature as President of Reserve Entertainment, LLC. The deal sounded perfect—connections, promotion, a shot at true global fame. All Zane had to do was sign, and the path to becoming the biggest star in the fighting world was his.

Across from him, Hannah sat with her phone in hand, excitement radiating off her. She was recording video blogs of herself for her own active social media.

"POV: When your man is about to sign a contract to get even *more* rich," she said as she angled her expertly painted face into the light.

Zane ran a brown hand through his curly blonde hair as he studied the document one last time. Then he grabbed a pen and signed his name at the bottom. The ink dried instantly.

Hannah leaned over, kissing his cheek. "We're going to be *huge!*" she gushed.

Four days later, Zane and Hannah sat on a private jet 42,000 feet over the vast plains of Texas. The city of Houston was fast approaching, and both of them were buzzing with excitement. Zane stared out the window, watching as the city skyline came into view, the buildings stretching upward like sentinels. It was quite different from the laid-back, sun-soaked vibe of L.A., but he was excited.

Beside him, Hannah scrolled through her phone, checking social media, and reading up on the upcoming fight. "This is going to be huge," she said for the hundredth time. "I mean, everyone's talking about you. The fight, the contract, all of it. It's blowing up. I really can't believe it."

Zane sighed. "Yeah, it's real now. We're here."

When they touched down at George Bush Intercontinental Airport, Zane and Hannah were greeted by a wall of heat as they stepped off the plane and onto the tarmac. The humid Texas air was thick, smothering them like a wet blanket as they made their way through the private terminal.

"Ew," Hannah frowned. "Why is it so hot?"

Waiting for them outside was an all-black Rolls Royce Phantom, its glossy exterior gleaming under the Houston sun. Standing beside it was Bishop, the Duke's towering bodyguard, his long dreads swaying slightly as he opened the back door for them.

Bishop gave them a nod as they approached. "Mr. Zane, Miss Hannah," he greeted them, his voice a deep rumble. "Welcome to Houston. Your luggage will meet you at the house."

They slid into the cool, leather-clad interior of the Rolls Royce. The contrast between the scorching Texas heat and the air-conditioned luxury was striking. Hannah let out a soft sigh as she leaned back against the plush seats, then immediately began taking photos of herself.

"So, what's next?" Zane asked as Bishop got behind the wheel and started the engine, the car gliding silently out of the airport parking lot.

"Now, we're headed to the world famous Gladiator Farm," Bishop replied, his tone professional. "The Duke wants to show you around the ranch, introduce you to the trainers and all that."

Zane glanced at Hannah, who was practically bouncing in her seat with excitement. "Sounds good to me," Zane said. "Let's do it."

The city of Houston rolled past as they wound their way out of the urban sprawl and into the rural outskirts where skyscrapers gave way to open fields and long stretches of highway. Zane watched the scenery shift, his mind already racing with thoughts of what the Gladiator Farm would be like. Michael had talked it up, calling it a place where legends were made.

After two hours of driving, they arrived. The ranch was vast, surrounded by rolling hills and thick groves of trees. They passed through the main gate and pastures filled with black cows standing in groups, chewing their cuds.

As they approached the entrance, Zane could see the outlines of the ranch's main facilities—a collection of training centers, fighter barracks, and even an outdoor sparring ring.

Bishop drove the Rolls Royce deeper into the ranch. "This is where the real work gets done," Bishop said as they passed a group of fighters running. "We take raw talent and turn them into killers."

Zane couldn't help but feel a surge of anticipation. He had trained hard his whole life, but this was a different level—this was where champions were born.

As they pulled up to the main house, Zane and Hannah stepped out, taking in the sight of the sprawling property. The Duke was nowhere to be seen.

Hannah squeezed his hand, her eyes wide as she looked around.

The tall wooden doors of the main house opened and out stepped a gentleman with gray at his temples but the quick, confident movement of an athlete. The Duke greeted Zane and Hannah with a warm smile. Dressed in a fine silk shirt, this one a deep emerald green, he exuded confidence and charm. His presence was magnetic, and Zane couldn't help but admire how the older man carried himself with such authority. Beside him, Hannah gave the Duke a polite smile, still taking in the grandeur of the estate.

"Welcome to Gladiator Farm," the Duke said, extending his hand to Zane. "I trust the flight was smooth?"

Zane shook his hand firmly. "Yes sir, all good. This place is incredible."

The Duke chuckled, his eyes glinting with pride. "It's a special place, no doubt. Come on, let me show you around."

They climbed into the all-black Range Rover, with Bishop at the wheel, the Duke in the passenger seat, and Zane and Hannah in the back. As the SUV rolled along the winding roads of the ranch, the Duke pointed out different parts of the sprawling estate. His voice was calm and friendly, like a gracious host showing off his prized possessions.

"This land has seen more blood, sweat, and tears than you can imagine," the Duke said as they drove past the open-air ring. "These boys come from nothing, but here, they become something. This is where we turn potential into greatness."

The Range Rover bounced gently along a dirt side road as they made their way toward the stables. The Duke gestured to the long, elegant stable house, its whitewashed walls gleaming under the Texas sun.

"We keep some of the finest horses here," the Duke explained as they passed by. "Thoroughbreds, quarter horses—you name it. I've always believed that training a fighter isn't just about brute strength; it's about control, grace, and discipline. Riding teaches all that and more."

Hannah's eyes widened as she leaned forward to get a better view of the horses. "Oh my god! I love horses," she squealed.

The Duke smiled. "Once y'all get settled, you two should go for a ride."

They continued on, the ranch sprawling in every direction. The Duke pointed out different sections—the outdoor workout areas, the barracks where the fighters stayed, the endless fields of land that stretched far beyond the horizon. Eventually, they pulled up to the heart of the Gladiator Farm: the main gym. It was an imposing structure, a massive metal building outfitted with every imaginable piece of training equipment. Fighters came and went, sparring, hitting heavy bags, and working with trainers on mitts.

"This is it. Your new home," the Duke said. Bishop parked the Range Rover, and they all stepped out. Zane and Hannah followed as the Duke led them inside.

The gym smelled of sweat and hard work, and the sound of leather hitting leather filled the air. Zane's adrenaline surged as he took in the sight of fighters working tirelessly. It was unlike anything he'd seen before. These weren't amateurs. These were warriors.

"I'll be honest with you," the Duke said, turning to Zane. "We've got some real talent here, but you? You're something special. I can feel it. You've got star power, and you're about to see what it takes to go from good to legendary."

The Duke led them out of the gym, and they walked a short distance along a paved path that eventually opened up to reveal an infinity pool surrounded by tall trees. Beside it was a stylish guest house.

"The VIP guest house. This is where you'll stay," the Duke said. "Make yourselves comfortable. We don't cut corners here, and neither should you. You're a guest, but more than that—you're family now."

Hannah gasped at the sight of the pool and the guest house. "This is unreal," she whispered to Zane.

Zane smiled, nodding in agreement.

The Duke chuckled, clapping Zane on the back. "Get settled in. Training starts immediately. I don't believe in wasting time, and you're going to need every second of preparation if you want to take down Mickie Donovan. The fight will be here before you know it."

Zane's face hardened with determination. "I'll be ready."

"Good," the Duke said, his voice suddenly more serious. "Because once you step in that ring, you'll either come out a king or a cautionary tale. And here at Gladiator Farm, we only crown kings."

With that, the Duke gave a final nod, leaving Zane and Hannah to explore their new home. As the Duke and Bishop drove away, Zane glanced around the property, feeling the pressure mounting, but also the excitement.

Hannah squeezed his hand, her eyes still wide with excitement. "This is amazing! I'm going to ride horses and swim every day. Can you believe it?"

Zane nodded, his gaze fixed on the horizon. "I don't know," he said, his voice steady. "It's pretty unbelievable."

7

Shadows and Secrets

GZD Training Center, Denver, Colorado, USA

Mason leaned back in his chair, the bright lights of the podcast studio casting a soft glow over his face. The GZD Training Center's media room was sleek and modern, outfitted with high-end equipment and soundproofed walls. His voice had just carried through another hour-long session discussing tactical training, mental resilience, and the ever-evolving world of private security. The podcast was one of many ways Green Zone Defense had expanded its reach—providing not just physical training but knowledge and insight into the rapidly changing landscape of defense and warfare.

Across from him, Alex, GZD's Director of Communications, wrapped up the episode. "And that's it for today, folks. If you're looking to sharpen your skills or dive into the world of tactical defense, you know where to go—GZD Training Center. Thanks again to Mason for sharing his wisdom."

Mason nodded, offering a quick handshake as he stood up. "Always a pleasure, Alex."

As the recording gear powered down, Mason stretched, feeling the familiar tug of old injuries. But the day never truly ended at GZD. There was always another challenge, another mission, another warrior to train.

He stepped out into the hallway, where the hum of activity continued as usual. GZD was alive with intensity. Mason thrived in this atmosphere—constant movement, constant improvement. He walked through a set of glass doors into the warm Colorado sun and strolled down a concrete sidewalk toward the Combatives Training Center, the gymnasium where most of GZD's hand-to-hand training occurred. He passed a pair of young trainees wearing dark green GZD t-shirts who smiled and said hello.

At the gym, he pulled open the green doors and entered. Inside, the open room was alive with the sounds of physical combat—grunts, thuds of bodies hitting mats, and the occasional bark of instruction echoing off the cinder block walls. Rows of trainees from the Salt Lake City Police Department stood in formation, their blue t-shirts soaked with sweat. The scent of rubber mats and determination filled the air.

At the center of it all was Mason's old friend, Benito. His presence dominated the room—a man forged by fire and sharpened by experience. His beard, grown to mask the reminders of an explosive ambush a few years back, only added to his imposing figure. Today, he was dressed in a black GZD t-shirt tucked into tactical cargo pants, his movements sharp and deliberate as he addressed the class.

"Alright, listen up!" Benito's voice cut through the murmurs, silencing the group instantly. He stood with his arms crossed. "You're not here to play grab-ass. You're here to learn how to survive—and not just survive but dominate."

From the sidelines, Mason leaned against the wall, his arms crossed, his eyes tracking Benito's every move.

Benito motioned for one of the trainees to step forward. A tall, fit officer in his mid-thirties with a buzz cut approached cautiously. Benito gestured toward him with a quick nod. "You. What's your name?"

"Benson," the man said.

"Alright, Benson," Benito said, letting his arms fall to his sides. "Show me your best defensive stance. Let's see what you've got."

Benson squared up, raising his hands in a boxing guard, his feet shoulder-width apart. Benito circled him like a predator sizing up prey.

"Not bad," Benito said. "But this is not a boxing gym. You're in a back alley, someone's coming at you with a knife, and you've got half a second to react. What do you do?"

Benson hesitated for a moment, and Benito rushed in. Benson threw a quick jab, but Benito was faster. He slipped, sidestepped, snatched Benson's wrist mid-punch, and twisted it downward. In one fluid motion, he swept Benson's leg out from under him, sending him crashing to the mat with a resounding thud. Benito dropped to one knee, pinning Benson's arm behind his back.

"This," Benito growled, his voice low and deliberate, "is what happens if you get distracted. Benson was expecting a knife. But what do you notice? There's no knife. Physicality is one thing, but psychology, awareness, and quick thinking are key. You can't let an opponent distract you. No hesitation. When you react, you react to end the threat you see, not what you imagine."

He released Benson, who scrambled to his feet, rubbing his shoulder with a sheepish nod. Benito turned back to the group. "Comabtives is about efficiency. It's about knowing when to strike and where to strike. You don't need ten moves. You need one or two done perfectly. Understood?"

"Yes, sir!" the group shouted in unison.

Benito gestured toward a red training dummy on the mat. "Now, let's break it down. This is what we call a stomp kick. When someone's rushing you, they're off-balance. You step back, stabilize your footing, and drive your heel straight into their knee. Think about it: how do you chop down a tree? From the top, or the bottom? From the bottom. Now, watch."

He demonstrated the kick with precision, his boot slamming into the dummy's knee joint with enough force to make the entire room flinch. "That," he said, straightening, "is how you stop momentum. They can't run at you if they can't stand."

One by one, the trainees stepped up to practice, their kicks ranging from hesitant to aggressive. Benito moved among them, adjusting stances, correcting form, and occasionally barking out praise when someone got it right.

"Good! Now follow it up. If they're still moving, you don't let them recover." He called over another officer and demonstrated a follow-up elbow strike to the dummy's head, his movements swift and decisive.

From the wall, Mason watched with a faint smirk. Benito was in his element, commanding respect and driving home lessons with the force of a drill sergeant.

Benito motioned for another trainee to step forward. This time, a shorter woman with a determined expression took the mat. "Alright," he said. "Once the forward aggression has been broken, we want to tie-up the opponent. The tie-up is about controlling their head and their hands. Doesn't matter how big they are. Size doesn't mean shit if you've got leverage."

He demonstrated, grabbing the trainee in a clinch, his forearm pressing against her neck while his other hand controlled her wrist. He guided her down to the mat in a controlled motion, his movements fluid yet forceful.

"See that? No brute strength. Just mechanics. Practice it until it's second nature."

As the trainees paired off to practice, Mason pushed off the wall, walking closer. "Not bad," he said quietly, standing next to Benito.

"Not bad?" Benito replied with a smirk, wiping sweat from his brow. "I'm out here making warriors, Mason. You just watching, or you want to show them how it's done?"

Mason chuckled, shaking his head. "You've got it under control. If they can survive you, they're ready for anything."

Benito grinned, clapping his hands to get the group's attention. "Alright, pair off. Three rounds of foot sweeps and tie-ups. No stomp kicks, or you'll all be limping out of here, but it's the same idea. And remember—this isn't just about looking good in the gym. Out there, it's life or death. Train like your life depends on it. Because one day, it might."

The room echoed with the sounds of practice, the thuds of kicks and the grunts of exertion. Mason watched as the trainees pushed themselves harder, their movements sharper, their focus unwavering.

Mason looked his friend up and down. Benito moved with a quiet intensity now, the weight of past battles etched into his expression. He was still stocky and fit, but thinner, his face more defined and angular. The beard he now wore covered the scars on his lower face that he'd earned in the ambush, the one they almost didn't make it out of. The man who stood before Mason now was a changed one—more serious, more dangerous.

Benito reached out for a handshake, his grip strong. "It's been a minute, man."

"Too long," Mason replied, clasping his friend's hand. "How're you holding up? How's your wife?"

Benito gave a nod, his dark eyes steady. "We're good, bro." He ran a hand through his beard. "Luckily, she digs scars."

Mason grinned. "It's good to see you, brother."

But the lighthearted, joking Benito was gone.

"I hear you've been training a lot recently," Mason said. "Good to see you back in the groove."

Benito nodded, his lips tightening beneath the beard. "Yeah, can't afford to slack off. Been running a lot of field ops lately, driving for VIP clients and such. But whenever I get the chance, I'm in here rolling. Can't let my guard down again."

Mason grinned. "You picked the right place to sharpen those edges."

"Damn right, bro," Benito said, his voice lowering slightly. "And I think we'll be needing those skills sooner than later."

Mason raised an eyebrow. "Oh, yeah? Why do you say that?"

Benito looked around, ensuring no one else was close enough to hear. "Frazier told me GZD got a call about a major event. There's a lot of buzz in the office. I think it's the big influencer fight in the news. Some big players are coming into Houston—celebrities, royals, people with serious money. Arab money, you know? Everybody is scrambling to hire security teams."

Mason nodded at the mention of Houston. "I've heard about that fight. Big deal. $450 million, I heard. Biggest purse in history. It's all over the news."

"Exactly," Benito said, nodding. "But that kind of money doesn't move without shadows. They announced this morning that that crooked boxing promoter, the Duke, is taking over Zane's management. Everybody knows that cat's a major gangster, so shit is already getting weird, bro."

Mason clenched his jaw. He had heard of the Duke. Everyone in the boxing, security, and law enforcement worlds had. The man wasn't just a boxing manager—he was a kingpin involved in everything: drugs, money laundering, extortion, murder. If Zane signed with the Duke without knowing the full score, there was a chance he'd end up in deep trouble.

"Zane seems to be a talented fighter," Mason said, thinking aloud. "But he doesn't know what he's getting into with the Duke."

Benito's eyes darkened. "And that's the problem. This isn't just about boxing. A guy like the Duke doesn't just want a cut of the fight. If Zane's not careful, he could end up caught in something way bigger than he's ready for."

Mason exhaled slowly, thinking. "Well, we can't get involved unless Zane reaches out."

Benito crossed his arms, the quiet intensity returning. "That's why I'm here, Mason. To train. Once Frazier told me they were already getting calls about security for the fight, I knew I needed to be ready. I mean, GZD is the premiere security firm in America right now. Whatever's coming, we're probably going to get a piece of it."

Mason nodded, thinking. "Yeah, you might be right."

Later, as Mason was sitting at his desk, the door creaked open, and Caleb stepped inside, his expression serious.

"Mason, got a minute? We've got something big," he said. "I just got a call. A VIP's interested in talking to us about some security work. High profile. They're flying someone in today to meet with us."

Mason raised an eyebrow. "Who's the client?"

Caleb leaned in, lowering his voice slightly. "A Saudi prince. His team reached out directly. Apparently, this is urgent."

"All right," Mason said. "Let me know when they arrive."

Later, they made their way to the helipad where the sound of a helicopter cutting through the air grew louder as it descended. Bud, Mason's Dalmatian, who was given free range of the facility after saving the day during a robbery attempt some years back, paced around anxiously. The dog had seen helicopters come and go before, but they still made him anxious. The sleek white and blue chopper, framed by the mountains in the distance, touched down smoothly, its blades kicking up wind as the door swung open. Out stepped a well-dressed man in a sharp navy suit, his features composed and confident, his dark hair and beard perfectly styled. Behind him, a second man exited the helicopter. Dressed in a black suit and dark sunglasses, he looked around with the intense but discreet bearing of a security professional.

Mason's eyes locked onto the second man, a flicker of recognition hitting him. The man's sharp gaze matched Mason's, but his face remained impassive.

The smiling representative in the suit approached first, offering a firm handshake to both Mason and Caleb. "Good afternoon. My name is Nasir al-Amri. I represent His Royal Highness Prince Omar bin Talal al-Mansour."

Mason exchanged a look with Caleb as they led Nasir and the security agent into the conference room. The atmosphere was formal, but there was an underlying tension that Mason couldn't shake, especially with the way the security agent kept stealing glances in his direction.

Caleb spoke first, his tone professional. "So, what can GZD do for the Prince?"

Nasir sat back, his fingers steepled. "My patron is producing a major boxing event between the social media influencer known as Zane and Mickie Donovan. Have you have heard about it?"

Caleb and Mason both nodded.

"It has come to the Prince's attention that Zane has signed a management contract with a man known as the Duke. This development has raised certain... concerns."

"Why is the Prince concerned?" Caleb asked.

Nasir leaned forward slightly. "The Duke is known as a dangerous man. He controls much of Houston's underworld, and while Zane is a talented fighter, he is not equipped to deal with someone like the Duke. The Prince is planning a significant investment in not just this event, but in Zane's career and future. He does not wish to see Zane fall victim to the same traps that many before him have by dealing with this... shady character."

Nasir continued, "The Prince wants to hire GZD's finest—specifically you, Mr. Mason—to provide close protection for Zane. You would be responsible for ensuring his safety and keeping him out of the Duke's grasp. The Prince is prepared to offer a significant sum for your services."

Caleb leaned forward, his curiosity piqued. "Well, Mason is our head of training and has a lot of duties here. Just this month we've got Miami SRT coming up for a week, plus ongoing training programs we run for Denver...."

As Caleb talked, Nasir smiled. He reached in his pocket and removed a notepad upon which he wrote a figure. He tore off the piece of paper and handed it to Caleb.

"As I said, a significant sum," Nasir repeated with a smile.

Caleb glanced at it and his eyes nearly bulged from his head. Mason noticed a slight shake in his hand as he laid the paper face down on the conference table.

"The Prince values Zane's potential—and he values expertise in security, as well."

"Yes, I see that. For that sum, I'm certain we could find someone to take over Mason's duties, at least for a short time," Caleb assured him.

"Why me?" Mason asked, his eyes returning to Nasir's. "You've got plenty of options for private security. What makes Prince Omar think I'm the right guy for this?"

Nasir didn't hesitate. "Because you have a reputation for handling the impossible. You're not just another bodyguard. You've been in the field. You've led operations and protected high-value targets in hostile environments. The Prince values experience over theory. Plus, his head of security recommended you."

Mason cut his eyes to the security man again.

Caleb spoke up, his voice steady. "Mason may need time to consider the offer."

Nasir nodded, his expression understanding. "Of course. But the Prince is eager to secure Zane's safety. Time is of the essence."

As they wrapped up the meeting, and while Caleb and Nasir chatted about details, the security agent slid over to Mason's side.

"When I first saw the footage of the shootout with the bikers, I didn't realize that was you. The long hair and the name almost threw me off. Travis

Mason. That's your real name, I suppose?" he said in accented English.

Mason looked into the man's dark eyes. He looked older yet somehow stronger than when he'd last seen him.

"Yep. That's me. And what about you? Are you still going by Ahmed?" Mason asked.

"No. My name is Karim al Rashid," the agent said. "After my father's brother. He was a falconer and bodyguard for King Abdullah the First."

"But didn't King Abdullah get assassinated?" Mason asked.

"Yes. My uncle was a great falconer, but a disgraceful bodyguard," Karim replied.

Mason chuckled, and the two men clasped hands.

"I never thought I'd be shaking your hand on American soil," Mason said.

Karim smiled. "We're a long way from Al-Mazar, my friend. I work for Prince Omar now, and his money grants access everywhere. Mostly just day-to-day protection. Nothing exciting. We're too old for the kinds of operations we used to run back when we were young, am I right, old friend?"

"You're telling me," Mason agreed. "How is it working for the Saudis instead of the Jordanians?"

"Eh," Karim said. "Royals are royals. How can a simple man like myself ever comprehend the mind of a king? I noticed your profile on the GZD website calls you 'former Delta Force.' I found that quite amusing. Do any of these people know the real truth about you?"

Mason rocked back and forth on his heels, his thumbs hooked in his pocket. He looked around warily.

"No," Mason said quietly, "and it's best for everyone to leave it that way."

Karim looked calm.

"I agree, my friend," he said after a pause. "In Arabia we say, 'A secret is like a dove: when it leaves my hand, it takes wing.' Your secret is safe with me."

Mason thought for a moment.

"This is because of you, isn't it? You set up this meeting?" Mason asked.

"As the prince's head of security," Karim answered, "it is my job to employ the best personnel available. I believe I am doing that by offering you this contract. You are the best in the USA. Maybe not in the world. Certainly not in Arabia. But for here, I trust you can handle the job."

Mason chuckled. "It's good to see you, old friend. You've always been a survivor."

"As have you. Peace be upon you, Mason," Karim said with a sly grin. "We will be seeing each other a lot until this circus is complete."

"Peace be with you, too, 'Karim'," Mason replied, and the two men parted ways.

As the helicopter lifted into the sky, Mason stood on the edge of the helipad and watched it go.

"What do you think?" Caleb asked, breaking the silence.

Mason didn't look away. "The Saudis want to hire us to protect a VIP from his own manager. How do you protect a primary from the same people he has to work with every day? I think Zane's in deeper than he knows. And if we take this job, we'll be in it with him."

Caleb nodded. "Big money though. *Huge!*"

Mason's jaw tightened. "Yeah. But we'll be going head-to-head with an entire criminal organization. Again. And that's not something we should do lightly."

Caleb laughed. "When have we ever done things lightly?"

Mason shook his head and chuckled. "Well, shit."

Two days later, Mason stepped off the plane at George Bush Intercontinental Airport in Houston wearing a worn ball cap, blue jeans, and a gray T-shirt. Dark sunglasses concealed his eyes as he scanned the crowded terminal. It had been a while since he'd been back home to Texas, and though the humidity hit him like a wall, the feeling of familiarity washed over him—the feeling of home.

Mason had to wait in the baggage claim area for over an hour before a woman in an airline uniform exited a side door pushing a flatbed dolly. On board, there was a travel kennel. He could hear Bud whimpering inside. Mason walked toward her, holding out his claim ticket, which she took and scanned with a handheld device. It beeped an approval, and she smiled as she handed him the ticket back.

"He's fine," she assured him. "Just ready to stretch his legs."

Mason smiled back.

"Thank you," he said. He opened the kennel and reached in to click a leash onto Bud's collar while the dog licked his hand excitedly.

Once he had Bud secured and the collapsible kennel broken down, the two made their way for the exit, Bud's nails clicking on the waxed floor as they went.

Outside, waiting at the curb was a glossy black Range Rover. Bishop, the Duke's towering bodyguard, stood by the open door, his massive frame impossible to miss. As Mason approached, Bishop gave him a curt nod, but Mason felt a flicker of tension.

"Dog has to go back in the box," the hulking bodyguard said. "In the back."

Mason sighed and looked down at his four-legged friend.

"Sorry, bud. His truck, his rules," Mason said. Bud tipped his head curiously at his words, and only whimpered a little as Mason loaded him back into the kennel and into the rear of the SUV.

With his baggage and dog stowed, Mason climbed into the Range Rover, and they made their way to Zane's training camp at the world-famous Gladiator Farm. As they drove, Mason's mind worked through the logistics of the task ahead. Zane would need round-the-clock protection, and Mason would have to navigate the delicate balance of keeping him safe while not stepping on the Duke's toes—at least, not yet.

Hours later, when they arrived at the sprawling ranch, Mason was impressed by the scale of it.

Zane and Hannah were waiting for him in front of one of the training areas. Mason exited the Rover carrying his duffle bag. He unloaded Bud, opened the kennel, and let the dog finally run free through the grass. The dog ran circles at full speed.

"Mason," Zane said, walking over to shake his hand enthusiastically. "Man, it's great to meet you. You're a living legend. I followed all the coverage of the ambush in Denver years ago. That shit was crazy!"

Mason gave him a firm handshake, assessing the young fighter. "Good to be here. We've got a lot to talk about. Are you ready?"

Zane nodded, his expression serious. "Yes, sure."

"The main thing is keeping you focused on the fight. I'll handle as much as I can, but we both have to be on the same page. Agreed?" Mason asked.

"Sure, yeah," Zane said. "I don't expect to go anywhere while I'm training. We've got everything we need on the farm, so I plan on just being here where it's safe."

At those words, Mason's jaw tightened while Bud was busy sniffing here and there suspiciously.

8

Tier 1

April 2003

Camp Dawson, West Virginia, USA

The crisp mountain air bit into Mason's face as he trudged along the steep, uneven trail. His rucksack felt like it was fused to his back, the 45 pounds of dead weight grinding into his shoulders with each step. The map in his hand, creased and damp with sweat, fluttered slightly in the breeze. His eyes scanned the terrain ahead, noting ridgelines, creeks, and a faint game trail that might save him a few steps—every inch counted.

Mason adjusted his pace, careful to keep it steady. He was hours into the Delta Force selection's infamous "Long Walk," a grueling 40-mile solo trek through the Appalachian wilderness. The terrain was unforgiving, the trails barely marked, and the only lifeline was the map, a compass, and his training. The instructors—ghosts in camouflage—were out there somewhere, watching. Judging. But Mason didn't look for them. He focused on his azimuth, trusting the compass dangling from his neck and the instincts honed during countless land navigation exercises.

"Trust the compass, not your gut," he muttered to himself, the words an echo of lessons drilled into him back at Fort Campbell. The Delta Force didn't care how fast you could run or how heavy you could lift; they cared if you could think under pressure, make decisions, and execute them flawlessly. This was a test of more than endurance—it was a test of will, judgment, and grit.

The faint whistle of the wind in the trees brought Mason back to the moment. He checked his heading again, adjusting slightly to avoid a false peak ahead. He could feel the sweat trickling down his back, soaking his shirt beneath the ruck. His legs burned with every step, but he leaned into the pain. It was familiar, almost comforting—a reminder that he was alive, pushing forward.

The steady rhythm of his boots on the trail brought his mind back to October 2001. He had been just 22, a newly-minted Green Beret assigned to Bravo Company, 2nd Battalion, 5th Special Forces Group—ODA 555, the "Triple Nickel." Their deployment to Afghanistan under Task Force Dagger had been a baptism by fire. Mason had barely unpacked his gear before he found himself on horseback in the rugged terrain of the Hindu Kush, working alongside Northern Alliance fighters to overthrow the Taliban.

Mason adjusted the straps on his ruck, the memory vivid enough to make him smile despite the strain. Riding a horse into battle in the 21st century had felt surreal, but it was also the kind of challenge he'd joined Special Forces for. ODA 555 had been tasked with coordinating airstrikes and leading ground operations—work that demanded precision, adaptability, and raw courage. Mason had thrived in the chaos, earning respect from his team despite being the youngest member.

One night in November 2001 stood out in his mind. They had been pinned down near Mazar-i-Sharif, the Taliban hammering their position with mortars. Mason had crawled through the dirt to reach a fallen Northern Alliance fighter, dragging the man to cover under fire. He had been terrified, but his actions had been instinctive. It wasn't the only close call he'd had in Afghanistan, but it was the one that stuck with him—the moment he knew he could lead, even under the worst conditions.

Mason's boots hit a patch of loose gravel, pulling him out of his reverie. He stumbled but caught himself, his legs screaming in protest. He paused for a moment to pull out the map, orienting it against the ridgeline in the distance. His next waypoint was a stream crossing a mile ahead, marked by a bend in the terrain. He checked his pace against his watch. He was ahead of schedule, but just barely.

"Stay sharp," he muttered, folding the map back into the pocket of his cargo pants.

The Long Walk wasn't just a test of endurance; it was designed to strip you down, to see if you could keep going when every fiber of your being screamed to stop. Mason had heard stories of men breaking down, collapsing just miles from the finish line. But he wasn't going to be one of them.

As the miles ticked by, his thoughts drifted to the reason he was here. The Delta Force recruiters had come to him not long after his return from Afghanistan. They had seen his work with the Triple Nickel, noted his calm under fire, his ability to adapt. At just 24, Mason had been one of the youngest candidates they approached. He had been proud, but also wary. Delta was a different level, a place where the best-of-the-best were constantly tested and failure wasn't an option.

"Why me?" he had asked the recruiter, a grizzled Master Sergeant with a scar running down the side of his face.

"Because you've got it," the man had replied simply. "And you're young and dumb enough to say yes."

Mason chuckled at the memory, his breath fogging in the cool air. Dumb enough, maybe, but also determined. He had something to prove—to himself, to his team, to the ghosts of Mazar-i-Sharif that still haunted his dreams.

He crested another ridge, his legs screaming with the effort, and paused to catch his breath. From here, he could see the landscape stretching out below—a patchwork of forest and open fields, bisected by a glinting ribbon of water. In the distance, he spotted a structure that looked out of place—a dilapidated warehouse sitting at the edge of a clearing. It wasn't marked on his map, but it caught his attention.

His instincts flared. In Afghanistan, they had learned to read the land like a book, to notice things that didn't belong. He didn't know if the warehouse was part of the course or just an abandoned relic of the past, but he noted its position before moving on. The Delta instructors were known for throwing curveballs, and Mason wasn't about to be caught off guard.

The sun was starting to dip lower in the sky, the shadows stretching long across the trail. Mason could feel the weight of the ruck pulling him down with every step, but he refused to slow. He thought of his team back at the Triple Nickel, the men who had trusted him to have their backs. He thought of the Delta recruiters, who had seen something in him he hadn't seen in himself. And he thought of the finish line, just a few miles ahead.

"Keep moving," he told himself, his voice a low growl. "One step at a time."

The Long Walk was a crucible, a trial by fire that would determine if he had what it took to stand among the best. Mason didn't know what the future held—only that he was willing to endure whatever it took to get there. He had faced the mountains of Afghanistan, the chaos of combat, the doubts and fears that had threatened to overwhelm him.

This was just another mountain. And Mason was going to climb it.

The final steps of the Long Walk were a blur for Mason. His body moved on pure willpower, his legs trembling under the unrelenting weight of the rucksack. The trail had given way to a dirt road lined with trees, their branches arching over him like a tunnel. In the distance, he could make out the faint outline of the checkpoint—a small clearing with a few vehicles, instructors standing casually, clipboards in hand.

His pulse roared in his ears as he forced his legs to keep moving, each step an act of defiance against the pain. He didn't think about the time, the distance, or the others who had started the trek with him. All that mattered was crossing the line.

As he stumbled into the clearing, an instructor glanced at his watch and made a note on the clipboard. Mason came to a halt, standing at attention despite the protest of his muscles, his chest heaving as he tried to catch his breath.

The instructor, a stone-faced Master Sergeant, looked up. "Number 24. Time: within the standard. Drop your ruck and wait over there."

Mason didn't respond, simply nodding as he unclipped the straps and let the ruck fall to the ground with a dull thud. The relief was immediate but fleeting. He knew this was just one step in a much longer process.

He joined the other candidates who had finished, their faces a mix of exhaustion and quiet determination. The Long Walk was over, but the real tests were just beginning.

The following days were a whirlwind of psychological evaluations. Mason found himself sitting in sterile rooms, answering endless questions from psychologists, behavioral specialists, and instructors. They dug into every corner of his mind, probing his motivations, his fears, his moral compass.

"What makes you think you're suited for this unit?" one evaluator asked, his pen poised over a notepad.

Mason met the man's gaze, his voice steady despite the fatigue that still clung to him. "I've been tested in combat. I know how to think under pressure, how to adapt. And I don't quit."

The evaluator didn't react, simply jotting something down before moving on to the next question. Mason could feel their eyes on him constantly, analyzing every word, every gesture. It wasn't just about physical endurance anymore—it was about proving he had the mental toughness and the psychological stability to operate in the most demanding environments imaginable.

At night, lying on a narrow cot in the barracks, Mason replayed the questions in his mind, wondering if he had said enough, or if he had said too much. But he forced himself to push the doubts aside. Worry wouldn't help him now.

When the list of candidates who had passed the selection phase was posted, Mason stood among them, his name inked on the page alongside a handful of others. The group had been whittled down from 100 men to just 8. The men who remained were a mix of battle-hardened soldiers and quiet professionals. He was one of them. He had made it to Tier 1.

The next phase was the Operators Training Course (OTC), a six-month gauntlet designed to turn raw recruits into Delta operators. Mason approached it with the same focus he had during the Long Walk, knowing that every moment was a chance to learn, to prove himself, to earn his place.

The final day of OTC was marked by a quiet sense of anticipation. Mason and the other candidates stood in formation, their faces sharp and their uniforms immaculate. They had spent months honing their skills—marksmanship, explosives, close-quarters combat, advanced land navigation, and a host of other disciplines that set Delta operators apart. They had been pushed to their limits and beyond, molded into something more.

A Colonel stepped forward, his voice steady and authoritative. "You've completed one of the most challenging selection and training processes in the world. You've proven that you have the skill, the endurance, and the mindset to stand among the best. From this day forward, you are no longer candidates. You are operators. Welcome to the Unit."

The words hit Mason like a bolt of lightning. He stood taller, his chest swelling with pride as the weight of what he had achieved settled over him. This was the culmination of years of training, of sacrifice, of pushing himself past every limit.

He had made it.

As the ceremony concluded, Mason felt a hand on his shoulder. He turned to see one of the instructors, a grizzled veteran who had barely spoken a word during OTC. The man's face was unreadable, but there was a glint of approval in his eyes.

"Good work, Mason," the instructor said simply. "You'll do well here."

Mason nodded, the words resonating deeply. He knew the journey wasn't over—far from it. Being part of Delta Force meant constant training, constant challenges. But for the first time, he felt like he was exactly where he was meant to be.

The next morning, Mason stood in the quiet confines of the briefing room, the air thick with anticipation. He was one of the newest operators in the Unit, fresh out of OTC, and today he would learn where he would be assigned. The room hummed with subdued energy as senior leaders filtered in, their presence commanding respect without a single word spoken.

At the front of the room stood Lieutenant Colonel Avery, the commanding officer overseeing Delta's selection and integration process. He surveyed the room, his steely gaze cutting through the silence.

"Congratulations to each of you," Avery began, his voice steady and deliberate. "You've completed a process few even dare to attempt. But make no mistake—this is only the beginning. You've been chosen because you meet the Unit's standard, and now you'll join the teams that carry out the missions no one else can."

He paused, letting the weight of his words settle over the room before continuing. "Assignments to the squadrons have been made. When I call your name, step forward."

One by one, names were read aloud, each operator stepping forward to receive their assignment. Mason stood motionless, his hands clasped behind his back, his expression neutral despite the anticipation burning inside him.

"Sergeant Mason," Avery called, his eyes meeting Mason's as he gestured toward him.

Mason stepped forward, standing at attention. Avery handed him a sealed folder, its weight symbolic of the responsibility that came with it.

"B Squadron," Avery said simply. "Report to your troop commander at 1300. Welcome to the Unit."

"Yes, sir," Mason replied, his voice calm but firm.

As he returned to his seat, the reality of the moment began to sink in. B Squadron—one of the Unit's most storied and active squadrons. He had heard the rumors, the legends about the operators who served there, their exploits whispered about in the quiet corners of military circles. Now, he was one of them.

At 1300 sharp, Mason stood outside the B Squadron ready room, the sealed folder tucked under his arm. The door opened, and a tall, broad-shouldered man with salt-and-pepper hair and a commanding presence stepped out. His name tape read "JENSEN," and his rank insignia marked him as a Master Sergeant.

"You Mason?" Jensen asked, his voice gruff but not unkind.

"Yes, Master Sergeant," Mason replied.

Jensen nodded, gesturing for Mason to follow him inside. The ready room was a hive of activity—operators in various stages of preparation, checking gear, running over maps, or sharing quiet conversations. The atmosphere was different from anything Mason had experienced before—focused, efficient, but with an undercurrent of camaraderie.

"This is your team," Jensen said, stopping in front of a group of men who were gathered around a table spread with maps and intel packets. "Triple Six Troop. They're a tight-knit bunch, but they'll break you in."

The men looked up as Jensen introduced Mason, their expressions ranging from mild curiosity to outright indifference. One of them, a wiry man with sharp eyes and a scar running down his cheek, stood and extended a hand.

"Name's Pierce," he said, his grip firm. "I'm your team leader. Welcome to Triple Six."

Mason shook his hand, nodding at the others as introductions were made. The team was diverse—each operator bringing a unique set of skills to the table—but there was a common thread of professionalism that bound them together.

The rest of the day was a blur of briefings and introductions, each moment driving home the reality of Mason's new role. B Squadron wasn't just a unit—it was a brotherhood, forged in the crucible of missions few would ever hear about.

As the sun set over Fort Bragg, Mason found himself sitting in the Squadron's quiet lounge, a cup of black coffee in hand. The weight of the day's events pressed down on him, but it was a weight he welcomed. He had earned his place here, and now it was time to prove himself all over again.

For Mason, this wasn't the end of the journey—it was the beginning of a new one. And he was ready.

9

A Cold Welcome

April 2023

River Oaks, Houston, Texas, USA

Michael drove his candy blue convertible 1985 Cadillac Eldorado Biarritz on 15-inch "swangas"—wire spoked rims that poked out from the whitewall tires—slowly down Westheimer Avenue. At the stoplights, he let the deep bass and smooth flow of Tre the Truth play loud, drowning out the buzz of the city while he ignored the stares of the wealthy soccer moms who passed in their luxury SUVs. He made a few turns down neighborhood streets lined with walls and immaculate grounds, then pulled through the main gate of his father's sprawling River Oaks estate. Michael parked near a fountain, got out, and strode toward the towering front doors. The massive white structure of his father's mansion loomed ahead.

The towering front doors were opened by servants. Inside, the air was thick with the scent of oil paint and cigar smoke. The soulful voice of Al Green echoed through the high-ceilinged spaces. Michael walked through the grand hallway, his polished shoes clicking against the marble floors as he made his way to his father's study. There, he paused at the doorway.

The Duke stood before a giant canvas at least 10-feet tall. His silk shirt, opened to the waist, was speckled with paint, and he held a long paintbrush in one hand and a glass of cognac in the other. His latest girlfriend—a 20-something model, as usual—sat poised on a velvet sofa like a house cat, her toffee-colored legs tucked under her, scrolling on her phone. A cigar sat smoldering in a marble ashtray on a table, and Bishop's hulking frame sat in a corner.

Bishop nodded at Michael when he walked in, cutting his eyes and tilting his head slightly toward the Duke. Michael followed his gaze as he strolled around to see what his father was working on.

He almost choked, then sighed and shook his head. On the canvas was a surreal, almost grotesque depiction of the Duke, bare-chested, kneeling behind a woman on all fours whose lower half was also bare. The Duke had a cigar in his mouth and was gripping her hips tightly as he thrust into her. His expression was one of gloating, as if he'd just won big at the crap's table, while her face was twisted in pain or pleasure, he couldn't tell.

Michael's fists flexed in frustration. "Pop! What the hell is that?"

The painting was detailed and accurate, so there was no mistaking who was depicted. It was the wife of a well-known Houston rapper, Big Caz, whose violent rivalry with the Duke had lasted for two years and claimed lives on both sides. Michael had negotiated a treaty between the Duke and the rapper just two months prior, and the painting was an obvious provocation.

The Duke didn't look up from his work, calmly dabbing paint onto the canvas. "I really captured her face, didn't I?"

Michael stepped closer, his voice rising in disbelief. "We agreed the problems with Big Caz were over, Pop. We squashed that beef. Why are you stirring it up again with this shit?"

"Shit? This is a motha' fuckin' masterpiece!" the Duke shouted.

Then, with a deep breath, he smoothed out his silk shirt and addressed Michael more calmly. "Michael, Michael, Michael. My only son. My only, only son. You still don't understand, do you? It's not about beef. It's about control. Big Caz may be safe, but this…" He gestured to the painting with his brush. "This reminds him I still own his as—and all this city."

"Pop, you're going to start some shit we don't need right now," Michael snapped. "This fight with Zane is bringing in millions. I've got a meeting about merchandising this afternoon. We don't need to be fucking with some rapper who's not looking for beef with us and truthfully is out the game anyway."

The Duke's eyes flashed with amusement. "You know what your problem is? You got a good mind and education and all that shit, but you don't got good instincts. Not like me. But that's because you grew up in the rich neighborhoods with the rick kids. When you grow up in the hood, like me, you learn different shit, shit they can't teach you in school. Only the streets can teach you this shit. See, you're smart, but you're too cautious. Treaties and alliances ain't about peace. They're about us knowing that the other side was too scared to keep fighting. A motha' fucka' like Caz will never scream 'Time out!' or 'Peace!' if he's winning the fight, ya' dig? If he's whoopin' yo' ass, he's gonna keep on whoopin' yo' ass. So, if he says he wants peace, it's because you whoopin' *his* ass. Peace treaties show weakness, and you supposed to attack your enemies at their weakest. Sun Tzu said that. But you don't even know who that is, with yo' soft ass."

Michael stared at his father, the growing tension between them threatening to explode.

"Of course, I know who Sun Tzu was, Pop. But I won't sit back and let you ruin the deal with Caz," Michael said firmly, standing his ground.

The Duke's gaze hardened. He dropped the paintbrush carelessly into the ashtray, then wiped his hands on his shirt. "You won't *'let'* me?" he repeated, his tone growing colder. "Boy, you don't *'let'* me do shit. Who do you think built all this?"

Michael took a deep breath, trying to control his anger. "You're right, Pop. My bad. So, what's the plan? You gonna send that painting to Big Caz and start a war right as the Zane fight is coming up?"

The Duke gave a low chuckle. "No. I changed my mind. Bishop, hang this in the front entryway so guests see it first thing when they walk in. It'll be a great reminder for everyone."

Michael ran a hand over his face in frustration. "A reminder of what?"

"That we're not just playing for money or titles," the Duke said, his voice menacing. "We're playing for respect. Because in this world, without respect, you won't hold onto that money or title for very long."

"And who said that?" Michael asked. "Machiavelli?"

The Duke smiled and took a sip of cognac.

"Nah, motha' fucka," he growled. "The Duke said that, and don't you fuckin' forget it."

Mason and Zane arrived at the Duke's mansion in Houston, pulling up in the black Range Rover the Duke had loaned them. As they exited the vehicle, Mason's sharp eyes scanned the grounds. The mansion was pristine, surrounded by manicured lawns and guarded by numerous video cameras. Zane, on the other hand, was more relaxed, his eyes wide as he took in the grandeur of the Duke's estate.

They were escorted inside by the Duke's bodyguard, a silent, hulking figure who led them down the marble-floored hallway into a large, elegantly decorated sitting room. The Duke and Michael were already there, waiting.

The Duke, dressed in another one of his signature silk shirts, leaned back in a plush armchair, his eyes sharp as they settled on Mason. Michael, standing by a window, glanced briefly at Zane but quickly shifted his gaze to Mason, a hint of displeasure flickering across his face.

"The legendary Mason," the Duke greeted him, his voice smooth. "I remember you from the news. I didn't expect to ever see you in my home."

Mason, ever the professional, gave a polite nod. "I'm here on request of the Prince for Zane's protection."

The Duke's smile didn't reach his eyes. "Of course. We all want Zane to be safe. But I can't help but feel you're a bit of an... over-extension."

Mason remained calm, his expression neutral. "When the stakes are this high, you can never be too careful."

Zane shifted uncomfortably beside Mason. "Look, I just want to make sure everything's good. Mason's here to help me stay focused on the fight. That's all."

Michael's eyes narrowed slightly, but he stayed silent, letting his father take the lead.

The Duke moved slowly across the room, his gaze never leaving Mason. "I've been in this game for a long time, Mason. I understand the need for protection. But I also know when someone's presence could be disruptive."

Mason didn't flinch. "I'm here to make sure Zane gets to the ring in one piece. That's all."

The Duke stopped in front of Mason, his posture relaxed but his presence imposing. "Let's hope you're a man of your word. Zane's future is tied to this fight, and that means he's tied to me. We all need to play our parts."

Mason locked eyes with the Duke, his tone unflinching. "I play my part better than most."

For a brief moment, the room seemed to freeze, the tension thickening as the Duke and Mason sized each other up. Then, just as quickly, the Duke's smile returned.

"Well then," the Duke said, his voice a touch lighter, his smirk as cold as the grave, "let's make sure Zane gets everything he needs. At the ranch, there's the apartment above the garage for you to stay in, and you've already got keys to a Range Rover. We want to make sure you feel right at home."

The Duke flashed a big grin, but Mason couldn't help but feel he was looking into the jaws of the big bad wolf himself.

10

Snow in the Tropics

The sky over Belize

The private jet sliced through the thick, humid air, its engines humming low as it descended toward Belize. Mason sat near the back quietly watching. His eyes scanned the horizon, then shifted to Zane, Hannah, and Michael seated up front. Michael was flipping through a magazine while Zane leaned back.

"We'll be on the ground soon," Michael said, closing the magazine. "Just follow me. Everything's taken care of."

The plane touched down at Philip S. W. Goldson Airport, the tires bouncing slightly before rolling smoothly to a stop. Zane shifted in his seat, glancing out the window at the jungle creeping up from the distance.

As they disembarked, a hulking, bald man with bulging muscles and a chrome pistol tucked into his waistband approached. He clapped hands with Michael.

"What's up, Tank?" Michael teased. "Damn, leave some creatine for the rest of us, big bro."

Tank didn't smile or react. His eyes, cold and detached, swept over Zane and then Mason.

"This is Tank, our head of security here in Belize," Michael said, still grinning. "He'll take care of you."

Zane nodded at Tank, who just stared back, expressionless.

Mason gave Tank a quick once-over. The man was built like his name, all right, but Mason noted the tension in his shoulders as well as the exposed 1911.

After a two-hour drive along the Western Highway, the Range Rover rolled to a stop in front of a white walled compound with tall wrought-iron gates. Mason leaned forward, eyes narrowing as the gates creaked open, revealing the Duke's Belizean estate. It was a fortress disguised as paradise, the jungle closing in on all sides, and high walls draped in vines that didn't quite hide the cameras and watchtowers perched above.

Mason's eyes flicked to the watchtower. A guard stood there, AK-47 rifle slung casually over his shoulder, scanning the grounds below. More armed men with radios strolled near the gate. Hannah didn't seem to notice, too distracted by the lush gardens and sparkling pool beyond. Mason's gut tightened.

"This place is incredible," Hannah whispered.

Tank parked near the grand entrance of the main house. Servants appeared instantly, helping them out of the vehicle with practiced, respectful movements. Mason stepped out last, taking a slow glance around the property. The security was tight—too tight for a mere vacation property. His eyes tracked the guards along the wall, the cameras sweeping silently, and his attention lingered on a large building, like a barn or storehouse, near the back of the compound. Something about all of it felt off.

"Welcome to paradise," Michael grinned, gesturing toward the pool where iguanas lounged casually. "Ignore the 'pool puppies'. They come with the territory."

Hannah squealed, already filming the reptiles on her phone. "Look at them! They're so cute!"

Zane gave a half-smile. He seemed uneasy. Mason watched him closely, noting the tension in his shoulders, the way his eyes kept darting to the armed guards. He wasn't the only one feeling it.

"Come on, man," Michael said, slapping Zane on the back. "I've got everything set up for you. Time to unwind."

They were led into the main house, and even Mason had to admit it was impressive. Marble floors gleamed under soft lighting, and tall windows framed stunning views of the gardens. The air smelled faintly of flowers and rich wood.

Hannah wandered ahead, awe-struck by the grandeur. "This place is amazing, baby! We're going to have the best time."

Michael led them to a wide terrace overlooking the pool. The jungle stretched out beyond the wall, dense and alive with the sounds of tropical birds.

Mason stood at the edge of the terrace, his back to the house. His eyes traced the perimeter. The walls were high, but the cameras could see everything. He noticed a single stone path leading away from the main building toward the warehouse. His instincts buzzed.

Later, after setting their bags in the guest rooms upstairs, they gathered in the high-ceilinged living room. Michael poured himself a drink from a tray. "Look, Zane. You've earned this. Time to relax."

Zane forced a smile, but Mason could see the wheels turning in his head. He was feeling the same pressure. Something wasn't right, but no one was saying it.

"To a great time in paradise," Michael toasted, raising his glass. Zane clinked glasses with him, but Mason hung back, observing.

A couple of hours later, the wind whipped through Zane's hair as the speedboat cut across the turquoise waters of the Caribbean. The late afternoon sun dipped low on the horizon, casting a warm golden light over the waves. Hannah was at the bow, laughing, her arms raised in the air as the boat skipped over the swells, her white bikini accentuating her curves. Michael was at the front with her, leaning against the rail, grinning broadly as his white linen shirt flapped in the wind. Mason sat in the rear wearing cargo shorts and a floral print shirt, watching silently. Due to international laws, he was armed only with a cell phone. Tank, on the other hand, sat across from him, the chrome pistol peaking from his waistband.

Ahead, the silhouette of a cay came into view, the white sand beach gleaming against the deepening blue of the ocean. When the boat finally slowed and pulled up to a wooden dock, Zane couldn't help but admire the scene. Palm trees swayed gently in the breeze, and a beachside restaurant with thatched roofs and twinkling string lights awaited them. The smell of grilling seafood and the sound of island music drifted across the water.

As they stepped off the boat, a waiter in a loose shirt and sandals greeted them, directing them to a table set right on the sand. It was like a postcard, and for a moment, Zane let go of his worries.

They sat at a long wooden table surrounded by torches, where platters of fresh lobster and grilled fish were brought out, the seafood smothered in butter and garlic. Cold tropical drinks arrived next, colorful cocktails decorated with slices of pineapple and umbrellas, and Zane found himself laughing with Hannah and Michael, the tension from earlier dissolving under the island's spell. Music played softly in the background, and for a moment, Zane thought of his father growing up in Jamaica.

"I could stay here forever," Hannah said, leaning into Zane with a blissful smile, a flower in her hair, her fingers toying with the stem of her drink.

Zane smiled and kissed her on the cheek, the sharp taste of rum and pineapple still on his tongue. "Me, too."

Michael, already a few drinks deep, raised his glass. "To paradise! This is what it's all about."

They clinked glasses, and Zane took another long drink, the alcohol buzzing through him, relaxing muscles he didn't even realize were tense. The seafood was perfect, and as the sun disappeared and the moon rose over the water, the atmosphere grew even more magical.

After dinner, they walked up the beach to a small bar where locals and expats mingled in the open-air space. Dance Hall music blasted from a set of old speakers, and a makeshift dance floor had formed on the sand. The bar was a mix of tourists and regulars, and the night was filled with laughter and dancing.

Suddenly, Michael grabbed Hannah's hand and stood. "Come on, let's dance!"

Hannah, looking surprised, stood up. Then, as an after-thought, she turned to Zane.

"Do you mind?" she asked.

"Nah, go ahead," Zane replied.

But before Zane could say more, Michael had dragged her— giggling— to the dance floor.

Zane chuckled, playing it off as cool as he could, but there was something about Michael's easy confidence that rubbed him the wrong way.

He grabbed another drink from the bar, sipping on it as he watched Hannah and Michael dance together. They moved effortlessly to the rhythm of the music, Michael spinning her and laughing, his hand on her waist. Hannah was having the time of her life, her face lit up with joy as the two of them swayed under the moonlight.

He sipped his drink, his eyes flicking back and forth between the crowd and the dance floor, trying to focus on anything other than the sight of Hannah laughing with Michael.

As the night wore on, the drinks kept flowing, and Zane found himself leaning against the bar, the tension slowly melting away with the alcohol. He couldn't deny the beauty of the place—the warmth of the night air, the sound of the ocean just beyond the sand, and the carefree energy of the locals and expats dancing under the stars. Mason made his rounds, evaluating the various guests, keeping a close eye on ones who seemed a little too drunk or a little too friendly. But he kept a closer eye on Tank, who mostly stayed near the boat.

Hannah eventually broke away from Michael, her face flushed and her eyes bright as she made her way back to Zane. "You okay, babe?"

Zane smiled and put his on her hip, pulling her close. "Yeah. Just enjoying the show."

She kissed him on the cheek, her breath warm with the scent of rum and fruit. "I'm having the best time."

Zane nodded, relaxing a little more as the night continued. The jealousy that had flared up earlier was still there, but it was quieter now, dulled by the drinks and the perfect tropical setting. Michael, meanwhile, was already back on the dance floor, spinning a local woman with the same effortless charm he always had. Mason watched from the shadows, sipping a bottled water, wondering why a fighter in training would need a vacation, but also remembering his place.

By the time they returned to the estate, the moon hung high in the sky, casting silver light over the sprawling property. Zane and Hannah stumbled up the steps, still laughing as they entered the grand living room, where dim lighting and cool air welcomed them back.

Michael dismissed Mason and Tank for the evening, assuring them all of the guests were in for the night. Uneasily, Mason agreed and headed upstairs to shower.

After releasing the bodyguards, Michael casually strolled into the living room with a wide grin. "You two are gonna love this," he said, moving toward a bar in the corner of the room.

Zane, still trying to sober up from the night, glanced at Hannah, who was twirling a strand of her hair and giggling to herself. She was still riding the high of the evening, her cheeks flushed, her eyes sparkling.

Michael returned, holding a glass dish in his hand, a mischievous glint in his eyes. He set it down on the coffee table and lifted the glass lid with a flourish, revealing a pile of shimmering white powder inside.

Zane's stomach tightened.

"Whoa," Hannah said, leaning in closer, her eyes wide. "Is that all...?"

Michael grinned and nodded. "You know it! Only the finest, purest powder. They call it fish scale because of how the flakes shine. Straight from Colombia."

Zane stared at the dish, feeling his good mood evaporate. "Seriously, man? I'm training for the biggest fight of my life, and you're pulling out cocaine?"

Michael chuckled. "Relax, Zane. Just hit a little bump. Trust me, it won't hurt your training."

Hannah, her eyes wide with excitement, glanced at Zane. "Come on, babe. It's just for fun."

But Zane shook his head, stepping back, feeling the weight of the night suddenly press down on him. "I can't. Not with everything coming up. I'm already under enough pressure."

Michael leaned forward, his voice dropping into a conspiratorial tone. "Zane, let me tell you something. You know how many belts I won, right?"

Zane frowned but nodded.

"Well, guess what? I was higher than New York rent every time I stepped into the ring." Michael's eyes gleamed with a wild energy. "How else do you think I stayed on top? Trust me, man. You'll feel like a god."

Zane felt his pulse quicken, his instincts screaming at him to walk away. "I'm good, bro."

Michael shrugged, nonchalant. "Your choice. But I'm telling you, every fighter's got something in their system."

Zane clenched his jaw.

"Nah, bro, I'm good," Zane said firmly, stepping away from the table. "It's bad enough I drank tonight. I've got the fight to think about."

Hannah hesitated for a moment, glancing between Zane and the dish. She was weighing her options, the temptation written all over her face.

Zane looked at her, his voice softening. "You coming with me, or...?"

But before Hannah could respond, Michael slid in, his grin as charming as ever. "She's just having fun, Zane. No harm in that. We're here to blow off some steam."

Hannah bit her lip, then smiled sheepishly. "It's just one night, baby."

Zane's chest tightened, but he allowed her a small nod.

Michael and Hannah snorted coke, laughed, and talked the night away. They tried to include Zane, but he wasn't interested and soon felt his energy wane. Eventually, he bid them goodnight. Hannah gave him a hug and promised to be along shortly. He could still hear their laughter behind him as he made his way down the hall to the staircase, and it grated on his nerves. He wanted to shake off the feeling—the jealousy, the worry—but it clung to him.

As Zane reached the bedroom, he lay down, staring at the ceiling. The sounds of the jungle outside were faint, almost drowned out by the distant murmur of Michael and Hannah's laughter from the living room. He closed his eyes, but sleep didn't come easily that night.

Just down the hall, Mason was standing at his window, mentally sketching out the layout of the compound, wondering what was inside the warehouse.

11

Mending Fences

Katy, Texas, USA

The sun had barely risen as Mason pulled the borrowed Range Rover off the road and into the parking lot of a diner in Katy, a suburb west of Houston. Bud rode in the passenger seat, sitting on a towel to protect the leather. He allowed Mason to leash him, then hopped out when he opened the door. Mason led the dog to the front of the restaurant, then secured him to a sign post next to the door. Bud loved to sit and watch cars and pedestrians go by.

The door chimed as Mason stepped inside, the inviting smell of sizzling bacon and fresh coffee greeted him, and he could hear the low hum of conversation and clinking dishes. The restaurant was brightly lit, the walls covered in photos of local little league teams and banners supporting the city's state champion high school football team. It was the kind of place where locals gathered for breakfast and lunch—nothing fancy, just good food and a laid-back atmosphere.

He took a seat at one of the wooden tables in the back. A laminated menu was already there, and he was browsing the options—omelets, pancakes, and patty melts—when he heard a soft voice.

"Hey, there."

Mason looked up. A waitress was standing next to him, a friendly smile on her face. She was brunette, around 30 years old, with soft features and warm brown eyes that sparkled in the light. Her hair was done up in a messy bun with a ballpoint pen stuck through it, and Mason couldn't help but notice how her jeans hugged her hips.

"Hi, I'm Lisa," she said. "You want coffee or maybe fresh squeezed orange juice?"

She gestured toward the menu with a grin. Her teeth were bright white, and her eyes tilted up when she smiled. The scent of her floral perfume drifted around him, enveloping him in a sweet cloud.

Mason's mouth went dry. "Coffee, please. Black."

"Coffee it is. I'll give you a minute to look over the menu."

She smiled again, her eyes twinkling as she held his gaze just a moment longer, then she turned and walked toward the kitchen. As she walked away, Mason found himself watching her hair bounce and her hips sway.

When she returned with his water, she stood beside the table, and Mason felt a lightness wash over him, as if he could float out of his seat.

"So," she said, glancing at the menu in his hand. "Figured out what you want yet?"

Mason looked at her, not thinking about the menu. Her perfume and the nearness of her body caused him to sit up taller in his seat. "I'm still deciding."

Lisa tilted her head, smiling playfully. "No rush. But I'd recommend the Colorado omelet—best in town."

"Yeah? You sound pretty confident about that," Mason said, matching her smile.

"I am. I would never steer you wrong," she replied.

Mason chuckled. "Alright. I'll trust you on the omelet then."

Lisa jotted down his order, but before she walked away, she hesitated, glancing at him with a curious look. "You from around here? I haven't seen you in here before."

Mason shook his head. "Just in town for work. But I'm liking it so far."

She gave him another warm smile. "Well, you've got good taste."

As Mason ate, he watched Lisa flitting about the diner, topping off coffee mugs and causing tables of older men in coveralls and flannel shirts to laugh uproariously. She left every table she visited with smiles and more than one old boy red-cheeked and flustered. Mason was amazed at her easy nature. After he was done eating, she strolled over with a playful look in her eye.

"Can I get you anything else, stranger?" she asked, her dimples lighting up her face.

"Well, now that you mention it," Mason said. "While I'm here, I'd love to see more of what the city has to offer. Do you have any suggestions?"

"Well," she said. "I may not be the best to ask. I don't get out to do fun stuff too often."

"Really?" Mason replied. "Why's that?"

"Work, work, work," she said, a strand of brown hair falling into her face. She gently brushed it behind her ear. "Plus, who would take me out?"

"Um, judging by the number of fans you have in here, I think this entire diner would love to take you out," Mason said.

Lisa laughed. "Well, I try to date men who were born *after* the Second World War. Most of these guys are like dads or uncles to me."

"Well, I'd be honored if you'd show me around," Mason said. "I bet both of us could use a break."

Lisa's cheeks flushed. She stood up straight, her eyes darting around as she struggled to respond.

"I mean...um..." she stuttered.

"Or I guess I can just eat here more often, if that's what it takes to see you again," he said.

"Oh, man," Lisa said under her breath. "I better get you your check."

With that, she spun and walked away to the register. Mason felt the butterflies in his stomach turn into a stabbing, icy fist. She's probably not single, he thought.

When Lisa returned to clear his plate, she handed him the check, her smile a little more reserved this time. "You know, I usually don't do this," she said, pulling out a pen and writing something on the check. "But if it turns out you might be sticking around a little longer, give me a call if you want some more suggestions of where to eat or whatever."

Mason looked down at the check, seeing her number scribbled in the corner. His heart skipped.

"Yeah, sure, I will do that," Mason said.

As he stood up to leave, Lisa flashed him one last smile. "Don't take too long though."

Mason smiled back, tipped the brim of his hat to her, then stood and walked to the cashier at the front to pay the bill. His body crackled with an energy he hadn't felt in years.

In the parking lot, Mason untied Bud and slipped him some bits of ham and sausage from a napkin in his pocket. The dog ate it greedily. They climbed into the Range Rover, the memory of Lisa's perfume still lingering when Mason's phone buzzed in his pocket. He pulled it out. The message snapped him back to reality.

"Check your secure email," the text message read. It was from an old friend, former detective and now FBI Special Agent Kim Wright.

His smile faded as the weight of his work came rushing back. Pretty waitresses would have to wait. Sitting in the quiet of the SUV, he retrieved a tablet from the glove compartment. His fingers tapped the screen as he opened his Protonmail account.

There was an email from Kim marked urgent.

"Immediate Threat Assessment—The Duke," the subject line read.

Mason's eyes narrowed as he opened the attachment and he scanned the text.

Profile Overview:

- Name: Luther Nathaniel Davis a/k/a "The Duke"

- DOB: September 12, 1958

- Affiliations: Fifth Ward criminal syndicate; extensive ties to Houston's underground

- Previous Convictions: Aggravated Robbery (First Deg. Felony): Sentence — 12 YR; Manslaughter (Second Deg. Felony): Sentence — 4 YR

- Suspected Criminal Operations: Money laundering, drug trafficking, extortion, robbery, kidnapping, murder.

- Notable Incidents: Multiple unconfirmed but suspected homicides.

Numerous reports of witness intimidation and suspected bribes to law enforcement.

- Recent Activity: Expanding influence into Belize under the guise of real estate and ranching operations. Intel suggests drug trafficking, human trafficking, and other high-risk criminal activity.

Following the report there were numerous pages of news articles, photos, and witness testimony about murders, robberies, missing people, and wars with other gangsters lasting years, causing death and destruction across Houston and the entire U. S. The Duke had connections from Sinaloa to Chicago. His entertainment management business had created several world champion boxers and platinum selling rap artists over the years. He rubbed shoulders with the highest in society as well as the lowest and had been considered the underworld boss of Houston for at least 20 years, a position he defended viciously.

Mason leaned back in the seat, his mind racing. He had known the Duke was dangerous, but the breadth of his reach and the severity of the violence was even more than he had expected. And now Zane was tangled up in the middle of it, unknowingly walking deeper into the Duke's web with every step.

He shut down the tablet. The interior of the SUV suddenly felt claustrophobic. Taking a deep breath, Mason put the device away and started the engine.

As he drove away from the restaurant, the morning sun beaming, Lisa's smile briefly crossed his mind, but it was soon drowned out by the urgency of the mission ahead.

Houston faded into Mason's rearview mirror as the cement sprawl gave way to towering pine forests. Highway 59 North stretched out like an asphalt river before him, flowing northeast into the Piney Woods of East Texas.

After an hour's drive, Mason exited the highway and turned down a narrow, red dirt county road leading through the woods to a modest farm. There was a simple brick house, a corrugated tin shed, and an old wooden barn tucked at the back of the property. Mason pulled the SUV to a stop next to a beat-up white Kenworth T2000 DayCab backed into the dirt driveway. The big truck looked like it hadn't moved in at least a decade.

Mason stepped out of the vehicle, opened the door for Bud to jump out, and walked toward the farm house, listening. Over the windchime clinking on the porch, he heard the sound of tools clanging from the backyard, the smell of diesel faint in the air. As he rounded the back corner of the house with Bud at his side, he saw him—an older man wearing blue coveralls. He was hunched over a tractor, his hands black with grease, his thin white hair standing up wildly. George Jones played on the radio, and a bottle of Jim Beam sat on a workbench next to a Mason jar.

Mason paused, watching the man work for a moment. His hands were shaking as he tried to screw the cup back on an external fuel filter without success. Cursing, the older man straightened up, wiped the back of his hand across his brow, and then squinted when he caught sight of Mason. He stared for a moment, then waved a liver-spotted hand at the tractor.

"Well, you gonna stand there all day, or you gonna get your ass over here?" the man said, his voice rough and gravelly.

Mason sighed then walked toward him. When he reached the tractor, the white-haired man pointed at a hydraulic hose.

"Hold that damn line out the way while I reattach the god damn filter," he ordered.

Mason didn't argue. He leaned over, holding the black hose out of the way as instructed, the smell of diesel filling his nostrils.

"Hold it steady," the man barked, wrenching the fuel filter into place.

Mason complied, keeping the line taut as the older man continued to mutter under his breath.

"Now, we've gotta bleed the line," he said, stepping back and wiping his shaky hands on a rag. "You still remember how to crank a diesel?"

"Yep," Mason replied.

He climbed up into the tractor's cab and plopped into the seat. He pressed the clutch, twisted the key, and the diesel engine cranked three times, then rumbled to life. It sputtered for a moment as the older man allowed the air to vacate the fuel line before tightening the filter cup the rest of the way. The engine evened out, filling the barn with a steady rumble.

The older man nodded to himself, a flicker of satisfaction crossing his face before he waved Mason off. "Alright, kill it."

Mason turned off the engine and climbed down. In the sudden silence, he could feel the tension between them thickening like the smoke from the engine. The older man tossed the rag onto the workbench. His gaze drifted toward the bottle of Jim Beam and the empty Mason jar on the work bench. For a moment, the only sound was the faint creak of the barn's metal roof popping as it warmed in the sun.

"Well," the older man grunted, wiping his hands once more before leaning back against the tractor, "you didn't say you was comin'. I only brought out one glass."

Mason just stood there, thumbs hooked in his pockets. The man in front of him hadn't changed much. His face was older, more lined, and his hair was pure white, but his tone and the hard set of his jaw was exactly as Mason remembered.

"I quit drinking," Mason said. "I was nearby. Figured I'd stop by and check on you."

The older man snorted. "Doin' fine without you."

Mason's jaw tightened.

"Maybe so," he said, "but I'm here now."

The man squinted at him, his lips pressed into a thin, disapproving line. He took a sip of his drink. Finally, the older man grunted again and turned his back, grabbed a pack of cigarettes from his shirt pocket, and lit one up. "Still got that look in your eye. The one that says you're running from something."

"I'm not running from anything," Mason replied.

The older man blew out a cloud of smoke, his eyes narrowing as he glanced back at Mason. "Then what are you doing here?"

Mason didn't flinch. "Just sayin' hello."

The older man shook his head, taking a long drag from the cigarette before flicking the ash into the dirt. "Well, you've said it."

Mason felt the familiar ache in his chest, the old wounds still raw after all these years. Still, he didn't let his frustration show. Instead, he let the silence stretch between them.

"You gonna stay this time?" the older man finally asked, his voice gruff but softer now.

"Not for long," Mason replied. "Just passing through."

Bud barked in the distance at a rabbit or squirrel.

"Got you another dog. What happened to the black one?"

"He died," Mason replied.

"Yeah, well, they do that," the older man replied, blowing out smoke.

"Yep," Mason replied.

"Well, you know where to find me," the man said with finality. "I'm not dead yet." Then he shuffled into the barn without another word.

Mason watched him go.

"Yeah, Dad, I guess I do," Mason muttered to himself, then turned on his heel to look around.

The place looked old and worn down, the passage of time apparent in every cracked board and missing shingle. Every building looked smaller than he remembered from his childhood. He noticed a long stretch of barbed wire laying on the ground, most of its old T-posts rusted and broken off, and he wondered if he should've come out to visit at all.

As Mason took the long drive back through Houston to the Gladiator Farm, he tried not to think about the old bars and honky-tonks he knew along the way and the burn of whiskey on his tongue, but it was hard not to.

12

Brother from Another Mother

Gladiator Farm, Fort Bend County, Texas, USA

Zane's muscles burned and his body was slick with sweat as he finished his last set of bicycle crunches. The morning had been intense—jump rope, bag work, then shadow boxing—leaving his arms heavy and numb. The gym echoed with the sounds of gloves smacking leather and jump ropes whistling through the air. Zane sat up panting and wiped his face with a towel his trainer handed him. His tank top and shorts were soaked with sweat.

"Alright," said the trainer, a middle-aged black man called Smurf. "Walk 5 miles on the treadmill to cool off, then hit the shower."

As he stood up, Michael strolled in and crossed the gym towards him. Dressed in a blue tracksuit and white sneakers, Michael moved with the confidence of a man who owned the place—or at least would someday.

"Smurf, how's our boy doing?" he asked with a huge grin.

"He's alright. Footwork ain't quite there, but as long as he don't quit, I'll get 'im right," the older man assured.

Michael's perfect white veneers flashed as he surveyed the gym. "I already know. With Papa Smurf on the job, we can't lose. But check it out, Zane, you can't be all work and no play, right?"

Zane finished swigging from a water bottle, then raised an eyebrow. "Party again?"

Michael sucked his teeth dismissively and stepped closer. "Just dinner, damn! What you worried about? I've got a great night planned for us. Houston's got a lot more to offer than what you've seen. Tonight, we're doing it big—upscale, VIP. You need to see how it really goes down in the H-Town."

Zane wiped the sweat from his neck. It had been three weeks since they'd returned from Belize. Three weeks of intense training, and the idea of unwinding for a night had its appeal. Still, he hesitated, thinking of how the last time had ended with Hannah and Michael partying until the next day.

"You sure that's a good idea?" Zane asked.

Michael grinned, unfazed. "Come on, man. You can't train twenty-four-seven. It's about balance. Trust me, after tonight, you'll feel more focused than ever."

Zane sighed. Michael wasn't someone you easily said no to, and part of him wanted to cut loose, even if just for a few hours.

"All right, cool. But I'm not going all out."

Michael laughed, slapping Zane on the shoulder. "I got you! Just get fresh and clean, my man. We roll out in style tonight."

Later that evening, Michael, Zane, and Hannah, along with Bishop and Mason, pulled up to a high rise building in a black Cadillac Escalade. Doormen with headsets opened their doors, and the guests filed out of the vehicles, into the building, and across the marble lobby. Mason and Bishop, both wearing black suits, led the way, making sure the path was clear. They took an elevator to the top floor. Zane could hear bass thumping down the shaft as they ascended. When the doors slid open, they were blasted with flashing lights, booming music, and the laughter of hundreds of partygoers.

"I thought you said, 'just dinner'?" Zane yelled over the music.

Michael laughed, patted Zane on the back, then motioned for Hannah to step out first.

The crowd boiled with excitement. Everyone was dressed impeccably. Zane had traded in his training gear for a black Amiri outfit, and beside him, Hannah looked stunning in a sleek black Dolce & Gabbana cocktail dress covered in crystals, the fabric hugging her tightly. Michael, as always, dazzled in a Versace blazer and matching slippers. Several diamond chains glittered around his neck along with a diamond pendant featuring the Reserve Entertainment logo. They were greeted by the VIP hostess, a stunning Latina with long shimmering hair and full lips. Her eyes lit up when she saw Michael. With a flirtatious flip of her hair, she gestured for them to follow as she led them through the crowd, her swaying hips leading the way.

Mason scanned the room for threats, but other than a few excited fans, the room seemed relaxed.

On the far side of the club, they approached a raised VIP booth. Hulking bouncers parted the velvet ropes as they approached. The nightclub was packed, the air filled with music, colorful lasers, and the scent of expensive cologne and alcohol. Bottle service girls in sequined minidresses wove through the crowd, carrying trays of champagne and spirits, sparklers blazing.

"This, my man, is how Houston gets down," Michael said with a big grin as they slid into the booth. The table was already set up with bottles of top-shelf liquor, mixers, and charcuterie.

Zane slid into the booth next to Hannah, who was smiling and bouncing to the music, her eyes wide with excitement. Mason and Bishop took discreet positions near the booth. Cocktail waitresses took drink orders, preparing them at the table from the array of bottles. The music vibrated inside Zane's chest.

Michael leaned in, handing Zane a drink. "You good? You look like you're still thinking about training."

Zane took the glass, swirling the clear liquid before taking a sip. "I'm good. Just focused, I guess."

Michael raised his glass with a grin. "Focus is good. But you also need to live a little. Remember, you're not just training for the fight—you're building the life that comes after."

Zane nodded. He glanced at Hannah, who was clearly in her element. The tension he'd been carrying from training began to ease.

As the night wore on, the trio settled into a rhythm. Drinks flowed and the music thumped through their seats as the glamorous crowd of Houston's elite frolicked around them. The bottle girls kept the drinks coming, and before long, Zane found himself slouching in the booth, feeling the warm buzz of alcohol through his body. Michael was in his element, effortlessly charming everyone around him, while Bishop and Mason kept watchful eyes on the surroundings. As friends and well-wishers stopped by to greet Michael and Zane, Mason let Bishop take the lead in who was allowed to pass the velvet rope.

The DJ played mostly Houston rappers such as Slim Thug and Megan the Stallion. Hannah pulled Zane to the dance floor where they swayed to the bass, the flashing lights casting alternating shadows across their faces. She grinded against him, her soft thighs and sweet perfume intoxicating. She looked into his face, her eyes big and glossy in the flashing lights. Zane went in to kiss her, but, in that moment, the music changed.

"Oh my god! This is my song!" she squealed, pulling her head away as Beyonce belted her latest hit through the booming speakers.

Zane smiled to himself.

By the time they returned to the booth, the night was a blur of lights and noise. Michael was still laughing and toasting with his entourage. He looked up as Hannah slid in next to him, followed by Zane.

"Ay! There y'all are," Michael beamed. "InZane in the house!"

He reached out to clasp hands with Zane, then told a waitress, "Yo, fix my man a drink. What were you drinkin' earlier? Vodka? Tequila?"

"Hannah probably wants a shot of tequila. I'll do a vodka and soda," Zane said.

"Tequila!" Michael cheered. "We all need to do a shot. Baby, line up that Patron."

"Woo! Tequila!" Hannah shouted, her arms raised in the air.

Michael leaned in close to Hannah, whispering something into her ear. Zane watched as she placed her hand on Michael's arm and laughed loudly at his joke.

As if on cue, a ripple of excitement swept through the club, drawing eyes toward the entrance. Zane glanced over just in time to see a figure make a grand entrance, striding into the room with an air of effortless confidence and flamboyance. The man wore a striking, tailored suit in a deep plum color, the fabric shimmering under the club's lights. His black shirt was unbuttoned most of the way, revealing chiseled abs. His hair was perfectly styled, and long diamond earrings dangled from his lobes.

"Who's that?" Hannah asked, staring at the newcomer.

Michael's face stiffened, the easy charm slipping for a moment as he caught sight of the man. His lips pressed into a thin line, the tension around him suddenly palpable.

"That's Mo," he sighed. "My half-brother."

Zane blinked in surprise, glancing between Michael and the slender man now making his way through the crowd with an air of theatrical grace. The contrast between the two brothers couldn't have been more stark. While Michael was smooth but masculine, his brother was flamboyant and unapologetic.

Mo approached their booth with a smile that was both mischievous and knowing, his eyes flicking from Michael to the others seated around him.

"Well, well, well," Mo said, his voice dripping with sass. "Look who's out slumming it tonight."

Michael's jaw tightened, but he forced a smile, though it didn't reach his eyes. "What's up, Mo?"

Mo's eyes gleamed as he slid into the booth with a dramatic flourish. His gaze swept over Zane and the others.

"And here I thought you'd forgotten how to have fun," Mo said with a lilt. "But I suppose even you need a break from being daddy's favorite."

Zane watched the exchange, feeling the tension rise between the brothers.

"You know how it is," Michael said, his tone forced but polite. "Some of us have responsibilities."

Mo let out a laugh, the sound high and mocking. "Ah, yes. The responsible son. Pray tell, how is the Duke these days? Still pretending I don't exist?"

Michael's face didn't react. "If you mean, is he still the same as he's always been, yes."

Mo flipped his hand dismissively. "Well, it's his loss. I'm doing just fine without his approval, thank you very much."

"I see you brought your attack dog with you," Mo said towards Bishop, then turned to Hannah. "But who are your lovely friends? Girl, this dress is *divine*!"

"Hi! I'm Hannah," she said. "I love your earrings!"

"Oh, girl, these old things. My ex bought me these after I caught him with a Brazilian soccer player. Or I guess they call it football in Latin America? Oh, dear, I don't know sports. But," Mo said, turning towards Zane, "I do know you. You're Zane."

Zane set his drink down. "Yes, and you're Mo. Michael's brother, right?"

"Michael's *estranged* brother, don't get it twisted. *Strange* and *estranged*, one might say," Mo laughed at his own joke. "Make no mistake, the Duke in all his primitive yet fragile masculinity could never embrace a queer son. Even Michael barely tolerates me these days. He never even calls."

"Don't do that," Michael said. "You know we've got the fight coming up. This is the first time I've been out since your birthday, like six months ago."

"Oh, poor Michael," Mo waved his hand. "Heavy is the burden of the crown prince. But I guess we can't all be the hot, delicious one. Somebody has to do the work part."

"What do you do?" Zane asked.

"Muah?" Mo asked dramatically. "Oh, my dear boy, I am designer to the stars. Did you see that dress Megan wore to the awards?"

"Um..." Zane began.

"Oh, never mind," Mo waved it away.

"Wait! The yellow one?" Hannah piped up.

"Yes!" Mo said excitedly.

"I saw it. Oh my god, to die for," Hannah said.

"Oh! Where did you find this precious doll?" Mo said, giving Hannah a hug.

Hannah and Mo hit it off, and soon Mo had dragged her away to meet friends at the bar.

Michael and Zane watched them walk away.

"So, if you couldn't tell, that's my gay brother," Michael said. "And no, you should never bring it up to the Duke. OK?"

"OK. But you two are cool, right?" Zane asked.

"Oh, yeah. We're good. But," Michael leaned in, "don't believe everything you hear. Mo is short for 'Motion', because that boy be having all types of motion going on. Mo's got more connections than I do. He's trouble. Trust me. Don't take all that fruity shit to heart. That shit is at least half smokescreen, you know what I'm sayin'?"

Zane glanced at Mo, who was introducing Hannah to a group of people at the bar. "Seems like he's just living his life."

"Living his life the wrong way with the wrong people," Michael said, his expression darkening.

From across the dance floor, Mo turned his attention back to Michael, raising an eyebrow as if sensing the whispered conversation. After a moment, he escorted Hannah back to their section, bid the party goodnight, and glided back into the crowd.

Michael let out a long breath, his jaw still tight as he turned to Zane. "Ignore him. He's been trying to drag this family down for years."

Zane downed his drink, then excused himself for the bathroom. Mason led as they worked their way through the crowd. Zane smiled, shook hands, and even granted a few photos along the way. Mason waited just outside the bathroom door. When Zane exited, they walked near the bar, and Mo suddenly turned away from the bar, grabbing Zane's arm as he passed.

"Taking the long way back to the section, I see," Mo teased.

Zane noticed a man leaning on the bar next to Mo. He was big and rugged, dark skinned, with a fade haircut and tattoos from his fingertips to his chin. He even had a tattoo of the Houston Astros logo on his cheek along with several teardrops. He stared at Zane menacingly.

Zane turned to Mo, not sure how to respond. "Just needed to get away for a minute, I guess."

Mo's eyes twinkled. "Yeah, I get that. Michael tends to do things... in excess."

There was a pause, and Zane noticed the way Mo's expression shifted, his playful mask slipping for a moment.

"Look, Zane," Mo said, leaning in closer, his voice dropping. "You seem like a decent guy. That's why I'm gonna give you some advice."

"OK," Zane replied.

Mo glanced over his shoulder, making sure Michael was distracted. "Stay on your toes around my brother and father. They're not who they pretend to be."

Zane's gut tightened.

Mo took a sip of his drink, his eyes scanning the room again, his expression a careful mix of concern and detachment. "Michael's smooth. He'll smile in your face, make you feel like you're his best friend, like you're in on something big... but trust me, it's always really about what he gets out of it."

Zane leaned against the bar. "And the Duke?"

Mo's smile faded, his tone turning serious. "Daddy dearest? He's even worse. The Duke cares about two things: power and more power. He'll do whatever it takes to get what he wants out of you. He sees you as a tool, Zane. Something to use. And when he's done with you, well, let's just say it won't end well."

Zane's eyes narrowed. "Why are you telling me this?"

Mo shrugged. "Because I know what it's like to get sucked into their world. They'll make you feel invincible, like you're part of something transcendent. But in the end, they only look out for themselves."

Zane looked over at Michael, who was still laughing and chatting with Hannah.

"And what about you?" Zane asked. "Aren't you part of their family?"

Mo laughed, though it didn't reach his eyes. "I'm not part of anything. Not anymore. The Duke cut me off because of who I am, and Michael, well, he's doing everything he can to be just like his daddy. But I know things they don't want people to know. And I can still stir things up when I need to, so they can't completely ignore me."

There was a moment of silence between them, the music from the club pulsing in the background. Everything about this world—the glitz, the money, the power—was starting to feel more dangerous than it had at first.

"Why do you care what happens to me?" Zane asked.

Mo's eyes softened for a moment, and he leaned in even closer. "Because I see what's happening to you. You're getting reeled in like a fish. And I don't want to see you destroyed the way they destroy everyone."

Zane nodded, the knot in his stomach tightening.

Before Zane could respond, Mo straightened up, his smile returning to its full brilliance, the mask sliding back into place. "Anyway," Mo said, his voice light again, "I'll let you get back to your night. Just remember what I said."

With that, Mo gave Zane a wink and turned back to his heavily tattooed friend at the bar. The gruff man sneered at Zane, but he noticed Mo place a calming hand on the brute's wrist.

Zane stood there for a moment, watching the club swirl around him, his mind racing. Then he straightened his jacket, then turned to walk back to the booth where Hannah was chatting away with Michael.

Mason watched the entire exchange, noting everything.

And then Zane saw it. Hannah doing a bump of cocaine from a key Michael held up for her. But that wasn't all. Michael's hand was firmly on Hannah's thigh. At first, Zane thought he was imagining it, but as Michael leaned in closer, guiding the key to her nose, then laughing and brushing a stray hair from Hannah's face, Zane felt a surge of heat rush through him. Hannah wiped her nose then laughed.

Zane's grip tightened around his glass. His mind flashed back to everything Mo had just said—about Michael, about the Duke, about the way they used people. And now, seeing Michael flirt with Hannah right in front of him, his gut twisted in rage.

He set his drink down and stalked toward the VIP booth, his pulse quickening with every step. His jaw clenched, and his fists tightened, every inch of him bristling. When he reached the table, Michael was mid-laugh, his hand still resting on Hannah's leg.

Zane didn't say anything at first—he didn't have to. The look on his face was enough to silence the conversation at the table. Michael looked up, catching the shift in the atmosphere. His smile faltered, but only for a second.

"What's up, Zane?" Michael asked, his tone too light, too smooth, as he casually pulled his hand away.

Zane's voice was low, tight with anger. "Did I miss something?"

Michael's eyes narrowed slightly, but he played it off, raising his hands in mock surrender. "You missed all the fun," he attempted to joke.

Zane's eyes flicked to Hannah, who looked between the two men, suddenly nervous.

"Fun?" Zane said, his voice rising. "Is that what you call touching my girl?"

Hannah's face paled, realization dawning on her. "Zane, it's not like that—"

But Zane wasn't listening. His focus was entirely on Michael, who leaned back in his seat, still trying to play it cool. "Zane, you're overreacting. We're all friends here."

Zane took a step closer, his voice dangerous. "Friends don't act like that."

Michael's eyes darkened, the casual smile slipping as he stood up to face Zane, now fully aware that the situation was escalating. "Don't make this into something it's not, bro."

"It is something," Zane growled, stepping chest-to-chest with Michael now, the heat between them palpable.

Bishop, noticing the rising voices, took a step closer to them.

Then Hannah stood, her voice frantic. "Zane, stop! Please, don't do this!"

But it was too late. The tension in the air had snapped, and Zane's patience had run out. Without thinking, he shoved Michael hard, sending him stumbling back into the booth.

The moment Michael's body hit the cushions, everything happened fast.

Bishop moved with lightning speed. Before Zane could move again, the hulking bodyguard had his hand around Zane's throat, lifting him off the ground like a small child. Zane's hands instinctively shot up to grab the bodyguard's wrist, but the man's grip was like steel, cutting off his air as he held him in the air.

"Bishop!" Mason's voice cut through the chaos, sharp and commanding. "Release him now!"

Bishop's eyes were dark and unreadable as he held Zane suspended, his massive hand crushing Zane's windpipe.

Without another word, Mason kicked Bishop in the back of his knee, causing his leg to buckle. Bishop faltered, lost his grip on Zane, then took a looping swing at Mason, which he slipped easily. Mason took a pivoting step between Bishop and Zane, prepared to fight the larger man. Bishop's face twisted in rage.

"Bishop! Stop!" Michael yelled, and instantly, the big man relaxed as if nothing had happened.

Zane coughed, gasping for air as he stumbled back, his chest heaving as he regained his footing.

Michael stepped forward, his expression calm again. "We're all too drunk, man. Shit got out of hand."

Zane glared at him, his fists still clenched, but the confrontation had drained some of the fire out of him. He couldn't take on Bishop, not here, not like this. But the rage still simmered beneath the surface.

Michael clapped a hand on Zane's shoulder, his tone casual again. "Let's all cool off. It'll be fine in the morning."

Zane shook off Michael's hand, his breath still ragged, but the fight had left him. Hannah eyes were wide with fear as she tugged at Zane's arm. Looking around, she noticed a few nearby clubgoers starting to pay attention.

"Baby, let's go," she pleaded. "Please."

Michael smirked, the tension between them already fading from his face as if it had never been there. "See? No harm, no foul. We'll laugh about this tomorrow."

Zane didn't respond. The party filed out of the booth and marched back to the elevator. Mason kept more than an arm's length between himself and Bishop, while Mo watched their every step from his perch at the bar.

13

Round One

Gladiator Farm, Fort Bend County, Texas, USA

The next morning, the rhythmic thud of Zane's fists slamming into the heavy bag echoed through the gym, pounding like the hangover that gripped his skull. Sweat dripped down his face and his muscles burned with every punch, but he welcomed the pain. It helped drown out the anger still simmering inside him from the night before. His mind replayed the image of Michael touching Hannah, the flirtatious smile, the way Michael had dismissed it all so casually afterward.

He growled as he threw another hard right hook, the bag swinging violently from the impact. His trainer, Smurf, stood nearby, watching, but keeping his distance. He could tell something was different today. Zane was pushing himself harder, his punches landing with more force, his movements sharp, like a man fighting more than just the leather bag in front of him.

A videographer lingered nearby, swooping in-and-out, his camera mounted on an elaborate gimbal, lights blazing as he captured clips for the never-ending marketing campaign to ensure ticket sales for the fight.

Outside, Mason was making his routine lap around the building. Bud scouted with him, sniffing at anything that caught his fancy. Mason's eyes scanned the area, looking for anything out of the ordinary.

After completing his sweep, Mason entered the gym, the cool air a stark contrast to the heat outside. Bud had taken to wandering on his own, so he let the dog explore outside. Mason leaned against the far wall, arms crossed, his eyes narrowing as he watched Zane hammer away at the heavy bag.

Just as Mason settled in to observe, the gym door swung open, and in walked Michael dressed in sweats. He was louder than usual, his voice echoing across the room as he greeted everyone with exaggerated enthusiasm. It felt forced, like he was overcompensating for the tension of the previous night.

"What's up, gentlemen?" Michael called out, clapping his hands as he walked toward the trainers. "Everyone ready to get to work?"

Zane barely glanced in his direction, his focus still on the bag in front of him, but Mason noticed the slight shift in Zane's posture—the tension creeping back into his shoulders as Michael's voice filled the gym.

Michael, pretending as if nothing had happened the night before, strode up to Smurf, talking to him with the same easy charm he always exuded. "How's our boy looking today?"

Smurf glanced at Zane. "He's been hitting the bag hard. Looks focused."

Michael's smile widened. "That's good. But you know how it is—if you're not sparring, you're not training."

Smurf nodded, wiping his brow with a towel. "We'll get some sparring in soon."

Michael's gaze shifted to Zane, who still hadn't acknowledged him. "Why wait? Let's get some rounds in now."

Smurf looked around the gym, scanning the fighters warming up. "OK. I'll get someone—"

"Nah," Michael interrupted, holding up a hand, "I'll do it."

That got Zane's attention. He stopped mid-punch, his hands dropping to his sides as he turned to face Michael, his eyes narrowing. Michael smiled, his voice casual but with a hint of challenge. "Come on, youngster. Let's see what you've got."

Zane stared at Michael. The challenge hung in the air. Mason watched closely.

Smurf glanced between the two men, hesitant. "I don't know if that's a good idea, Michael. Zane's been working hard, and—"

Michael waved him off, his grin widening. "Relax. We're just gonna have a little warm up. Nothing serious."

Zane stepped forward, his fists still wrapped, his expression hard. "You want to spar? Let's do it."

Some other nearby trainers exchanged glances.

Smurf sighed, looking uneasy, but nodded. "Alright. But keep it clean."

Zane didn't say a word as he turned, stormed over, and slipped into the ring, his movements deliberate. He could feel the anger rising in his chest, the frustration from the night before bubbling just beneath the surface.

"Papa Smurf, wrap me up," Michael said, holding his hands up as he began to jog lightly in place, the smile never leaving his face, his eyes never leaving Zane.

When Smurf was done wrapping his hands, Michael reached into his pocket and pulled out a mouthguard. In the ring, another trainer helped Zane into headgear and a groin protector. Michael climbed into the ring, passing through the ropes smoothly. He slipped into a groin protector but waved Smurf off when he approached with headgear.

"Just bring me those 14-ounce Reyes gloves," he said instead.

"Michael, what are you doing? We spar with headgear and 16-ounce gloves in this gym, always. You know that," Smurf whispered.

Michael ignored him and continued jogging in place. "Just get the damn gloves," he growled through his mouthguard.

Mason watched calmly from the sidelines as Smurf retrieved a pair of red boxing gloves. He knew this wasn't going to end well, but there was nothing he could do now. This was something Zane needed to handle on his own.

Smurf slipped the gloves onto Michael and laced them up. Other fighters and trainers had begun to circle the ring, and tension filled the room thicker than the humidity outside.

Smurf, acting as ref, brought the opposing fighters to the center of the ring.

"Box clean. No holding. Keep your head up and protect yourself at all times. Break when I signal. If you hear 'stop,' immediately stop punching. Now, go to your corners, and touch gloves when you come out," he said.

Michael and Zane glared at each other. Sweat was already beading on Zane's face, but Michael was calm and cool. They went to their corners, the bell rang, and the fighters squared off in the center of the ring.

Michael moved first, light on his feet, his hands up in a classic boxing stance. He threw a few quick jabs, testing Zane's reflexes, but Zane didn't back down. He kept his guard up, moving with precision, blocking the shots, and waiting for his moment.

"You still mad about last night?" Michael taunted, his voice low enough for only Zane to hear. "Come on, man. We were all drunk. It didn't mean anything."

Zane's jaw tightened, but he didn't respond. Instead, he threw a sharp jab, catching Michael off guard and making him take a step back. The smile on Michael's face faltered for a second, but he quickly recovered, moving in again.

"Don't be so serious, Zane," Michael said, his voice taunting. "It's all just a game."

But Zane wasn't playing. He stepped forward, unleashing a series of quick punches—jabs, hooks, and a cross that forced Michael to cover up.

The trainers and other fighters watched in silence as the tension between the two men escalated. Zane wasn't holding back.

Michael threw a hook, but Zane slipped it easily, countering with a hard right that knocked Michael off balance. For the first time, Michael's cocky grin wavered, and Zane saw it.

Michael's face twisted into a smirk, but there was something darker in his eyes now. He moved in, throwing a series of fast punches, but Zane was ready. He blocked them, but then a slick uppercut caught him under the chin, snapping his head back.

With Zane dazed, Michael began to walk him down, trapping him into a corner. He lowered his lead hand and wrapped his right around his mid-section, assuming a Philly Shell guard.

Zane, sensing an opening, feinted a low left to Michael's midsection, then an overhand right to his head, which deflected harmlessly off Michael's lead shoulder. Michael answered with a counter left-right combo of his own, his gloves smacking sharply against Zane's headgear.

Rattled, Zane took a step back and brought his guard back up. Michael waited for another chance to counter, flinching, and jabbing at Michael, attempting to bait him again. Zane changed levels, dropping low but swinging high, then pulled back slightly to dodge Michael's counter. Then, in a blur, Zane pivoted and rocked Michael with a sharp check hook to the mouth, catching the taller, older fighter completely by surprise.

Michael stumbled, his smile gone, replaced by a cold glare. He wiped blood from his lip, his voice cold. "Alright, Zane. Let's see what you've really got."

The gym held its breath. Mason found himself silently cheering for Zane.

Zane braced himself, his fists up, his breathing steady. His anger had been fueling him, but he realized that Michael wasn't a fighter to take lightly. Despite his smooth-talking charm, Michael was dangerous, and not just outside the ring. He moved like someone who had spent years honing his craft, and Zane felt the weight of that experience pressing down on him.

The bell rang at the end of the round, and the fighters broke and went to their corners. Smurf squirted water into Zane's mouth and told him to keep working feints and watching for counters, while another trainer, Smurf, rubbed petroleum jelly on Michael's cheekbones. The fighters glare at each other the whole time.

The bell rang again, signaling the start of the next round, and this time Michael charged straight at Zane like a furious bull.

Zane threw the first punch, a sharp jab aimed at slowing Michael's advance, but Michael slipped it with ease, ducking and pivoting out. Before Zane could reset, Michael was on him with quick, controlled punches. A hook to the ribs, a cross to the chin. Zane grunted, his guard slipping as he tried to keep up with the speed and precision of Michael's strikes. The blows were fast, but more than that—they were calculated. Michael wasn't just sparring. He was showing Zane who was in control.

"Come on, Zane," Michael taunted, his voice calm as he danced around him, darting in and out, landing punch after punch. "You're supposed to be the next big thing, right? Show me what you've got."

Zane swung wide with a right hook, hoping to catch Michael off guard, but Michael saw it coming. He dodged effortlessly, stepping inside Zane's guard and delivering a brutal uppercut to his jaw. Zane's head snapped back, and he stumbled, blinking away the stars that filled his vision.

Michael didn't give him time to recover. He pressed the attack, throwing a series of body shots that left Zane gasping for breath. Every punch hit harder, faster, and Zane found himself retreating, his body screaming in pain as he tried to keep his guard up.

"Is that all?" Michael sneered, his voice mocking. "All pissed off, and this is what you've got?"

Zane swung again, desperate to land a solid hit, but it was no use. Michael's footwork was too fast, his movements too controlled. He slipped Zane's punches effortlessly, countering with punishing blows to Zane's ribs and jaw. Each hit sent a wave of pain through Zane's body, sapping his strength and slowing his reactions.

The trainers watched in tense silence, knowing this had gone far beyond a simple sparring match.

Zane could feel the fight slipping away from him. His body was slowing down, his punches losing power. He was out of his depth, and Michael knew it.

With a sudden burst of speed, Michael feinted left, then came in hard with a right hook that caught Zane square in the temple. The world tilted, and Zane's legs buckled beneath him. He hit the canvas hard, his vision swimming as the gym lights blurred overhead.

For a moment, the world was silent, save for the ringing in Zane's ears. He blinked, trying to focus, but his body refused to respond. His arms felt like lead, and his chest heaved as he struggled to catch his breath.

Above him, Michael stood, breathing hard but composed, his gaze cold and indifferent. He glanced down at Zane, his expression unreadable, then turned away as if the fight had been nothing more than an inconvenience.

Zane groaned, rolling onto his side, his body aching from the punishment he had just taken. He had been outclassed, beaten soundly by a man who had barely broken a sweat.

Michael didn't look back as he walked to the edge of the ring, leaning on the ropes. "Get up when you're ready," he called over his shoulder, his tone casual, as if they hadn't just fought.

His work done, Michael climbed out of the ring, calmly chatting with his trainer as if nothing had happened. He was back to being the charming, confident leader, while Zane stood in the middle of the ring, his fists still clenched at his sides, trying to swallow the bitter taste of defeat.

Mason stood nearby, leaning against the wall, watching Zane quietly. He pushed off the wall and made his way over to Zane, his boots making soft thuds against the gym floor. Zane didn't look up as Mason approached, but he could feel his presence.

"You alright?" Mason asked as he reached the ring's corner.

Zane let out a frustrated sigh, running a hand through his sweaty hair. "I'm fine."

Mason sat in silence for a moment while Smurf helped Zane out of his padding and gloves.

"Listen," Mason finally said, his voice low and steady, "I don't want to overstep, but the truth is, sometimes the people around you aren't looking out for your best interests."

Zane's gaze shifted, glancing over at Michael, who was still charming the trainers. His jaw tightened. "You think I don't see that?"

Mason leaned in slightly, his eyes locked on Zane's. "You see it, but you're not doing anything about it. And that's the problem."

Zane scowled, his frustration bubbling to the surface. "What am I supposed to do, Mason? Walk away? I've got a fight coming up, and everything's tied to him now. I can't just walk away. I've got a contract."

Mason's voice remained calm, but there was a seriousness in his tone that Zane couldn't ignore. "You can, and you should. Look, I've seen people like Michael and the Duke before. They're not in this for you. They're in it for themselves. You're just another pawn on their chess board."

Zane's eyes flashed with anger, but Mason didn't back down.

"And Hannah," Mason continued, his voice softer now. "I don't know what's going on between you two, but I've seen enough to know that whatever it is, it's not good for you. Her mind is somewhere other than yours, and if you're not careful, she's going to drag you down with her."

Zane swallowed hard, the weight of Mason's words settling in his chest like a heavy stone.

"You've got to think about your future—what you want, who you want to be," Mason continued. "And if you keep walking this path, it's going to end badly."

Zane leaned forward, his elbows resting on his knees as he recovered his breath.

Mason stood up, his presence still calm but commanding. "Look, I'm not telling you what to do. But I've seen enough to know that if you don't make some changes—and soon—you're going to lose more than just a fight."

Zane looked up at him, the weight of the decision heavy in his eyes.

Mason gave him a small, understanding nod. "Think about it, Zane. You're stronger than this. Don't let them control your future."

With that, Mason turned and walked toward the door, leaving Zane alone in the gym, the echoes of his footsteps fading into the distance.

Zane sat there, the silence of the gym pressing in on him, his thoughts racing.

14

Pills

Mason sat behind the wheel of the Range Rover, the soft hum of the engine filling the quiet night as he glanced over at Lisa. She was in the passenger seat, her brunette hair catching the faint glow of the streetlights as they passed. Her warm smile had a way of cutting through the tension he seemed to carry everywhere with him. It had been years since he had felt this light.

Tonight, he had picked her up from her home for their first official date, and for once, Mason wasn't thinking about work. Her brown hair hung in loose curls around her face, and she was wearing a black dress that accentuated her figure in ways that made Mason's heart pound. Her large brown eyes shimmered, and her skin glowed softly in the golden light of the setting sun.

"Steak or seafood?" he asked.

"Um, I like both," she replied.

"Good, because we're going to Truluck's by the Galleria. They've got both. That way, you don't have to choose."

"Oh, wow," she said. "I've never been there. Only heard of it."

"Have you ever been to the Water Wall?" Mason asked, her eyes sparkling with curiosity.

She raised an eyebrow, glancing over. "The Water Wall?"

118

"Yeah, it's this huge fountain by the Galleria. It's like a giant curtain of water."

"Oh, yeah," she said smiling, recollection striking her. "I haven't been there since I was little."

After that, they drove in silence for a while. Mason turned on the radio to ease the mood. He took a guess and put it on a country station.

After a while, she said, " Do you listen to anything other than country?"

Mason chuckled. "I mean, I prefer rock, to be honest."

"Oh, thank God," she said. "Please put something else on. Country is too sad for me."

Mason pressed play on a Chevelle CD, and the mood instantly lifted. Lisa chatted away for the rest of the drive, telling him about her life. She was born and raised in Cypress. Her family was not too well off. Dad was not in the picture much. Mom had some health issues. She didn't have kids, but there was an ex-husband, but he had moved away a couple of years ago with a new wife. She was working her way through veterinary school, but it was hard to keep up with work and studies. He realized that he liked the Texas twang in her voice, and the way she moved her hands when she talked.

Dinner at Truluck's, a white table cloth restaurant serving fresh seafood and prime steaks, did not disappoint. She had a glass of white wine with her lobster tail, but didn't bat an eye when he ordered iced tea with his dry-aged ribeye. He was happy to let her carry the conversation. They both complimented the scalloped potatoes and complained about being too full after their plates were cleared.

The valet retrieved the Range Rover, and a few minutes later, they pulled into a parking spot near Gerald D. Hines Waterwall Park, an oasis tucked away in the midst of Houston's urban sprawl. The 64-foot tall, semicircular fountain loomed ahead, its cascading waters creating a peaceful roar that drowned out the noise of the city. The mist from the fountain filled the air, cool and refreshing in the warm night air.

As they stepped out of the SUV and walked toward the towering wall of water, Mason glanced over at Lisa. She looked happy. She smiled when she caught him looking and looped her arm through his.

They stood at the base of the fountain, the sound of the rushing water creating a sense of privacy, as though they were in their own little world. The water cascaded down the limestone wall in perfect sheets, illuminated by soft lights that reflected off the surface, making the whole place glow.

She turned to face him, her expression playful yet sincere. "So, mystery man. You swing into town in your fancy car and take a small town girl like me to a fancy date in the city, but you haven't told me a thing about yourself. Are you married?"

Mason almost choked. "Married? No, no. Not me. Never had time for that."

"So, what do you do?"

"Well, I'm a partner in a private security company in Colorado. I do some training. Mostly police and military. And I do a little bodyguard work, but not often."

"Oh, wow," she said, honestly impressed. "A man of action. I can get into that. You said you live in Colorado, but you sound like Texas."

"Yeah, I'm from here originally, but I don't make it back very often" he replied. When he saw her smile start to falter, he quickly added, "But I'll be here for a few months for work. I'm not going anywhere any time soon."

"What are you doing here? Training the police?"

"No, VIP protection. Have you heard of the boxing match with the internet kid, Zane? The one all over the news?"

"The YouTube fighter? With the curly blonde hair? Yeah," Lisa said.

"I'm here with him. I'm actually his bodyguard," Mason said. "For the duration of the fight, anyway."

Her eyes got even wider.

"Oh, wow! So, you're like a *big time* bodyguard. What were you, like, a Navy SEAL or something?"

He laughed.

"Well, not a SEAL, but yeah, I was in the Army for a long time."

"Oh, OK," she replied.

They stood for a while, looking at the waterfall.

"So, you don't have a girlfriend back in Colorado?" she asked.

Mason laughed.

"No," he replied, looking into her eyes. "No girlfriend. Just a lot of work. And a dog."

"What kind of dog?"

"A Dalmatian. His name is Bud."

She smiled and pulled his arm a little closer.

"I have two dogs," she said. "A pug named Puddin' and a Yorkie named Frisco. They're my babies."

Mason smiled. They strolled for a moment around the fountain, then Mason said he had to get back to work.

"Oh, yeah. I guess you're always at work, Mr. Bodyguard."

"Not always. I will be busy until the fight is over, but I'll be able to slip away here and there."

"Good," she said.

Before he could respond, she stood on her tiptoes and pressed a light kiss to his cheek, her lips brushing against his beard. It was a simple gesture, but it sent a jolt of warmth through him, the kind of warmth he hadn't felt in what seemed like a lifetime.

Mason blinked, caught off guard, but he didn't pull away. Instead, he let himself enjoy the moment.

At her house, he walked her to the door. She thanked him for a great night and kissed him on the cheek again. He held her hand for just a moment longer. After years of holding weapons, he was amazed how small and soft it was.

When they said goodnight, he realized that he wished the night could go on and on.

The next morning, the Duke's black Rolls-Royce Phantom glided through the streets of Fifth Ward, a quiet storm in a city that knew no rest. As the Duke drove deeper into the heart of his old stomping grounds, a familiar tension crept into his chest. It had been years since he'd moved on from this place—years since Luther Davis had become "the Duke". But Fifth Ward was where it all began, and no matter how high he climbed, it would always pull him back. Especially now.

He pulled up to a modest brick home, one that stood out from its weathered neighbors for its well-kept appearance. The flowers in the front yard were bright, and the grass neatly mowed. He made sure of that.

As the Duke stepped out of the car, a middle-aged woman in scrubs came to the front door and stood waiting for him. She greeted him with a tight-lipped smile, but there was tension in her eyes.

"She's in a mood today," Sharon, his mother's nurse, warned as the Duke approached the door. "It's been worse than usual. She's been asking for her pills since yesterday. Keeps saying Michael promised them to her."

The Duke raised an eyebrow. "Pills? From Michael?"

Sharon nodded, glancing back into the house. "Yes, sir. I'm not sure what she means. I haven't given her any new medication, and I've checked with her doctor. Everything she's on is accounted for, but she insists there's something else."

The Duke felt a prick of unease but forced it down. "Alright, I'll talk to her."

He stepped inside the house, the scent of old wood and the soft drone of the television hitting him. The living room was dimly lit, and his mother, Ethel Davis, sat in her favorite armchair by the window, her frail frame hunched forward as she stared blankly at the flickering TV screen.

"Luther," she muttered as soon as he entered, her voice sharp and biting, even before she looked at him. "You're late."

The Duke paused. She hadn't called him by his first name in years. She hadn't called him *anything* except for cold curses and complaints since the dementia had begun to eat at her mind.

"I'm here now, Ma," the Duke said, stepping closer. He had learned not to take her words too personally. Not anymore. "What's going on? I hear you've been asking for some pills."

Ethel's eyes snapped to him, her face contorting into a mix of anger and confusion. "I need them. Michael promised me my pills. He always brings them. You should be helping him, not running around doing whatever it is you do."

The Duke suppressed a sigh and took a knee beside her chair, his large hand resting gently on the armrest. "What pills, Ma? You don't need anything new. The nurse is taking care of you."

Her eyes flashed with a sudden fury, and before the Duke could react, she grabbed a small bottle off the table beside her and hurled it at him with surprising strength for someone so frail. The bottle hit his chest and fell to the floor, rolling a few inches before coming to a stop.

"There! *Those* pills!" Ethel spat, her voice trembling with frustration. "Michael promised me. He takes care of me—better than you ever did."

The Duke picked up the bottle from the floor. He turned the bottle over in his hand, inspecting the faded label. It was an unfamiliar name, not something prescribed by her usual doctors.

"What are these?" he asked, unscrewing the cap and peering inside. It was empty. His mind raced with questions. Why would Michael give her these? And why hadn't he known about it?

Ethel watched him, her face twisted into a sneer. "Oh, you don't know anything. Michael knows. He takes care of everything while you sit in your fancy house pretending you're someone important."

Her words stung, though the Duke knew they weren't entirely her own. The dementia twisted her memories, turned her bitterness into cruel jabs.

"Where did these come from, Ma?" he asked, his voice low. "Who prescribed these to you?"

Ethel's expression softened, her confusion returning as quickly as it had vanished. She blinked, looking at the bottle in his hand as if seeing it for the first time. "Michael... Michael said I need them for my arthritis. He always brings them... Where is he? Why aren't you helping him?"

The Duke stood slowly, turning the bottle over in his hand again, the weight of it heavy in his palm. The questions swirled in his mind, but there were no answers here. His mother's mind was too far gone to explain anything. He would have to ask Michael himself.

Ethel had already begun to drift away again, her gaze returning to the television, her muttering turning incoherent. The moment of clarity—or what passed for clarity—was gone.

The Duke clenched his jaw, slipping the bottle into his pocket. He leaned down and kissed his mother's forehead, though she barely noticed. "I'll be back soon, Ma," he whispered.

As he walked out of the house and back into the humid Houston air, his mind raced.

The Rolls-Royce hummed to life as Bishop put it into gear. They pulled away from the curb, the pill bottle bulging in the Duke's pocket. Whatever was going on, he wasn't about to let it slip under his radar. Not in his world. Not in his family.

And Michael—his charming, smooth-talking son—had some explaining to do.

Inside Gladiator Farm's outdoor training area, Zane's fists hammered against the weathered punching bag, each blow sending ripples through the thick leather. Sweat poured from his body, his muscles burning as he pushed himself harder, faster. But no matter how hard he hit, he couldn't drown out the thoughts swirling in his head.

Focus on the fight. Just focus on the fight.

That's what he kept telling himself, but it was getting harder every day. The steady rhythm of his training—the hours spent sparring, running drills, and conditioning—had once been the only thing on his mind. But now, there was something else gnawing at him. Or rather, someone.

Hannah.

Zane slammed another punch into the bag, his jaw clenched tight as frustration coursed through him. Hannah had been spending more time with Michael. It had started off subtle—just a few laughs shared over dinner, the two of them exchanging stories. But lately, she had been going out with him every night, partying with celebrities and influencers, rubbing elbows with the kind of people Zane had never really cared about.

At first, he tried to ignore it. He knew Hannah loved to have fun, and Michael—being Michael—was always at the center of attention. But there was something about the way she lit up around him that made Zane's stomach turn. The revealing way she dressed when she knew they were going somewhere. The way she'd come back to the guesthouse late at night, smelling like expensive perfume and alcohol, laughing about how crazy the night had been.

And Michael... Michael didn't help. He seemed to go out of his way to flaunt the attention he got, always making sure Zane knew he was taking Hannah to the hottest clubs, introducing her to famous athletes and musicians. It was as if he enjoyed watching Zane squirm. But then he was always playing innocent, like he was just trying to be a good friend and host.

Stay focused, Zane told himself again. *You've got a fight coming up. This is your chance—your moment.*

But even as he tried to focus on the fight, the jealousy burned in his chest like a fire he couldn't put out.

"Zane!"

The voice of his trainer, Smurf, broke through his thoughts. Zane stopped, panting as he turned to face him. Smurf, a grizzled veteran of the fight game, stood with his arms crossed, his sharp eyes assessing every move Zane made.

"You're not here, kid," Smurf said, his voice stern. "Your body's moving, but your head's somewhere else. I can see it. You need to dial in, or you'll get crushed out there."

Zane wiped the sweat from his brow, trying to steady his breathing. He knew Smurf was right. His mind was a million miles away, and that wasn't going to cut it when he stepped into the ring against Mickie Donovan. The Irishman was no joke—tough, experienced, and hungry. There was no room for distraction.

"I'm fine," Zane muttered, his voice a little too sharp.

Smurf raised an eyebrow, not buying it for a second. "You sure about that? Because from where I'm standing, you look like you've got a lot more on your mind than just this fight."

Zane's eyes flicked toward the house where he had last seen Hannah. He bit the inside of his cheek, trying to suppress the anger rising inside him.

"It's nothing," Zane said, turning back to the bag, his fists tightening around the wraps. "Just... stress."

Smurf gave him a long look, his mouth tightening into a line. "I've been around long enough to know when a fighter's distracted. And right now, you're distracted. You're thinking about her, aren't you? Or maybe I should say, *them?*"

Zane's shoulders tensed. He hated how easily everyone saw through him, but there was no point in lying.

"I can't help it," Zane admitted, his voice low. "She's spending all her time with him. Going out, partying, doing God knows what. And I'm stuck here, training like my life depends on it."

Smurf sighed, rubbing the back of his neck. "Listen, son, I've seen this before. Fighters lose focus when they let shit into their heads. Women, money, fame—it'll all be there after the fight. But if you don't stay locked in now, none of that's going to matter. You'll get chewed up and spit out."

Zane nodded, but the jealousy was still there, gnawing at him. He could try to push it down, but it was always just under the surface, ready to explode. Every time he thought about Hannah and Michael together—about the way Michael looked at her, the way she laughed at his jokes—it twisted the knife deeper.

He slammed his fists into the bag again, the thud of leather hitting leather echoing through the training yard.

Smurf watched him for a moment, then stepped closer, lowering his voice. "Look, I know it's hard. Michael's got that charm. But don't let him get in your head. He's testing you, trying to mess with you, and if you let him do that, he's already won."

"Isn't he supposed to be on my team though?" Zane said, punching the bag angrily. "Who treats their teammates like that?"

Smurf nodded sympathetically. "Boy, the one thing you need to learn about life is it's just like boxing: when you step in that ring, you'll be there alone. If you don't start thinking about your what's good for you, you're going to blow the biggest opportunity in your life. Ya' dig?"

"Yeah. I think so," Zane said finally, though the words felt hollow even to him.

Smurf patted him on the shoulder. "Good. Because this fight is your big shot, and not everybody gets one of those. Don't let anything—or anyone—take it from you."

As Smurf walked away, Zane stood there, his fists still clenched, staring at the bag in front of him. He tried to clear his mind, to focus only on the fight, but the image of Hannah with Michael kept creeping back in, like a virus he couldn't shake.

That night, after training, Zane sat alone in the guesthouse, staring at his phone. He had texted Hannah earlier, asking when she'd be back, but there was no response. His stomach churned as he scrolled through social media, looking for any sign of her night out with Michael.

And there it was—photos of them together at some high-end nightclub partying with celebrities. The jealousy flared again, stronger this time, burning hotter with every photo he saw.

Zane's fingers hovered over his phone screen, hesitating for a moment. Then he scrolled through a social media app, searching for someone. He found who he was looking for and typed a private message.

Need to talk. Can we meet?

A few minutes passed, then Zane's phone buzzed.

Sure. Meet me at Marfreless at 10.

Zane raised an eyebrow. Marfreless wasn't a place he was familiar with, but after a quick search, he found it—an underground lounge hidden away in River Oaks, known only to locals and the few who sought it out.

He got dressed, walked to the main house, and found a servant. He made up a story about needing to go to the store real quick. The servant looked uneasy, but with a little reassurance, eventually retrieved a set of keys to one of the Range Rovers. Zane unlocked the car with a beep of the key fob, and climbed in.

A couple hours' drive later, Zane made his way down Shepherd Drive in the heart of Houston, then turned onto West Grey. Marfreless was difficult to find, tucked away with its plain white brick façade, like an old speakeasy. Zane approached the door, his heart beating a little faster as he walked in. The interior was dark and smoky, with an air of mystery clinging to every dark corner. The warm light from the chandeliers barely illuminated the room, giving it an almost dreamlike quality.

Mo sat at a small table near the back, a martini glass on the table before him, his posture relaxed but alert. He was dressed in a deep maroon blazer with gold brocade on the lapel and rings on every finger.

Zane slid into the chair opposite him, and for a moment, neither of them spoke. The silence hung between them like the cigar smoke that filled the air. Zane glanced around the club, doing a double-take at a patron sitting at the bar. It was the man with the Astros logo face tattoo and the surly attitude he had seen with Mo before.

"You made it," Mo said finally, taking a sip of his martini. "I didn't expect you to reach out."

Zane shrugged, though the frustration in his voice was clear. "Had to. I guess I needed to talk."

Mo studied him for a second, his eyes narrowing. "Let me guess. Michael?"

Zane nodded, leaning forward, his elbows resting on the table. "It's more than that. It's everything. Michael, the Duke, even my girlfriend. I feel like I'm getting pulled into something I don't understand. And every day, I'm wondering if I made the wrong choice coming here."

Mo let out a low chuckle and shook the ice in his glass. "Yeah, well, you're not the first, and you won't be the last."

A waitress came by in a short black dress, and Zane ordered a water. She raised an eyebrow at Mo, cutting her eyes toward Zane, intrigued, but Mo shooed her away.

Zane clenched his fists under the table. "I don't know how to deal with it. Michael's messing with me—messing with Hannah. He's playing some type of game, but I don't get it. I don't know what his goal is."

Mo took another drink, his gaze distant for a moment before he looked back at Zane. "The thing with Michael... it's never just one game. It's layers of manipulations, love. He makes you feel like you're part of something big, something special. But it's all about control. And if you're in his way, if you become more of a liability than an asset, he'll cut you loose without thinking twice."

Zane's jaw tightened. "OK, but what about the Duke?"

Mo's eyes darkened. "The Duke's an entirely different breed. He doesn't bother with games. He controls everything outright—fear, intimidation, and *especially* violence. Michael learned some tricks from him, but he is *not* him. Where Michael manipulates from the shadows, the Duke is not afraid to get his hands dirty. *Very* dirty."

Zane sat back, letting the words sink in.

"What about Hannah? Why mess with her?" Zane asked, his voice quieter, as if he didn't want to hear the answer.

Mo paused, swirling the liquid in his glass. "I don't know her like that, but from what I've seen, that child is caught up in the same web you are, she just doesn't see it. Michael's got a way of charming people, of making them feel like they're the center of his world. She thinks it's fun and games, when really it's all smoke and mirrors. Poor baby doesn't even realize how deep she's in."

Zane felt a pang in his chest, his stomach tightening.

"So, what am I supposed to do? I've got a contract and a fight in just a few weeks?"

"You need to make a decision," Mo said. "Are you going to keep letting Michael and the Duke run your life, or are you going to take control of it?"

Zane met Mo's gaze, the weight of the question settling heavily on him.

"And what about you?" Zane asked, leaning in. "Why are you still around if you hate them so much?"

Mo smiled, but it was a sad, knowing smile. "I don't have a choice, Zane. Houston is my home. But you, you can still get out."

Zane shook his head, frustration clear on his face. "It's not that simple. I signed the contract. I'm tied to them now."

Mo leaned forward, his eyes locked on Zane's. "Contracts can be broken. You've just got to be willing to deal with the consequences."

They sat in silence for a while, the hum of quiet conversations and clinking glasses filling the gaps between them.

"Thanks for meeting me," Zane said finally, his voice low. "I don't know what I'm going to do. But I should get back before they miss me."

Mo nodded, his expression softening slightly. "Don't mention it. Just... be careful, Zane. The Duke and Michael—they're not the kind of people you walk away from easily."

15

Ground Branch

October 2009

Fort Bragg, North Carolina, USA

The bar just outside Fort Bragg was dimly lit, the air thick with the scent of spilled beer and aged wood. It was the kind of place where soldiers could lose themselves in the haze of camaraderie and liquor, forgetting the weight of the missions they carried for a little while.

Mason sat at the bar, nursing a whiskey neat. He'd spent enough nights here after long deployments to know its rhythm, the ebb and flow of conversation, and the occasional burst of laughter that cut through the low buzz of voices.

"Holy shit, Mason!" a voice called out from behind him.

Mason turned on his stool, his sharp eyes narrowing before breaking into a rare smile. "Pierce?"

Pierce, his old commander from when he first joined B Squadron, strode over, a wide grin on his face. The man looked just as Mason remembered— wiry, with a scar down his cheek. They clasped hands, pulling each other into a brief hug.

"Man, I haven't seen you since Kandahar," Pierce said, pulling up a stool beside him. "How the hell have you been?"

Mason shrugged, taking a sip of his drink. "Same old. You know how it is."

Pierce leaned in, his voice dropping. "Yeah, but I heard some stories about you. Iraq, right? Fallujah?"

Mason sighed, setting his glass down. The memories of Fallujah were like a weight in the back of his mind—always there, always heavy. He nodded slowly. "Yeah. Fallujah."

Mason recapped the story for him.

The streets of Fallujah were chaos. The city, once a bustling hub, was now a war zone, its buildings reduced to rubble, and its streets littered with the remnants of battle. It was nighttime. Mason was perched on the second floor of a bombed-out building, his sniper rifle resting on a makeshift stand of sandbags and debris.

The headset crackled in his ear as his spotter, a fellow Delta operator named Chase, scanned the streets below with his binoculars. "That Marine squad is pinned down, fifty meters east of the intersection. Enemy sniper's got the high ground. Third floor, beige building, window on the left."

Mason shifted his night vision scope, his trained eye searching the building Chase had called out. It didn't take long to find the sniper. He was well-hidden, his rifle barrel just barely visible in the shadows of the window. Mason's heart rate slowed as he steadied his breathing.

"Got him," Mason said, his voice calm, almost detached. "Range?"

"Five-fifty meters," Chase replied. "Wind's light. Maybe one click left."

Mason adjusted the scope, his finger brushing the trigger. Below, the Marines were pinned behind a crumbled wall, one of them waving desperately for support. Mason zeroed in on the sniper, his focus narrowing until the chaos around him faded into nothing. It was just him, the rifle, and the target.

"Taking the shot," Mason murmured.

He exhaled slowly, his finger squeezing the trigger with practiced precision. The rifle cracked, the sound echoing through the empty building. Through the scope, Mason saw the enemy sniper slump forward, the rifle falling from his grasp.

"Target down," Chase confirmed, his binoculars still trained on the building.

Mason's eyes shifted to the Marines below. They wasted no time, surging forward to regroup with another fire team. A short, stocky Marine paused briefly, glancing up at the building where Mason was stationed. He couldn't see Mason, but he gave a small, grateful salute toward the sniper's position before disappearing into the fight. Mason and Chase would end up covering the same Marines for many more days and weeks, and he would get to know that stocky Marine well. His name was Benito.

Pierce whistled low as Mason finished recounting the memory, his eyes fixed on his drink. "Hell of a story," Pierce said. "Benito owes you a few beers for that one."

Mason shook his head, a faint smile tugging at his lips. "He'd have done the same for me."

Pierce leaned back, studying his old friend. "You ever think about how much we've done? How many lives we've touched, saved, or... you know."

Mason's smile faded as he looked into the amber liquid in his glass. "Every damn day. Every damn day."

They sat in silence for a moment, the weight of their shared experiences filling the space between them. Outside, the hum of passing cars and distant voices carried on, indifferent to the men inside who bore the unseen scars of their service.

"Here's to making it back," Pierce said, raising his glass.

Mason clinked his glass against Pierce's. "And to those who didn't."

Pierce downed the last of his beer, wiping the foam from his beard with the back of his hand. The two men sat in a comfortable silence, the noise of the bar swirling around them. For Mason, it was rare to feel this kind of ease, even with someone like Pierce, who had been through the same hells.

"So," Mason said, swirling the remnants of his whiskey in the glass, "what about you? What have you been up to?"

Pierce smirked, leaning back on his stool. His eyes darted around the bar for a moment before he leaned in closer, his voice dropping just enough to be heard over the noise. "I'm a spook now."

Mason arched an eyebrow, giving a faint smirk. "CIA, huh? I never figured you for that type."

Pierce shrugged, the faintest grin tugging at the corner of his lips. "Yeah, well, someone's gotta do the dirty work. Still boots-on-the-ground stuff, just... quieter."

"Ground Branch?" Mason asked, his tone knowing.

Pierce chuckled. "You're sharper than you look, brother."

Mason leaned back, his expression unreadable as he considered Pierce's words. He knew enough about Ground Branch, the CIA's paramilitary arm within its Special Activities Division (SAD/SOG), to understand what Pierce wasn't saying. It wasn't just covert work—it was shadow wars, deniable missions, and operations that didn't exist on paper.

"You like it?" Mason asked, his voice neutral.

Pierce nodded slowly. "It's different. Missions are faster. Smaller teams. A lot more autonomy. And let's just say Uncle Sam's pockets are deep when it comes to resources."

Mason tilted his head slightly. "Sounds messy though."

Pierce's grin widened. "You'd be surprised how clean it can be. Or maybe you wouldn't."

They fell silent again, Mason turning Pierce's words over in his mind. He had always been the type to follow orders, but in Delta, he'd learned the value of flexibility—of thinking outside the box. If what Pierce was saying was true, Ground Branch was a natural progression. A way to keep doing the work without being shackled by red tape.

Pierce broke the silence. "Listen, Mason. You ever think about what's next?"

Mason's eyes narrowed slightly. "What do you mean?"

"I mean Delta's got its limits, man," Pierce said, leaning in. "Sure, we're the best of the best, but we're still part of the machine. With the Agency, you're not just a cog—you're the whole damn mechanism. You pick your fights, make real changes. No bureaucracy. No politics."

Mason's jaw tightened, his mind flashing to the countless times he'd been held back by rules or orders that didn't make sense. Missions where lives could've been saved if not for waiting on approval from higher-ups.

"I've got a good thing with the Unit," Mason said, though his tone lacked conviction.

Pierce nodded, his expression understanding but persistent. "I hear you. But think about it—what we do in Ground Branch? It's all the stuff Delta trains you for, but with even more freedom. Plus..." Pierce's grin turned mischievous. "You get to disappear. No public record, no glory hounds. Just the mission."

Mason stared at his empty glass, the amber liquid long gone but the weight of Pierce's words sinking in.

"And if I were interested?" Mason asked after a moment, his voice low.

Pierce leaned back, his grin spreading wide. "I might know a guy. Let's just say the Agency's always looking for people like you."

Mason didn't respond immediately. He let the idea hang in the air, his mind already working through the possibilities. It wasn't just the promise of autonomy or the allure of disappearing from the radar. It was the idea of doing something different, something that mattered in ways the world would never know.

Pierce clapped him on the shoulder, breaking the tension. "No pressure, man. Just think about it."

As the night wore on, Mason and Pierce drifted into easier conversation, the weight of the past slipping away with every shared story and laughter. But in the back of Mason's mind, the seed had been planted.

When they parted ways, Mason walked into the cool night air, his mind racing. The glow of the bar's neon lights cast long shadows on the pavement, and Mason found himself standing still, staring at nothing.

Ground Branch.

The idea lingered, gnawing at him like an itch he couldn't scratch. For the first time in years, Mason felt the pull of something new, a challenge that was calling his name.

And he wasn't the kind of man to ignore a call.

16

Too Big for His Britches

June 2023

Gladiator Farm, Fort Bend County, Texas, USA

Darkness had fallen over Gladiator Farm hours before. The horses in the stables were quiet, and the air was thick with the smell of hay. Tucked away from the main house, a large, wooden barn stood, its beams creaking softly in the wind.

Inside, the Duke paced slowly on the barn's dirt floor. He was dressed in a blue silk shirt, the pristine fabric out of place in the dingy, dimly-lit stables, the sleeves rolled up his rippling forearms.

In front of him, tied to a wooden chair, was a man—one of his own, a mid-level henchman. His face was bruised and swollen, his clothes torn and filthy, and sweat poured down his face as he squirmed in the chair.

The Duke stopped in front of him, his cold eyes narrowing. "You've got one more chance, Marcus. One. Where did the pills come from?"

Marcus coughed, his voice shaky and hoarse. "I—I told you, Duke, I don't know. I swear I don't—"

Before he could finish, the Duke backhanded him across the face with a sickening crack. Marcus's head snapped to the side, blood spurting from his split lip.

"Don't lie to me," the Duke growled, his voice low and menacing. "The nurse told me you've been dropping off packages at mama's house recently. Who gave you the pills? What are they for?"

Marcus whimpered, and blood trickled down his chin. Three other men, including Bishop, leaned against the stable walls.

"I—I swear, Duke, I didn't know what they were for," Marcus stammered, his voice breaking. "Michael... Michael gave them to me to drop off. Said it was for his grandma. I didn't ask questions, I just did what he told me. Please, you gotta believe me—"

The Duke took a step closer, his hand resting on the hilt of the filleting knife tucked into a sheath behind his belt buckle. Marcus trembled, his eyes darting around the room as if searching for an escape, but there was none. The barn was quiet, the air thick with blood and fear. The Duke turned away for a moment, his eyes closing as he fought to keep his rage in check. When he turned back to Marcus, his voice was a low growl.

"How long?" he demanded. "How long has this been going on?"

Marcus gulped, shaking his head. "I don't know exactly. A couple months. Michael kept it quiet, didn't let too many people know."

"What kind of pills are they?" the Duke asked. "What are they for?"

"Come on, boss. I just do what I'm told... " Marcus pleaded.

"Answer me!" the Duke yelled and raised his fist again.

"Fentanyl," Marcus whispered, looking down. "They're fentanyl pills."

"Fentanyl?" the Duke looked shocked. "Ain't that the shit the dope fiends use? Why would he give mama that?"

"For pain, boss. Michael said it's to help with her arthritis. That's all, boss, I swear."

The Duke's eyes narrowed as he thought for a moment. He looked over at Bishop.

"That's what fentanyl is for? Pain?" he asked his most trusted bodyguard.

"I believe so, boss," Bishop responded.

"But how did Michael get them? And why would *he* give them to mama and not the doctor?" the Duke asked.

Bishop shrugged and slowly shook his head. "I couldn't tell you. First I've heard of this."

"This the same shit the dope fiends get high off of though, right? The shit that's all over the news?" the Duke asked again, his face tight with anger.

"That's right, boss," Bishop repeated.

"Well, damn," the Duke said. He turned back to Marcus and stared at him for a while as he thought. Then he exhaled and let the tension out of his shoulders. He chuckled, then grinned. He turned to face the man bound to the chair.

"It's all good, brotha'" he said. "You was just doing your job, right?"

"Yeah...yeah...that's all," Marcus said, a nervous but hopeful grin forming on his swollen lips.

In a flash, the Duke drew the knife from his belt, the blade gleaming in the dim light. Marcus's eyes widened in terror, his body going rigid as he realized what was about to happen.

"No—no, please, Duke! I told you everything, I swear!" Marcus screamed, thrashing against the ropes that bound him to the chair, twisting his face away.

But the Duke was beyond listening. His hand moved in a blur, and the knife slashed across Marcus's face, severing his nose. Marcus cried out. Bishop frowned.

The Duke leaned down and picked up the severed nose. He held it in front of Marcus, who had blood gushing down his chin and dripping onto his shirt.

"This is what happens when you stick your nose in my family's business," the Duke said.

He threw the nose into Marcus's face, who cried out on agony, then in one clean sweep of his hand, he slashed Marcus across the throat from his ear to just under his Adam's apple. Blood sprayed across the barn floor from his severed carotid artery. Marcus's screams choked into a wet gurgle, and his body convulsed for several seconds before falling still.

The Duke calmly wiped the blood from the blade on the dead man's shirt, his expression unreadable.

"Bring him in," the Duke said with a wave of the knife.

Bishop and the two other henchmen stepped out of the stall, leaving the Duke alone with Marcus's corpse leaking blood into the straw and dirt. He heard the heavy doors of the barn creak open, then voices, then a moment later, Bishop stepped back into the stall. His long dreads framed his broad face. He was followed by the two other bodyguards who each held one of Michaels arms, dragging him in behind them.

Michael looked different. Gone was the smooth confidence, the effortless charm that he wore like a second skin. In its place was a guarded wariness. His eyes darted around the barn, taking in the sight of the mutilated body and the spreading pool of blood on the dirt floor.

"Yo, what the hell is this?" Michael asked, wrenching his arm free from Bishop's grip. "What's going on, Pop?"

The Duke stood in the center of the barn, his arms crossed over his chest, his face carved from stone. He didn't speak immediately, allowing the silence to stretch, the weight of it crushing. Bishop stood behind Michael, a silent shadow, his eyes never leaving the Duke.

"You gonna say something?" Michael asked.

The Duke took a slow step forward, his boots crunching on the barn's dirt floor. He pulled the pill bottle from his pocket and held it up, his eyes locked on Michael's.

"Tell me what this is," the Duke growled, his voice low and dangerous.

Michael blinked, caught off guard for just a second before his usual facade slid back into place. He chuckled, though there was no real humor in it. "Come on, Pop. It's just some meds for Grandma. Doctor's orders. She's been getting worse, you know that."

The Duke's hand tightened around the bottle, his knuckles white. "Don't lie to me, boy. I've already talked to your homeboy here." He pointed the knife at Marcus's leaking remains.

Michael's eyes flicked to the side for a moment, his smirk faltering again. "Marcus? That idiot? What the hell did he tell you?"

The Duke took another step forward, the fury in his eyes barely contained. "He told me about the pills, Michael. How you've been giving them to mama. Fentanyl."

The word *fentanyl* hung in the air like a bomb waiting to explode.

Michael's face paled, and for a moment, his usual cocky demeanor cracked. "It's not—" he started, but the Duke cut him off, his voice rising.

"You gave my mother *fentanyl*? You've been feeding her poison, and you didn't think I'd find out?" the Duke's voice was thunderous now, his anger palpable.

Michael raised his hands in mock surrender, trying to defuse the situation. "Whoa, whoa, calm down, Pop. It's not like that. I'm not giving her anything that's gonna hurt her. It's... controlled. She's fine."

"Controlled?" the Duke spat, his eyes blazing. "You've been giving her dope that kills people, Michael. And for what? She's your grandmother, *my* mother!"

Michael's smirk was completely gone now, his eyes darting between his father and Bishop, who stood silently behind him like an executioner waiting for his cue.

"I had to do something, Pop," Michael said, his voice quieter now, almost pleading. "Her hands were getting worse. The pain was driving her crazy."

"Oh, and you're a doctor now? Where did you get this shit?" the Duke demanded. "And don't lie to me!"

Michael's eyes flashed with anger, but he held his tongue. He had learned long ago that challenging his father head-on was a losing game.

The Duke took another step forward, his voice dropping to a deadly whisper. "You better tell me right now that you're not dealing fentanyl, boy. Because if you are—"

"I'm not dealing!" Michael snapped, his temper flaring. "Jesus, Pop, I'm not stupid. I know what that shit does. I'm not messing with that. It was just for her pain."

The Duke's eyes narrowed, searching his son's face for any sign of deception. He wanted to believe him, but the problem with Michael was that he had always been slippery—always playing both sides, always with a trick up his sleeve.

"You're not dealing?" the Duke repeated slowly, his voice still dangerous.

Michael shook his head, his expression hardening. "I swear. I'm not dealing. This was about helping her with her pain. That's all!"

The Duke stared at him for a long moment, the barn silent except for the creak of the old beams in the rafters.

"Bishop," the Duke said quietly.

Bishop stepped forward, his massive frame looming behind Michael. Michael flinched, though he tried to hide it.

"Take him back to the house," the Duke ordered. "But keep an eye on him. I'm not convinced yet."

Michael scowled, his usual cocky bravado returning now that the immediate threat seemed to have passed. "Pop! This is how you treat me?"

"I don't know what you're up to," the Duke said coldly. "But if I find out you've been lying to me about any of this—about the pills, about dealing—I'll make sure you never lie to anyone again. You understand me?"

Michael's jaw clenched, his eyes flashing with anger, but he nodded. "Yeah, I get it."

The Duke's gaze didn't waver, his eyes hard as steel. "Get out of here. And don't think for a second I won't be watching your every move."

With a grunt, Bishop grabbed Michael's arm and dragged him toward the barn doors, his footsteps heavy as they exited into the night.

As they disappeared, the Duke stood alone in the dim barn, the weight of everything pressing down on him. He had always been in control—of his empire, of his family. But now he suspected his eldest son was getting too big for his britches.

17

Something Real

Discovery Green, Downtown, Houston, Texas, USA

Over the next few weeks, Mason and Lisa found themselves spending more time together. What had started as a casual connection had quickly blossomed into something deeper, something neither of them had expected. For Mason, it felt like a slow, steady unraveling of the walls he had spent years building.

They explored Houston like tourists, taking in parts of the city Mason had long ignored. Lisa had a knack for finding hidden gems, and she dragged him along with her boundless energy, always laughing, always making him feel... lighter.

One Friday evening, they found themselves at Discovery Green, a lush park in the heart of downtown, filled with live music, art installations, and the soft hum of people enjoying the summer afternoon. Mason had never been much of a "park guy," but the place had a calming effect, especially with Lisa by his side.

They wandered the park together, passing groups of friends lounging on blankets, kids chasing each other near the playground, and couples picnicking under the trees. The golden hues of the setting sun bathed the park in warm light, making the moment feel even more surreal.

Lisa pointed to a small lake in the middle of the park, where a few paddleboats floated lazily across the water. "Ever tried one of those?" she asked, her smile teasing.

Mason chuckled, shaking his head. "Can't say I have. You?"

"Oh yeah," Lisa replied with a grin. "I used to come here all the time with my cousins when I was younger. They'd always make me do all the paddling while they just sat there."

Mason gave her a sideways glance, his own smile playing at his lips. "You're saying we should get one? You planning on making me do all the work?"

Lisa's eyes sparkled. "Depends on how strong you are."

A short while later, they were gliding across the water in one of the park's bright yellow paddleboats. Mason, true to his word, did most of the paddling, but he didn't mind. The water was calm, the air warm but pleasant, and every now and then, Lisa would lean back with her feet up on the edge of the boat, laughing about how much fun it was to make him work.

"See? You're not so tough," Lisa teased as she splashed her fingers in the water, the ripples spreading out in gentle waves. "You're basically my chauffeur right now."

Mason smirked. "Is that right? You're going to regret saying that."

Before Lisa could respond, Mason gave the boat a hard turn, causing it to tip slightly. Lisa squealed, grabbing onto the sides of the boat as it rocked, her laughter bubbling up as she clung to the seat.

"Okay, okay!" she cried, still laughing. "You win! You're stronger, tougher, all of that!"

Mason grinned, slowing the boat as they drifted peacefully in the middle of the small lake. The setting sun reflected off the water, casting everything in shades of orange and pink. For a moment, the world seemed to still, and they were the only two people who existed.

Lisa looked over at him, her laughter fading into something quieter, more intimate. "You know, you're not what I expected, Mason."

He raised an eyebrow, intrigued. "Oh yeah? What did you expect?"

She smiled, soft and genuine. "Someone tough. Someone guarded. And you are, don't get me wrong. But you're also... more. There's kindness in you.

I like that."

Mason's heart tightened at her words. He hadn't let anyone in for so long—hadn't allowed anyone to see the parts of him that weren't hardened by war. But with Lisa, he didn't have to hide.

"You've got a way of bringing that out in me," he admitted, his voice quiet.

Lisa's eyes softened, and she reached out, her hand resting lightly on his arm. "I'm glad."

For a moment, they sat there in the paddleboat, the air between them charged with something unspoken. The sounds of the park faded into the background as the sun dipped lower, casting long shadows across the water. It was a perfect moment, and Mason could feel it—the pull, the connection.

He leaned in, hesitating for just a second, searching her eyes for any sign that she wasn't ready. But all he saw was warmth and openness. She leaned in too, closing the distance between them until their lips met in a soft, tentative kiss.

The world seemed to stop.

Mason's heart pounded in his chest, but it wasn't from fear or adrenaline this time. It was from something much deeper, something real. The kiss was gentle, sweet, and for the first time in a long time, Mason let himself enjoy the moment without second-guessing, without worrying about what came next.

When they finally pulled back, Lisa smiled at him, her eyes sparkling. "I was wondering when that would happen."

Mason chuckled, feeling a warmth spread through him. "Me too."

They sat there in the boat, the setting sun casting a golden glow over everything, their hands now intertwined. The world seemed far away, and for once, Mason didn't mind.

He had spent so long living in the shadows, surrounded by danger and darkness. But with Lisa, there was light. And for the first time in a long time, Mason felt like he was moving toward something good. Something worth holding onto.

18

Feeding the Hogs

Gladiator Farm, Fort Bend County, Texas, USA

The knock pounded against the silence of the guest house, persistent and sharp. Zane blinked awake, his body sore from the prior day's training, but something deeper gnawed at him, a raw frustration that had been building for days.

He groaned, scrubbing a hand over his face as the knocking grew louder, more insistent. The clock on the nightstand showed it was early. Too early for anyone to be at the door. He reached out instinctively, expecting to find Hannah beside him. But the bed was cold. Empty.

Zane's brow furrowed as he sat up, the ache in his muscles nothing compared to the irritation bubbling inside him. Swinging his legs over the edge of the bed, he stood, exhaustion weighing down on him like a lead blanket. The knocking continued, but he ignored it. He needed to see where Hannah had gone.

Stepping into the hallway, Zane felt the frustration when he saw her. Sprawled on the couch, still in last night's clothes. Makeup smudged, her breathing shallow. On the coffee table, a small mirror sat, dusted with a line of cocaine. A trickle of blood had dripped from her nose, staining the couch.

He walked over and felt her forehead. Still warm. She was alive. Zane's fists clenched. His jaw tightened as he stared at her, the anger coiling in his gut.

The knock came again, louder now, but Zane barely registered it. His eyes stayed glued to Hannah, her face slack, her body limp in the haze of whatever high she'd chased the night before.

The pounding on the door finally snapped him out of it. Zane took a deep breath, trying to calm the storm building inside him. He turned away from the couch, heading for the door, each step heavy with frustration.

He yanked the door open, the early morning light casting long shadows across the floor.

Michael stood there, dressed sharp as ever, but his usual grin was gone. Behind him, Bishop stood, a silent wall of muscle. Zane's gut twisted when he saw the Duke, sitting in the front passenger seat of the black Range Rover parked in the driveway, watching through the windshield.

The tension hit Zane like a gut shot.

"Get dressed. We've got something to show you," Michael said flatly.

Zane's muscles tensed, his eyes narrowing as he scanned the group in front of him. "What's this about?"

Michael didn't blink. "You'll see soon enough. Go throw some clothes on. You don't want to keep the Duke waiting."

Zane hesitated, then nodded. He stepped back inside, grabbing a hoodie and jeans, his pulse hammering in his ears.

When he stepped back outside, Michael gestured to the waiting SUV. "Let's go."

Zane climbed in, wedged between Michael and Bishop. The Duke didn't say a word as they pulled away from the guest house.

Instead of exiting the property through the front gate, they veered off the main drive onto a dirt road that headed into the ranch. They crossed a cow pasture before winding through the wilderness, bumping across shallow creeks and deep ruts, until they reached a small, run-down house deep in the woods.

"Get out," Michael said.

The air was thick with humidity, and the stench of decay hit Zane the second he stepped out.

In front of the house, standing on a rotting porch, was a wiry, old woman with wild, gray hair. Her eyes were sunken, her Mahogany skin leathery, and behind her, the sounds of snorting and splashing animals drifted from dilapidated pens.

"We've got a little demonstration for you," Michael said as they walked.

Zane followed in silence, his senses on high alert. They rounded the house, and the source of the noises became clear—pens filled with wild hogs and alligators, the animals snarling and snapping in their cages. Buzzards circled above in the early morning sky. It was like a menagerie from hell. Zane's skin crawled, and the stench was overwhelming.

The Duke still hadn't say a word as he led their small procession across the yard toward one of the pens. Momma Heloise stared at him as they passed. He held her gaze, and he could see her trembling with fear or excitement, he couldn't tell which.

As they got closer to the pens, Zane felt he could go no farther.

"Damn, it stinks," he protested as he covered his nose with his hand.

"Come on," Michael ordered. Bishop grabbed Zane's arm and nudged him forward toward the foul-smelling cages.

His sneakers squished in the foul mud as cicadas buzzed in the distance. He heard frogs ribbiting from the trees, and all the way his stomach sank lower and lower.

And then he saw it.

In one of the pens lay the dismembered remains of a man—a henchman Zane vaguely remembered seeing around the ranch. His limbs were torn apart. Blood and flesh clung to the ground in a grotesque mess. A hog ate hungrily at the man's organs.

Zane's stomach turned, the scene hitting him like a punch to the gut. His hands trembled as he looked away, but Bishop gripped his arm even tighter.

Finally, the Duke turned and looked Zane dead in the eyes. "This is what happens when people don't listen," he said, his voice calm, but dripping with menace. "You've got decisions to make. About your future. About who you trust."

Zane stayed silent, the knot in his throat tightening. Bishop's grip on his arm was like a vice. He felt the blood draining from his face, and he thought he would faint.

The Duke continued, his voice smooth. "I've been thinking about how to best handle your career. You've got talent, but like fire without purpose, talent without management achieves nothing but destruction."

Michael stepped closer, his eyes gleaming. "You're going to sign an exclusive contract with us. You're going to sign over 85% of your earnings. Fights, endorsements, sponsorships, social media, future deals, everything."

Zane looked up in shock. "What?"

Michael leaned in. "You heard me. We control everything. You fight, we make you a star. You refuse? You end up in there."

The Duke's voice was low, cutting through the air like a blade. "This is your future, son. You take the deal, or you feed the hogs. It's your choice."

Zane's heart pounded in his chest, rage bubbling beneath the surface. He was trapped, backed into a corner. And he knew now—there was no walking away from this.

19

Under the Thumb

Gladiator Farm, Fort Bend County, Texas, USA

Three times a day, Mason walked the perimeter of Gladiator Farm with Bud by his side, scanning the grounds, eyes sharp for anything out of place. It wasn't something he thought about much; it was second nature. But today, the tension was different. It buzzed in the air, something dark and off-kilter lingered over the ranch.

The late afternoon sun was dipping low. Zane was taking a break after another brutal training session, the air still heavy with the sounds of distant grunts and leather hitting bags. Mason's boots crunched over the gravel as he continued his usual sweep.

Everything seemed calm until he neared the barn. He heard voices through an open window. Low, urgent—voices that didn't want to be overheard. He glanced down at Bud. The dog was standing stiffly, ears perked, staring toward the building. Mason moved closer, staying in the shadow, his instincts sharp. As he drew closer, he could hear the voices more clearly.

"You sure about this? We've gotta keep this shit tight, bro," a deep voice muttered.

Mason recognized it—Rico, one of Michael's henchmen. The guy was always close to Michael.

There was a pause, then Michael's voice cut through the air, cool and measured. "Of course, I'm sure. This shit moves fast, and we're making a killing. We've already flooded Fifth Ward and South Dallas."

Mason pressed closer, ears straining.

"This shit is dangerous, bro. Overdoses are up. Got the cops sniffing around. Plus, now your pops," Rico muttered.

Michael's chuckle was low and dark, sending a chill down Mason's spine. "That's why we keep it tight. No one's tracing it back to us. The Duke doesn't even know about half of it. This is my operation, and it's making us a fortune. Besides, we're moving it so fast, they won't know what hit 'em."

"Still risky, man," Rico muttered. "We already lost one of the mules. Cops found him OD'd with a stash the other night."

Michael's tone darkened. "Yeah, that shit was sloppy. But let me worry about the risk. You just keep moving the shit. I've gotta head back down South in a few days to meet with the sugar man and get this payment process smoothed out."

Mason backed away from the wall, his mind racing. As he walked back to the gym, he walked round the corner and caught sight of Zane. He was in the gym, pounding the heavy bag, each punch harder than the last. The sweat, the aggression—it all spoke of a man on the edge. Zane was unraveling under the pressure.

Zane finally stopped, breathing hard. He leaned against the bag and looked over as Mason walked in, their eyes locking. They were both caught in this mess, but only one of them knew just how deep the trap went.

Mason walked over, his expression tight. When he reached Zane, he leaned against the wall and took a casual look around to see who might be listening, but the other trainers and fighters were busy.

"I can't keep doing this," Zane muttered, his voice low and raw.

Mason crossed his arms, eyes narrowed. "What do you mean?"

Zane stared at the floor, his breath coming in slow, controlled waves. "They're extorting me, Mason. Michael and the Duke. They told me to sign over everything—my fight money, endorsements, even my future deals—or I'm dead. Fucking threatened to feed me to the pigs."

Mason straightened, his mind already racing. He had suspected things were bad, but this? Zane was trapped, and Michael's fentanyl racket made it all the more dangerous.

"How long's this been going on?" Mason's voice was steady, but the anger simmered just beneath the surface.

Zane scoffed, shaking his head. "Honestly, it started as soon as I signed that fucking contract. They made it sound like a great deal at first. Now, they want 85% of everything I make. Fuck, man, Michael is even taking my girlfriend right in front of me. It's like they brought me down here just to take everything from me."

Zane punched the bag hard, tears of frustration mixing with the sweat running down his face.

Mason's jaw tightened.

"And they threatened you directly?" Mason asked, keeping his voice low.

Zane squeezed his eyes shut hard, as if to block out a vision. "There's an old lady. Back in the woods. They feed people to animals, man. I saw a fucking body."

Mason clenched his fists. His voice came out calm, but inside, the fury burned. "You're not signing anything, Zane. You hear me?"

Zane's eyes flickered with doubt. "I don't have a choice, Mason. These guys don't take no for an answer."

Mason stepped closer, locking eyes with him. "You always have a choice. You're not alone. I've dealt with guys like this before. Worse. Fear's their weapon. But it only works if you let it."

Zane stared at him, the weight of the situation pressing down. But for the first time, Mason saw something in him—something that said he was ready to fight.

"Alright," Zane muttered. "What's the plan?"

Mason took a deep breath. "First, we get you out from under their thumb. Then you leave the rest to me."

The next morning, before the sun was up, Zane slid out of bed without waking Hannah. They had hardly spoken all week. She spent most of her days lounging around the pool or having one of Michael's goons drive her to the Galleria to shop. Zane slid on jeans, sneakers, and a t-shirt, then made his way to the kitchen where he ate a quick breakfast of fruit and a protein shake. When he was done, he brushed his teeth and was walking out of the bedroom when Hannah rolled over and opened her eyes.

"Hey," she said.

He stopped and looked at her. As much as he was growing to resent her, he couldn't help but feel a pain in his chest.

"Hey," he said back.

"Can I get a kiss before you go, my hard-working man?" she asked, her voice thick with sleep, her blond hair spilling across the pillow.

Zane hesitated a moment, then walked over and sat on the bed next to her. She snuggled close to him, and he felt the warmth of her body and the softness of her skin. She took his hand in hers and kissed his knuckles gently.

"I know you're busy training," she said, her eyes puffy from sleep, "and I never get to see you anymore. But I want you to know that I'm proud of you, and I miss you."

He sat for a moment, caught between the warmth of her caress and the anger building in his heart. In the end, he decided honesty was the only way.

"I wish I could say the same about you."

Hannah stopped kissing his hand.

"What does *that* mean?" she asked, confused.

"It means just what I said. I'm surprised at you. We came down here to accomplish something together, but all I see is you pulling away from me. Or getting pulled away, I can't tell."

He felt her body tense, then roll away.

"Are you serious right now?" she demanded. "All I've been doing is sitting here waiting for you all day while you get to go do your thing. You think this is fun for me?"

"It seems like you're having plenty of fun to me," Zane replied, his temper rising. "Partying day and night but then acting like you're suffering. I don't even know what to say."

"Uh, say *thank you*. Thank you for standing beside you while you pursue *your* dreams. Thank you for being in your bed every night when I could be back in L.A. where my entire life is. I came here to be with you. I can't believe you're acting this way."

Her voice was rising in agitation. Zane stood and walked to the bedroom door.

"Nobody's keeping you here. You're just causing a distraction anyway. And blood stains on the couch. If you're going to use coke, at least stuff some tissue up your nose, or something," he said.

"Oh, fuck you!" Hannah screamed and threw a pillow at him.

"Yeah, I thought you'd say that," Zane said, then walked out of the room.

Mason was waiting for him in the driveway, leaning against the Range Rover with sunglasses on, drinking coffee from a paper cup.

"I thought I was going to have to come in there and get you," he said. "We're late."

"Sorry about that," Zane said, still fuming. "Overslept a little bit."

"It's all good," Mason said. "You're going to need the extra rest anyway. Load up. We've got a drive ahead of us."

Mason steered the Range Rover through the gates of Gladiator Farm, down the country road, and eventually out to I-10 headed back into Houston. They skirted the city using the Grand Parkway as they made their way to Highway 59N leading into the Piney Woods of East Texas. Mason let the radio play old rock and roll hits. Zane rode quietly, staring out the window, and Bud rode happily in the back seat, his tongue hanging as he watched the passing cars.

"Some kind of life you've got," Mason broke the silence. "How does one end up an internet star?"

Zane wiped his hand down his face, as if changing masks.

"Man," he said, "it just happened. My buddies and I used to make prank videos on this one app. We were really just messing around, trying to be popular in school or whatever, but shit just blew up. I guess it was easier to go viral back then. Now, everybody wants to be a celebrity."

Mason sipped his coffee.

"Not all it's cracked up to be though, huh?" he asked.

"Shit," Zane said, exhaling. "I mean, it was. I used to think I was on top of the world. But now, shit, man... I don't know what the fuck."

"Yeah, I know what you mean. After the incident in Denver, I went from nobody to being on the 5 o'clock news overnight. I still had stiches in me when they were trying to book me for morning talk shows. I never asked for it. Never wanted it. But overall, it's been a blessing. The trick is taking time away to reconnect with yourself. To get back to an older time, before being a celebrity was a concern."

"Is that why you're taking me out into these woods?" Zane asked. "To connect with my primal self?"

Mason chuckled.

"Something like that," he said. "You need to get away from that place, but you still need to train. Think of this as old school training."

They drove for a while away from the concrete jungle and into the jungle of pine forest that laid just beyond the city. Then they turned down a dirt road that led to an old, one-story house with a dirty 18-wheeler parked out front. Mason parked, and they got out.

"Nice," Zane teased.

"We're a long way from Malibu," Mason teased back.

Zane started toward the front door, but Mason waved for him to follow, and they made their way around the house.

"No need to knock," he said. "He's not inside."

As the two men and the dog circled around to the back, the sound of old country music carried on the humid air. The sun was fully up, and Zane could smell cow manure and pine needles.

The door to a run-down barn stood open, and Mason walked over to it, removing his sunglasses as he stepped in.

His father was there wearing his grease-stained cover-all's, leaning over a work bench. The engine of a gas-powered trimmer was there disassembled, and his father was blowing carburetor cleaner into it. He looked up over the edge of his glasses as Mason and Zane walked in, his thin white hair standing out in various directions.

"Good morning, Pop," Mason said. "This is Zane, the young man I called you about."

"The fighter?" his dad said skeptically. "Now, George Foreman, that was a real fighter. He came up from nothin' to be one of the greatest. Back then, people were dirt poor. That's how we all grew up. Made us tough. They don't make 'em like that anymore."

Mason chuckled. "I guess not, Pop."

"What is it you said you wanted to do out here?" his father asked, frowning.

"We came to fix the fence," Mason replied, hooking a thumb over his shoulder.

"Fix the fence? He don't look like no fence builder. Mexicans build the best fence. Are you Mexican?"

"No, uh, sir," Zane replied. "I'm Jamaican."

"*Jamaican?*" Mason's father exclaimed. "They got barbed wire in Jamaica?"

Zane stuttered, and Mason laughed.

"Where's the fencing tools at?"

His father scowled, then waved the spray can dismissively toward a corner of the barn.

"There's a T-Post driver and some fencin' plyers over there. There's a few T-Posts and some wire around back. You'll probably have to cut them out of the dewberry vines though. I've got to get this damned trimmer going. Stupid thing acts like it's not getting air."

"You'll get it," Mason assured him with a smile. "We'll gather what we need and get out your hair."

"Ha! I ain't got no damn hair left," he said back.

He reached down for a glass, took a sip of whiskey and coke, then went back to muttering to himself and fidgeting with the motor.

Mason waved Zane to follow him to the corner where he pointed out the tools they would need: a T-Post driver—a piece of metal pipe welded shut on one end with handles on both sides used to hammer steel posts into the ground; a fence stretcher with a ratcheting lever that could be cranked to put tension on the wire; and a specially designed pair of fencing pliers. He pointed to a sack of galvanized fence clips used to attach the barbed wire to the T-Posts and a pair of worn work gloves laying on the ground.

"You're going to need those," Mason said.

They gathered the fencing tools, and Mason grabbed a machete that was leaning against the wall, then they headed out of the barn and made their way around the back. There was a pile of green-painted steel T-Posts laying across some boards at the back of the barn to keep them out of the dirt, and four spools of barbed wire sitting on top. Dewberry and thorny greenbrier vines were tangled all around them.

"Put those gloves on and start pulling those vines back," Mason pointed.

Seeing the thorns, Zane looked hesitant.

"Listen," Mason said, "this is Texas. Everything has a thorn on it. You're gonna get scratched today no matter what. Put the gloves on, pay attention to where you grab, and let's get to it. You pull them away, and I'll chop them. And watch where you step. There's probably a snake around here somewhere."

Zane's eyes got wide.

"A snake? Like, a poisonous one?"

"I mean, not *that* poisonous," Mason laughed. "Come on, the day is wasting. Let's get going."

With a deep breath, Zane went to work ripping the vines away from the pile of fencing supplies while Mason chopped them near the base with the machete. As they cleared the vines, Bud sniffed at everything. In short time, they had cleared the tangled obstructions out of the way, and Mason instructed Zane on how to pick up the spools of barbed wire without getting scratched. Zane was surprised how heavy the spools of galvanized steel wire were. Together, they began moving the supplies about fifty feet from the back of the barn to the fence line Mason had noticed was dilapidated during his previous visit. It didn't take long before Zane's clothes were soaked with sweat, and his arms burned from the exertion of moving the heavy supplies.

"Alright," Mason said. "Now, we have to roll up this old wire and pull up the old posts that are too bent or rusty to keep."

The fence line was overgrown with grass, saplings, and more thorny vines. Together, they yanked the old rusty wire from the brush and hacked the overgrowth away with the machete. It was only about a fifty foot stretch of fence from a gate post to a corner, but Zane was amazed how much work it took to pull up the old fence.

"Damn, Mason," Zane said, panting. "You used to do this when you were little?"

"All the time," Mason replied. "We used to build fence in high school for a couple bucks a foot during the summer."

"This is some hard ass work," Zane said.

"Shit, we're just getting started," Mason replied.

After the old rusty wire was spooled up and set aside, Mason went along and decided which old T-posts were too bent or rusty to keep. On the first rejected post, he taught Zane how to pull the old posts out using the post driver as a lever. Even with the mechanical aid, pulling the posts out of the dry, packed clay was no easy task, and Zane began to feel his shoulders burning.

After that, it was time to start stringing the new fence. Mason rolled out the first strand of wire from the gate all the way to the corner post, which was as thick and round as a power pole. Using the wire as a guideline, he walked along and laid fresh T-Posts where the old ones had been. Then he showed Zane how to stand up the new T-Posts and bang them into the hard earth using the two-handed T-Post driver.

"Alright," Mason said, handing the heavy steel driver to Zane. "Now, it's your turn."

Zane stabbed the first post into the ground, then slipped the post driver over the top, and just like Mason had shown him, began to lift the driver up and slam it down onto the top of the post with both hands as hard as he could. The impact sent shockwaves through his arms. Each post took dozens of whacks to drive home, and soon his shoulders were on fire.

The two men spent the rest of the morning and the better part of the afternoon driving new T-Posts, then stringing and stretching fresh barbed wire while Bud had a day filled with chasing rabbits. Finally, Mason showed Zane how to attach the wire to the posts using clips and the fencing pliers. By the time they were done, Zane was more exhausted than he'd ever been. He had drained ten or more water bottles but was still thirsty, and he couldn't feel his arms except for the sting of the sweat that ran into the innumerable scratches all over his forearms. His clothes were ripped and torn from getting snagged, and despite the gloves, his hands were covered in blisters.

"This is crazy," he said, out of breath. "And the fence goes on and on for miles. You do all this just for some damn cows?"

Mason was standing back, sipping a bottle of water, and admiring their work through his dark sunglasses. Blood ran down his arm from a deep scratch, but he didn't seem to notice.

"Cows?" Mason said. "What cows?"

Zane's jaw dropped.

"What the hell?" he shouted. "We did all this and there aren't any cows?"

Mason chuckled.

"I never said there were."

With that, he motioned for Zane to start gathering up the tools, and together, the two of them made their way back to the barn.

The sun had crossed over the sky's midpoint, and the old radio was still playing. They replaced the tools, but Mason's father was no longer in the barn. He noticed that the trimmer motor was still disassembled on the work bench. He walked back out with Zane trailing behind and saw the back door of the old house was open with only a screen door to keep the wasps and horseflies out.

"Wait here," Mason said, opened the screen door, and walked in.

Inside the mud room, he stomped his boots on the rug to get the dust off, then made his way into the kitchen. The sink was hardly used except for a few old cups and glasses, but he saw the trashcan was overflowing with paper plates.

He heard a television playing from the living room, and he could smell the pungent reek of cigarette smoke in the air. He walked toward the sound and smell, his boots clonking on the old linoleum floor. In the living room, he found his father asleep in his worn leather recliner, mouth wide open, snoring loudly.

He watched him for a moment, then looked around the room. There were old photos of his father as a younger man next to a pretty, smiling woman, and a young boy. He hardly recognized himself as a child, and he didn't remember his mother ever looking that happy in real life. He saw photos of himself in his football uniform, kneeling on the field for school photos, and more of him in his Army uniform. There was a black and white photo of his father as a young man, shirtless, holding an M14 at a firebase somewhere in Vietnam, dog tags hanging on his skinny chest, ribs showing, a cigarette dangling from the corner of his mouth, a green beret on his head, standing before a sign bearing the MACV-SOG emblem. The house looked the same as it had his whole childhood, as if he had stepped back over 30-years into the past.

He looked to make sure his father's cigarette was in an ashtray and not smoldering in the chair cushion, then quietly made his way back out through the kitchen. He closed the door, then eased the screen door so it wouldn't slam.

"Everything good?" Zane asked.

Mason nodded. "All good."

At the front of the house, they climbed back into the Range Rover and started the drive back to Houston.

"You hungry yet?" Mason asked.

"Holy shit, I never thought you'd ask," Zane responded.

"Good. Let's go get some real bar-b-que."

20

The Arab Spring

February 2011

Al-Mazar, Jordan

The rhythmic chanting of protesters echoed off the sandstone buildings lining the narrow streets of Al-Mazar. From his vantage point on the roof of a dilapidated apartment block, Mason could see the crowd swelling in the distance. Thousands of people packed the city square, their voices rising in anger and hope as banners fluttered in the cool February breeze. Below, the maze-like streets pulsed with tension—young men clustered in groups, shopkeepers closed their doors, and the Jordanian military maintained a cautious presence on the fringes.

Mason adjusted the collar of his worn jacket, blending into the city's muted hues. His beard was longer than usual, and a keffiyeh was loosely draped around his neck. He looked like any other expat navigating the chaos of a city in turmoil. But the Glock tucked inside his waistband and the encrypted phone in his pocket told a different story.

"Eyes on target," came the voice in his earpiece. It was Pierce, stationed in a café across the street, his tone as calm as ever.

Mason raised the cheap binoculars he'd picked up at a bazaar, scanning the scene below. The target—a mid-level officer of the Muslim Brotherhood—stood near a shuttered spice shop, casually smoking a cigarette. He wore a dark blazer over a disheveled shirt, his hair slicked back.

"Confirmed," Mason muttered, his voice low but clear. "Target is at the spice shop. Looks relaxed."

"Copy that," Pierce replied. "Let's see if he stays that way."

The operation was simple in theory: track the officer, identify his contact, and gather intel on their plans. But Mason had been in the field long enough to know that no mission was ever simple—especially in a city teetering on the edge of revolution.

Jordan was a pressure cooker. Protests over rising food prices and stagnant wages had filled the streets for weeks, inspired by the uprisings in Tunisia and Egypt. The Arab Spring, the State Department was calling it, but Mason and the other SAD/SOG operators weren't so sure about that. King Abdullah II had promised reforms, but the people were impatient, their frustration bubbling over into mass demonstrations. While Uncle Sam was OK with regime change in certain countries—Syria, for example—they were not so keen to see the Jordanian throne fall to Islamists. Between the Muslim Brotherhood, whose influence was spreading rapidly from Egypt to Bedouin tribesmen secretly funded by wealthy Wahhabis in Saudi Arabia, to Shiite agitators tied to Iran, and the two million Palestinian refugees living in Jordan who dreamed of driving Israel into the sea, there were more powers pulling in more directions than anywhere else on earth. Meanwhile, with the Global War on Terror raging, the CIA had a vested interest in stomping out fires before they got carried away. This kind of milieu is what Ground Branch had been created for.

For Mason and his team on the ground, the unrest was both a cover and a complication. The chaos made it easier to move unnoticed but it was also unpredictable—one wrong move, and they could end up as collateral damage in someone else's fight.

The target stubbed out his cigarette and glanced at his watch. Mason watched as the man shifted nervously, scanning the street before stepping into the shadow of an awning. A moment later, another figure emerged—

a wiry man in his forties with a duffle bag slung over his shoulder. They exchanged brief nods before disappearing into the alley behind the shop.

"Movement," Mason reported, already on his feet. "They're heading into the alley. I'm following."

"Careful," Pierce warned. "These guys are jittery. Don't spook them."

Mason slipped down the building's crumbling cement steps, exiting in a narrow passage that reeked of diesel and spices. He kept his pace steady, his footsteps blending with the city's ambient noise. The alley twisted and turned, each corner revealing another layer of Al-Mazar's underbelly—abandoned crates, stray cats, graffiti scrawled in Arabic.

Ahead, the two men stopped near a heavy wooden door. Mason ducked behind a stack of barrels, watching as the messenger bag was exchanged for a thick envelope. The wiry man opened the bag, revealing the unmistakable outline of an FN FAL rifle. Mason's jaw tightened. This wasn't just about money—these were weapons destined to fuel the chaos gripping the region.

"Pierce, we've got a rifle in play," Mason murmured.

"Copy that," Pierce said. "You want us to move in?"

Mason hesitated. The safe play was to let the deal go down and track the players. But every instinct told him this was more than a routine exchange. The protests had already drawn international attention, and the introduction of weapons could turn a volatile situation into a bloodbath.

"Stand by," Mason said, pulling his Glock and screwing on a suppressor. He crept closer, his body low and silent, until he was within striking distance. The officer was speaking in rapid Arabic, his gestures animated as he pointed toward the rifle.

Mason waited for the right moment. His breathing slowed, his focus narrowing until the noise of the city faded away. When the officer turned his back, Mason surged forward, pressing the Glock against his temple.

"Don't move," he growled in Arabic.

The man froze, his hands shooting up instinctively. The wiry man spun, reaching for something in his bag, but Mason was faster. A single, muffled shot dropped him where he stood, the sound barely more than a whisper in the crowded city.

The officer stammered, his words spilling out in a panicked rush. Mason shoved him against the wall, keeping the Glock pressed firmly against his head.

"What's your plan with the rifle?" Mason demanded, his voice low and lethal.

"I don't know!" the man protested, his eyes wide with fear. "I just deliver them!"

Mason gritted his teeth, his mind racing. There wasn't time for an interrogation—any second, someone could come down the alley and blow his cover.

"Pierce," Mason said into his mic, "I've got the officer. The messenger's down."

"The crowd is moving. Cops are closing in from the east," Pierce replied. "You've got maybe two minutes before this place is crawling."

Mason glanced at the dead man on the ground, then back at the officer. With a sharp motion, he pulled the man's phone from his pocket, shoving it into his jacket.

"You're lucky today," Mason muttered, releasing him with a shove. The man stumbled, his legs barely holding him up as he bolted down the alley.

"Time to go," Pierce said, his voice urgent.

Mason melted into the shadows, his movements quick and practiced. By the time the police arrived, he was already blocks away, blending into the crowd of protesters filling the streets. The city was alive with energy, the people's chants reverberating through the air as Mason disappeared into the chaos.

Later, back at the safe house, Mason and Pierce pored over the contents of the officer's phone. By plugging it into a CIA laptop, they were able to download, decrypt, and examine every message ever sent, every call made, every GPS location. Two other Ground Branch operators hung out waiting for instructions.

"We don't have a lot of time to figure this out," Pierce said, "but there's more than one mention of the courthouse here in Al-Mazar. We need to get surveillance up on that building. Mason, you and Shawn head over there. Keep me posted."

"Roger that," Mason said.

Shawn, another Delta-operator-turned-spook, slid an automatic pistol in the back of his pants, wrapped a keffiyeh around his head, and stood to follow. "Sounds like fun," he said.

It was getting late, and while the streets of Al-Mazar were normally quiet at this hour, the chaos of the day hadn't subsided. Streetlights cast pale yellow halos over the uneven pavement, and men could be seen milling about the streets, pumping their fists and chanting against the regime. Mason adjusted his earpiece, pulling his jacket tighter against the cool night air as they loaded into a white Toyota Hilux and began the drive to the courthouse building.

After a few turns, they took Highway 35 North for a couple of miles, then exited and took more side streets until the courthouse, a low, dusty concrete building, came into view. A small contingent of six Jordanian Gendarmerie were gathered with two Toyota trucks in front of the building, nervously eyeing a crowd of protestors who seemed agitated, but were keeping their distance.

"Well, shit," Shawn muttered. "Nothing to see here."

Mason chuckled, then pushed the PTT button for his radio.

"Fox 1, Coyote. We're on location. There's a crowd of savages here, and they look hungry, over."

"Roger that, Coyote," Pierce's voice came through. "Stay out of the way and keep me advised, over."

"Roger, Fox 1, out," Mason replied.

The night simmered with tension as Mason and Shawn leaned against the Toyota Hilux parked a block from the courthouse. From their vantage point, the scene had shifted. The once agitated but controlled crowd now swelled with raw energy, a mass of bodies fueled by frustration and adrenaline. Their chants had grown louder, angrier, echoing off the crumbling sandstone buildings.

"This doesn't look good," Shawn muttered, nodding toward the courthouse steps, where a few protestors had gathered, shouting at the Jordanian Gendarmerie officers. "You think it's going to pop?"

Mason adjusted his jacket, keeping his Glock hidden but accessible. "It always does," he replied flatly. "The only question is when."

The officers stationed near the courthouse exchanged nervous glances, gripping their rifles tighter as the crowd edged closer.

A fiery glow flickered within the crowd as a Molotov cocktail arced through the air. It smashed against the courthouse facade, erupting in flames. The crowd roared as the fire licked at the building's concrete walls, smoke curling into the night sky.

"Here we go," Mason said, his voice steady despite the surge of chaos.

The Gendarmerie sprang into action, shouting warnings in Arabic and advancing with riot shields raised. The protestors didn't scatter. Instead, they pushed forward, emboldened by the flames and their own numbers. Another Molotov flew, this one crashing into the line of officers, forcing them back as the fire spread across the ground.

Shawn shook his head, muttering under his breath. "This is about to get ugly."

With batons and shields, the few police tried to push back the mass of protestors, but little by little, they were forced to give up ground. Mason could see their commander shouting into his radio, probably calling for help. Suddenly, the sound of breaking glass carried, and a car parked along the street went up in flames. The crowd cheered louder. Rocks and paving stones began to rain down on the Gendarmerie, so they pulled together and raised their shields overhead like a Greek phalanx. Random protestors broke free of the crowd and ran up the steps of the courthouse, only to be tackled by police.

Finally, three more Toyotas pickups came barreling up the street from behind Shawn and Mason, each loaded with police. They spilled out and joined their colleagues in trying to stop the crowd's push.

"Looks like they're trying to get to the courthouse," Shawn observed.

"I think you're right," Mason agreed.

"Fox 1, Fox 1, shit is boiling over down here at the courthouse. We're probably going to need to make a move pretty quick, over," Mason said.

"What's the situation?" Pierce radioed back.

But before Mason could answer, a shot rang out, then three more. They seemed to be fired into the air. Shawn and Mason ducked and moved to the back of the Hilux.

"We've got rifle fire, over" Mason called back.

The situation escalated in seconds. While the police were panicking, a group of protesters broke free of the crowd and charged toward the courthouse. Men with keffiyehs around their faces broke windows and forced their way into the courthouse, shoving aside a few scattered barricades. The officers fired warning shots into the air, but it only spurred the crowd on. Mason and Shawn stayed behind their pickup, observing as the mob surged forward, their chants now drowned out by the shattering of glass and the crackling of flames.

Then, a sharp crack split the air. The distinct sound of a rifle. Mason's stomach dropped as he saw another Jordanian officer stumble, clutching his chest before collapsing onto the steps. Blood spread across the man's uniform as his comrades dragged him back, their panic visible even from a distance.

"Shit," Shawn hissed. "They're firing back now."

"We've seen enough. Time to go," Mason ordered.

The two men moved quickly but calmly, slipping into the cab of the truck. Mason started the engine, his eyes flicking to the rearview mirror as the fire consumed more of the courthouse. Protestors swarmed inside, and the officers fell back, regrouping near their vehicles.

Shawn checked his sidearm, his jaw tight. "What a mess."

Mason nodded grimly, steering the Hilux away from the scene. "Let's not add to it. We've got what we need."

The drive back to the safe house was tense, the streets alive with sporadic chaos. Small groups of protestors roamed the city, setting fires and clashing with police. Mason kept the headlights low, navigating through side streets to avoid trouble.

By the time they reached the safe house, the adrenaline had settled into a cold resolve. Mason parked the truck in the narrow alley behind the building, cutting the engine and scanning the surroundings before they stepped out.

Inside, Pierce and the other operators were waiting, their faces shadowed in the dim light of the room. A laptop hummed on the table, its screen glowing with surveillance feeds and maps of Al-Mazar.

"What happened?" Pierce asked, his voice sharp.

Mason dropped into a chair, running a hand through his hair. "They sacked the courthouse. Protesters stormed it and set it on fire. One Gendarmerie officer's dead. The crowd's armed."

Pierce frowned, crossing his arms. "That's going to ripple. The Jordanians won't take that lightly."

"They'll crack down," Shawn added, leaning against the wall. "And hard. It's about to get a lot worse out there."

Mason met Pierce's gaze, his expression grim. "We need to move fast. That rifle exchange we interrupted earlier? It's not the only one. If this spreads, they'll have more firepower in the streets. We can't let that happen."

Pierce nodded, his mind already working through the next steps. "Agreed. Let's focus on the leads we've got from the officer's phone. If there's another weapons shipment, we need to intercept it before it hits the ground. I've got a call into Jordanian intelligence. They're sending a case officer in the morning to help."

Mason stood, his resolve hardened. "Let's get to work."

The team dispersed, diving into their tasks with practiced efficiency. Mason sat down beside Shawn, reviewing the intel from the phone. The chaos in Al-Mazar was far from over, but Mason knew they still had a chance to steer it—if they acted quickly and with precision.

The sun rose over Al-Mazar with a haze of smoke lingering in the air. Mason, Pierce, and Shawn gathered in the safe house's main room, poring over maps and intelligence gathered from the stolen phone. The tension was palpable—whatever the next move was, it had to count.

A knock at the door drew everyone's attention. Mason's hand instinctively went to his Glock as Shawn peered through the peephole. Satisfied, he unlocked the door, revealing a Jordanian man dressed in local garb, blending in, his eyes scanning the room with the practiced precision of a seasoned operator.

"Good morning," the man said in accented but fluent English, stepping inside. Behind him were two Jordanian operatives wearing cargo pants and plate carriers, both armed with M4 carbines. The Jordanian officer nodded toward the table, his demeanor all business. "I am Ahmed. We need to talk."

Pierce gestured to the seat across from him. "Ahmed, I'm Pierce. I'm the OIC for our operation. This is Mason and Owens. Let's hear it."

Ahmed placed a slim manilla folder on the table, opening it to reveal grainy surveillance photos and handwritten notes in Arabic. He pointed to an image of a man exiting a nondescript sedan.

"His name is Adnan al-Bahri," Ahmed said, his tone clipped. "He's a mid-level operative in the Muslim Brotherhood, known for handling sensitive logistics. Last night, during the courthouse chaos, documents were stolen from a government archive. Those documents contain intelligence on our undercover agents, their families, and our current operations."

Pierce leaned in, his expression hardening. "How bad are we talking?"

Ahmed's jaw tightened. "Bad enough that if those documents get out, it could destabilize the entire region. Lives are at stake. These papers cannot fall into the wrong hands."

Mason glanced at the photos, committing every detail to memory. "You've got a lead on where they are?"

Ahmed tapped another photo, this one of a run-down apartment block in the outskirts of the city. "We've tracked Adnan to this safehouse. It's used by the Brotherhood for storing weapons and intelligence. We believe the stolen documents are there. Adnan is likely inside, along with at least four other operatives. Our mission is to retrieve the documents and neutralize any threats."

Shawn whistled low, studying the building layout in the folder. "Looks like a fortress."

Ahmed nodded. "It's well-guarded. Armed men patrol the perimeter, and the apartment itself is reinforced. But we've got the element of surprise, and with your team's expertise, we can hit them hard and fast."

Mason crossed his arms, his mind already calculating. "We'll need to move at night. Keep it clean and quiet until we're inside. What's the terrain like?"

Ahmed flipped to a hand-drawn map. "The building is surrounded by alleys and a small courtyard. There's a single road leading in and out, which means we'll need to secure our exfil route before the raid. We'll set up a diversion to draw attention away from the area."

Pierce nodded, tapping the map. "We'll need eyes on the place before we hit it. Shawn and I can set up overwatch positions here and here." He pointed to two rooftops overlooking the courtyard. "Mason, you'll lead the entry team with Ahmed's men."

Mason's face was stone, but his eyes were sharp. "What's the plan for handling Adnan if he resists?"

Karim's voice was cold. "Then he doesn't leave the building alive."

The operators spent the rest of the day preparing. Ahmed's men assembled their weapons with clinical precision, while Mason and his team checked their gear—suppressed rifles, sidearms, flashbangs, and breaching charges. Mason inspected every piece of equipment twice, his movements deliberate and focused.

As the sun dipped below the horizon, the team loaded into two vehicles—a beat-up van and a nondescript sedan. The drive to the safehouse was tense, the streets eerily quiet after the previous night's violence. The operators didn't speak much, their minds on the mission ahead.

When they arrived at the staging area a few blocks from the target, Pierce and Shawn broke off to set up their overwatch position on top of a two-story carpet merchant's shop two blocks over while Mason and the assault team waited in the van. After fifteen minutes, Peirce's voice called over the radio.

"Guards on the roof and at the entrance," he whispered. "AKs. They're on alert, over."

"Roger that, Fox 1," Mason called back. "We're getting ready to move, over."

"Ahmed, now would be a good time for that distraction," Mason said.

Ahmed pressed the PTT button on his radio and said something in Arabic.

Mason caught the word "kahraba'"—electricity. Within moments, the light spilling though the van's tinted rear window went dark as power was cut to the entire area, causing the street lights to go dark.

Mason, Ahmed, and the rest of the six-man entry team lowered the GPNVG Ground Panoramic Night Vision Goggles attached to their FAST helmets, racked rounds into their M4s, and climbed silently from the rear of the van. They trotted down the sidewalk, sticking to the shadows close to the building as they approached the apartment block with Ahmed at point.

Ahmed paused near an alley, his eyes scanning the building's exterior.

Mason nodded, signaling for the team to hold. He keyed his radio. "Pierce, you in position?"

"Roger," came the reply, crisp and calm. "We've got eyes on the rooftop and courtyard. Two tangos on the roof, three at the entrance. No sign of the target."

"Copy that. Stand by." He looked up and down the street one last time before keying his radio. "Kick it off, Fox 1."

The operation began with precision. Pierce and Shawn silenced the rooftop guards with simultaneous suppressed shots, the faint cracks echoing through the night.

"Rooftop clear," Pierce's voice carried.

Then there were more muted cracks as Pierce and Shawn dropped the front door guards before they had time to react.

"Two down at the front, one still up and shielded," Pierce transmitted.

"Roger, Fox 1. Entry team moving now," Mason sent back.

With that, the assault team stormed toward the building. The one remaining guard at the front was shouting in panicked Arabic when Ahmed shot him twice in the upper chest, silencing him by collapsing his lungs instantly.

Ahmed led the entry team forward, their movements fluid and silent as they crossed the courtyard. At the building's entrance, Ahmed signaled for the team to stack up at the door. The Jordanian breacher moved up from the back and placed a breaching charge against the lock, his hands steady despite the tension.

The charge detonated with a muffled thump, and the team surged inside. Mason led the way into an office to the right, his rifle sweeping the room. Muffled shots rang out as the team dropped two bodies. Mason flowed through a door into the next room, a Jordanian operator right beside him. There was movement in the green view of his night vision goggles, a rifle barrel from a doorway, so Mason fired. A man's body tumbled forward and thumped on the ground. The entry team never said a word, working like ghosts in the darkness.

The sound of muffled voices came from upstairs, and the team moved quickly but carefully, their boots silent on the worn concrete steps. On the second floor, they encountered resistance. A burst of gunfire erupted from a doorway, forcing the team to take cover. Mason lobbed a flashbang into the room, the deafening blast disorienting the occupants. He entered a moment later, taking down two armed men with precise shots.

In the next room, they found Adnan. He was scrambling to grab a pistol from a desk, but Mason closed the distance in an instant, butt stroking him with his carbine and slamming him against the wall. Ahmed entered behind him, his expression cold as he pulled a bag from his vest.

"Haqibat lah," he ordered, stepping back as his men subdued the target. "Bag him."

Efficiently, the team zip tied the Muslim Brotherhood operative's hands and slipped a black bag over his head.

The stolen documents were laid out on a table in the corner of the room. Ahmed inspected them briefly before nodding. "This is it. Let's move."

The team led their prisoner back down the steps and out into the street. The van slid to a halt the moment they stepped through the door, so they loaded up and exfiltrated without incident. The sedan picked up Pierce and Shawn, their vehicles disappearing into the night before anyone could react.

Back at the safe house, they debriefed quickly, the tension easing as the success of the mission sank in.

Ahmed approached Mason, his face solemn. "You've done good work here," he said. "This could have ended very differently."

Mason gave a small nod, his expression unreadable. "It's not over yet. This city's still ready to burn."

Ahmed nodded. "The entire region is ready to burn. We are merely firefighters. We extinguish the flames we can. The rest is up to Allah."

21

Round Two

July 2023

Gladiator Farm, Fort Bend County, Texas, USA

They made it back to Gladiator Farm just after dark. Mason dropped Zane off, bid him good night, then drove the Range Rover to the garage apartment where he'd been staying.

Exhausted from building fence all day, Zane strolled to the back door of the guest house. He heard music playing—he recognized a Houston rapper's voice, not the pop music Hannah normally listened to—and immediately his stomach tightened. He pushed open the door, and the sight inside made his blood boil.

Sure enough, Michael was there, sitting on the couch with Hannah. She was perched next to him, laughing softly at something he'd said, a wine glass dangling from her fingers. Michael's arm was draped casually across the back of the couch, his posture relaxed, comfortable.

Hannah's eyes were half-lidded. The mirror on the coffee table was covered in remnants of white powder.

Michael looked up, noticing Zane's entrance, and that same cocky grin spread across his face.

"Hey, champ," he said casually, his voice dripping with arrogance. "You're just in time to join us."

Zane's fists clenched at his sides, his body tense as he stepped further into the room. He looked from Michael to Hannah, her disheveled appearance only adding fuel to the fire burning inside him. She looked up at Zane with glassy eyes, but didn't say anything—too far gone to realize the situation unfolding.

"Get the fuck out," Zane growled, his voice low and filled with barely contained fury.

Michael raised an eyebrow, feigning innocence. "Whoa, take it easy, man. We're just having a little fun. No need to get all worked up."

Zane stepped closer, his heart pounding in his chest. "I'm done with this, Michael. I'm done with your threats, and I'm done playing your game."

The tension in the room shifted instantly. Michael's smile faltered for a split second, but then it returned, colder this time, more calculating. He stood up slowly, adjusting his shirt as he moved to face Zane head-on.

"Big talk," Michael said, his voice dripping with condescension. "But you and I both know you don't mean it. There's no walking away from this. You've got too much to lose."

Zane's jaw tightened as he fought to keep his temper under control. "I'm not signing your contract, I'm not giving you 85%, and I'm sure as hell not letting you run my life."

Michael chuckled, shaking his head. "You really don't get it, do you? This isn't a negotiation. You're going to sign that contract, and you're going to do it with a smile. Because if you don't..."

His voice trailed off, and he lifted his eyebrows to remind Zane what he'd seen at Mama Heloise's.

Zane's heart raced as the words hung in the air. He could feel the room closing in around him.

"You don't scare me, Michael," Zane said, his voice steady, but full of defiance. "I'm not playing these games anymore. If you want to take me out, then do it. But I'm done letting you and the Duke control me."

Michael's eyes darkened, his smile vanishing completely. He took a step closer, his voice a low growl. "You're making a big mistake."

Zane squared his shoulders, his muscles taut. "I'm not scared of you."

The room fell into a tense silence, the only sound the soft hum of the air conditioning. Hannah's eyes were wide and her mouth was moving, but she couldn't seem to form words. Michael's expression hardened, and for a moment, it looked like he might lash out, but then he took a step back, regaining his composure.

"Cool," Michael said, his voice smooth again. "Have it your way. Champ."

He turned to Hannah and placed the wine glass back on the table. "Have a good night, Hannah."

Without another word, Michael strode out of the guest house, his footsteps heavy as he left Zane standing there in the living room, the tension still crackling in the air.

Zane let out a slow breath, his hands trembling with adrenaline. He turned toward Hannah, who was now slouched on the couch, staring blankly at the floor. The anger he'd felt moments ago was replaced by something else— exhaustion, frustration, and a deep sadness.

He crouched down in front of her, his voice soft but firm. "Hannah, you need to get it together. This isn't you."

She looked at him, her eyes hazy with the remnants of the drugs. "I'm fine," she mumbled, her words slurred.

Zane shook his head, the weight of everything pressing down on him. "No, you're not. And I can't keep doing this. You've got to help yourself."

For a long moment, they just sat there, the room silent except for the faint sound of the wind outside.

She started to sob quietly, her tears dripping eyeliner down her cheeks and onto the expensive white rug. Zane's heart ached as he watched her, knowing she was slipping further and further away from the person he had fallen in love with.

As the door closed behind Michael, Zane glanced over his shoulder, knowing he had drawn the line. There was no going back now.

The night was still, an eerie calm settling over Gladiator Farm. Zane lay in bed, staring up at the ceiling, his mind a swirling mess of thoughts. The confrontation with Michael earlier had left him raw—angry, but also uncertain. He had drawn a line in the sand, refused to bend to the Duke's threats, but the weight of that decision was heavy.

Next to him, Hannah was absent again. He had been too tired to argue with her after the mess with Michael, hoping she'd crash on the couch like before and sleep off whatever binge she was on. The drugs were wearing her down, pulling her further into Michael's world, and Zane didn't know how to save her from it—or even if he could. At some point, exhaustion consumed him, and he faded into darkness.

When he woke the next morning, the house was quiet. He got out of bed and walked into the living room, hoping to find Hannah passed out on the couch like she had been so many times before, but she wasn't there. The living room was empty. The mirror on the coffee table had been wiped clean, the bottle of wine gone. Zane's gut twisted. He called out her name, but there was no answer. He checked the rest of guest house, then stepped outside, checked the back patio and pool, and scanned the property for any sign of her.

Nothing.

Zane grabbed his phone and dialed Hannah's number. The call went straight to voicemail. He dialed again, then again. Still nothing.

As Zane paced the living room, his phone buzzed. It was Michael.

"Don't worry about her. She's with me now," Michael said.

Zane's heart slammed in his chest as he read the message. His fingers trembled as he typed back a response.

"What the hell does that mean? Where is she?" Zane demanded.

The reply came almost immediately.

"We took a trip South," Michael replied.

Zane's blood ran cold. Belize, the Duke's ranch deep in the jungle.

"What are you doing? What the fuck is this?"

"Let's just say she's on vacation with me while you consider your best option."

Zane's jaw clenched as he gripped the phone tighter, his mind racing.

"Listen to me. If you hurt her, I swear to God, Michael..."

"You swear to God what?" Michael laughed. "No one's hurt. Yet. But you've got a decision to make. No need to worry about her. You need to worry about signing that contract."

Zane's heart pounded in his chest. His pulse roared in his ears as the reality of the situation sunk in. Hannah wasn't just gone—she had been taken, and they were using her as leverage to force his hand.

"I'll come for her," Zane said coldly.

Michael was calm.

"I'd like to see you try, little boy. You've got 24 hours to make your choice. There's all kinds of animals in these jungles. You ever seen what a jaguar can do to a girl?"

Then the phone clicked and went silent.

Zane stood in the center of the guest house, his phone clutched tightly in his hand. He felt trapped, cornered like never before.

His mind raced, trying to find a way out. He couldn't trust the police— Michael had too many connections, too many people in his pocket. And with the Duke involved, things could escalate fast. He couldn't sit back and do nothing, but he couldn't just sign over his life to these people either.

Zane's phone buzzed again, and he glanced down at the text message.

Michael: Clock's ticking. I'm going to need that answer tonight.

Zane swallowed hard, his jaw clenched tightly. He needed help. He couldn't do this alone, and there was only one person he trusted right now.

Without hesitation, Zane dialed Mason's number. It rang twice before Mason's gruff voice answered on the other end.

"Mason."

"It's Hannah," Zane said, his voice tight with barely contained panic. "Michael took her. Kidnapped her. They're in Belize. I need your help."

22

When Words are Too Soft

Gladiator Farm, Fort Bend County, Texas, USA

Mason couldn't be sure the garage apartment wasn't bugged, so he stepped outside, went down the stairs, and walked across the yard, his phone clutched tightly in his hand. Bud followed close behind. He'd just finished talking to Zane who sounded like a man on the brink. Michael had taken Hannah to the Duke's compound in Belize. The stakes had gotten much higher.

He stood next to the barbed wire fence separating the main estate from the cow pastures. The quiet hum of the ranch felt unnaturally calm compared to the storm raging inside his head. He drew in a steady breath and hit the first number on his call list: Caleb.

Caleb picked up. "Mason, what's up?"

"It looks like the Duke's son kidnapped Hannah, Zane's girlfriend," Mason said, keeping his voice low. "It sounds like he took her to their ranch down in Belize."

A brief silence on the other end, then Caleb's tone grew sharp. "That escalated fast. You sure?"

Mason glanced at the main house, where the Duke's men roamed the grounds like watchful dogs. "Zane got the message straight from Michael. She's a hostage. They're using her to force him into signing away his fight earnings."

Caleb cursed under his breath. "We can't let that stand. So, what's the move? Take one of theirs hostage? Make an exchange?"

"Nah," Mason replied. "We have to stay within the law. I think we have to extract the girl."

"OK. I can have QRT ready to move, but we need a plan. You have any intel on the ranch?"

"Some," Mason replied. "It's a fortress. Walls, armed guards, gun towers. We'll need every advantage."

"What about legal authority in Belize?" Caleb asked.

"Let me work on that," Mason replied. "Can you start pulling resources?"

"I'm on it," Caleb said. "Give me two hours."

The line went dead. Mason stared at his phone, the next call weighed heavy on his mind.

He dialed Karim, Prince Omar's head of security, the phone's ring echoing in the still air. It picked up sooner than he expected.

"Mason." Karim's voice was calm, laced with an accent that rarely betrayed emotion.

Mason kept his tone level. "We have a problem."

A pause. "Aha. Go on."

"It's Michael, the Duke's son," Mason said, his jaw tensing. "They're trying to extort Zane for his prize money. He kidnapped Zane's girlfriend to use as leverage. They're holding her at the Duke's ranch in Belize."

Another silence, just the faint sound of breathing on the line. Then Karim's voice turned steely. "That's a serious situation."

"Serious enough to need your help," Mason replied. "My people have men, but the Duke's strong, and Michael's cunning. They're both dangerous. We need resources in Belize, and we need them fast. And we need legal authority of some sort."

Karim exhaled slowly. "Prince Omar won't like hearing about kidnappings. Especially if it threatens his interests."

Mason glanced around the ranch again, verifying no one lingered close enough to overhear. "Zane's on the brink. He can't fight this alone. Neither can I. We need your team, your gear, your connections."

Karim didn't hesitate. "Understood. I'll consult with the Prince. Get me details—maps, guard numbers, everything you can gather. We'll come to you in Houston. Where are you exactly?"

"I'm at the Duke's ranch."

"You'll have to meet us at one of our safe houses. Can you slip away without raising alarms?"

"Yes," Mason said.

"Good. Don't raise any suspicions but get ready to move. I'm already in town," Karim said.

A flicker of relief crossed Mason's face. "Roger that. Thanks, Karim."

"I'll be in touch," Karim replied.

The line clicked dead. Mason took a moment to gather himself, breathing in the thick Texas air.

He slipped his phone into his pocket, mind racing with the next steps: gear, transport, intel. Zane would need reassurance, but Mason couldn't sugarcoat this.

Things were about to get real hot, real fast.

After dropping Bud off at his father's house in the country, Mason drove into Houston, taking the 610 loop around to the Westheimer exit. He assumed the Duke's vehicle had a tracker on it, so he parked the Range Rover in the parking garage of the Galleria mall, then walked up the ramp and summoned an Uber. The Uber arrived quickly and in half an hour he made it downtown. There, the driver deposited him on the curb.

Mason glanced up at the towering glass building. A discreet sign marked it as Saud International Investments, but he knew better. This wasn't just another high-rise.

Karim, flanked by two serious looking security men wearing dark suits, met him inside the opulent marble and gold lobby. They shook hands and walked quickly. They rode a private elevator in silence to the top of the building. The polished doors slid open onto a spacious, modern penthouse. Floor-to-ceiling windows revealed the Houston skyline, and the furniture was sleek and modern.

Inside, Caleb and Benito stood around a large table. Other men were either standing around the table with them, leaning against a bar, or sitting on a couch nearby. He recognized three of them from GZD, but judging by their dark complexions, the other men were Karim's men. Saudis or Jordanians, most likely.

"There he is," Caleb said as Mason approached.

They clasped hands warmly.

"What's up, bro?" Benito asked, clasping Mason's hand and clapping him on the back.

"Didn't expect to see you here," Mason said.

"What? Man, you can't go to the tropics without me," Benito teased. "I packed my board shorts and everything. I'm trying to get some sand between my toes, homie."

"I don't know how much surfing we'll get in. I hope you brought your Chloroquine though, because if this goes how I think it will, we'll be headed into the jungle," Mason replied.

He looked down at the table and noticed a large aerial photo of the Duke's Belizean compound.

Mason exhaled, steadying himself. "Alright. Time is of the essence, so let's get down to it."

Karim walked over.

"As soon as we learned Zane had signed on with the Duke, we began gathering intel and preparing option packages. We had our people in Belize City ask questions around the airport there. Michael arrived with the girl about eight hours ago and left with his usual entourage. We assume he went to the family compound west of the city, but I'm waiting for confirmation now. We have people headed out there to recon the compound, but as you see in the photo, it's surrounded by a wall and therefore difficult to surveil."

Karim gestured to the photo. "The Duke's estate is deep in the jungle. High walls, armed patrols, spotlights, watchtowers. He keeps it guarded like a fortress."

Caleb tapped a satellite image. "Most likely, Michael's hiding Hannah somewhere inside. We don't know exactly where, but intel suggests the main guest quarters are here."

"Yeah, that's right," Mason agreed. "I've been there. Once. I can walk you through the internal layout."

"Good," Caleb nodded.

Benito folded his arms, brow furrowed. "Well, we can't just walk in without an invitation. Assume we're going in high speed?"

Karim nodded. "Prince Omar has obtained authorization for a small team of operators. We'll handle the perimeter and the exfil. GZD, you will handle the extraction. In and out, no alarms triggered. We move fast."

Mason rubbed the back of his neck. "The Duke will have a lot of firepower. Michael needs Hannah as leverage, so it does him no good to execute the hostage. Nevertheless, we can't give him that chance."

"We won't," Caleb said, voice firm. "We'll coordinate with local contacts for a quick extraction. We'll need a chopper for medevac though."

Karim nodded. "We will infil half the unit by automobile on the main road to somewhere around here. The other half will infil by boat along the Belize River here. Both teams will finish the insertion by foot, approaching from the north and the east. The main gate faces east. We can create a distraction there, neutralize these towers, then come over or through the wall. As soon as we find the girl, we have to assume she can't climb, so we'll have to take her out through the main gate or a breach in the wall. Then we use the same vehicles to drive or boat back out."

Benito's gaze flicked from the map to Mason. "We do this right, we're out before they know what hit 'em."

Karim studied each man in turn. "Belize City is only a two hour flight. We launch at dawn. That only gives us a few hours to finalize details, check gear, and get to the airport."

Mason eyed the aerial photo one last time. His eyes were drawn to the mysterious warehouse in the back of the property.

"We get Hannah out and we get everyone home safe. No half-measures."

A silent agreement passed among them.

Karim placed a small folder on the table. "These are your diplomatic clearances, courtesy of Prince Omar. Do not waste them. This is a one-shot deal."

Mason picked up the folder, glancing at the papers inside—special permissions, travel documents, discreet weapons clearance. The cover was a legally complex top secret drug interdiction mission in coordination with the Drug Enforcement Agency under Title 22 of the United States Code mixed with a training mission in accordance with a Status of Forces Agreement under Title 10. The Prince's reach was vast indeed.

"Alright, gentlemen," Karim said, snapping the folder shut. "We prepare tonight. Rendezvous at 1000. From there, we head to the airport, and we don't stop moving until we meet back here. Understood?"

The men all voiced their agreement.

Mason squared his shoulders. "Let's get to work."

Meanwhile, Mo stood at the wrought-iron gates of the Duke's River Oaks mansion, heart thudding as the gate swung open. He had never been here, to his own father's house.

He strode up the long driveway, past the manicured hedges and imported statues. The house loomed ahead, a pristine monument to the Duke's success. But Mo knew about the shadows behind those walls, the secrets and sins that no amount of marble could hide.

He used the iron knocker on the massive front door, and a towering bodyguard in a black suit opened it without a word, stepping aside to let Mo in. He gestured for Mo to turn around and hold his arms out so he could pat him down for weapons.

Mo followed the guard through the entryway, past a colossal, grotesque painting of his father, shirt open, grinding behind some naked woman. It was the most disturbing thing Mo had ever seen. They walked to the study, passing more oil paintings and relics of the Duke's rise to power—a dozen gold and platinum records his label had earned, even more photos of the Duke with boxers, pro athletes, and local politicians.

He found his father standing by a floor-to-ceiling window, hands clasped behind his back as he gazed out over the garden, a cigar smoldering in his clenched fist.

The Duke turned slowly, a flicker of disdain crossing his face. "What do you want?"

Mo braced himself.

"Mom is sick," Mo said, his voice tight. "She needs help."

The Duke's eyes narrowed. "Not my concern."

Mo took a deep breath.

"You cut her off because of me. Don't blame her for who I am. She stood by you for years, and now you're discarding her? All because you can't accept who I am? It's not her fault you can't stand me."

A cold chuckle slipped from the Duke's lips. "You want honesty, Mo? Fine. You're not my son. I don't have a son who"—he paused, sneering—"acts like you."

Mo's jaw clenched, hurt mingling with fury. "You can't erase me just because I'm gay."

The Duke advanced, eyes steely. "Watch me. You turned your back on everything I built. You could've had power, wealth, respect—but you chose to be *this*."

Mo's heart pounded, a raw ache cutting through his anger. "I didn't *choose* anything. I am who I am. So, you're punishing her, too? She's sick. She needs care, and you know she can't afford it."

His father shrugged, cruel indifference etched on his face. "I owe her nothing. She made sure of that when she chose you over me."

Mo took a shaky breath, the words slicing deep. "You can hate me all you want, but don't pretend you ever cared about her. All you ever want it to control everyone."

"Control is what keeps this family alive," the Duke spat, voice low. "And you lost your claim to this family the day you threw everything away."

Silence weighed heavy. The house felt colder, the air thick with the finality of this rift. Mo forced himself to stand taller, refusing to crumble under the Duke's disdain.

"You're a monster," he said, tone measured but trembling at the edges. "I don't know why I bothered coming here. One day, you'll choke on all that cruelty."

The Duke's lips curled in a sneer. "Get out. And don't come back."

Mo stared at the man who had once been his hero, now a stranger wrapped in arrogance. Hurt twisted in his chest. But he wouldn't let the Duke see him break.

Without another word, Mo turned and walked away, footsteps echoing through the marble hall. Outside, the humid Houston night enveloped him, but it felt less stifling than the mansion he left behind.

He climbed into his G-Wagon, fingers gripping the wheel as he stared at the grand facade. Tears threatened, but anger burned them away. The Duke had cut off him and his mother—but Mo vowed this wasn't the end.

Not by a long shot.

Soon after, a black Mercedes S-Class pulled through the gates of the Duke's River Oaks mansion. The same Saudi emissary who had first visited Zane, Nasir al-Amri, stepped from the back of the car and knocked on the front door. The Duke's bodyguard opened it. After a pat down, the emissary followed the henchmen down the marble hall into the Duke's study with its dim lights, expensive rugs, and the reek of cigar smoke. The Duke sat behind an imposing desk dressed in one of his silk shirts, eyes burning with a cold fury when he looked up at the Arab. Bishop's hulking frame was deposited in a corner watching calmly.

"What the hell do you want?" the Duke snapped, clearly in a foul mood.

The emissary steadied himself, locking eyes with the man who thought he held all the cards. "I am here on behalf of His Royal Highness Prince Omar bin Talal al-Mansour. I am here to talk about Miss Hannah. The Prince would like to see her returned safely to the United States so Mr. Zane can focus on his training—to all of our mutual benefit."

The Duke's face didn't move.

"You think this is a negotiation?" the Duke spat. "Zane is *my* fighter. Nobody tells me what to do with *my* fighters."

The Arab emissary didn't flinch. "The Prince believes Miss Hannah has nothing to do with the business we are attempting to conduct. However, he has received numerous distressed phone calls from Mr. Zane. The Prince believes this matter is placing undue strain on the business at hand and wishes a quick and peaceful resolution."

"Peaceful?" the Duke exclaimed. "What are you talking about? Who said things weren't peaceful? That some kind of threat?"

"No threat, sir. Just a polite request with the backing of a powerful man," the Arab replied.

The Duke stared again. Finally, slowly, he reached into a drawer and pulled out a chrome 1911 .45 pistol and set it on the desk between them.

"You motherfucker," the Duke said. "You come to my city, my country, *my house*, and threaten me. Well, guess what? *I'm* the powerful man in this town. Tell the Prince that I'll handle my fighters, and he doesn't need to worry about it anymore. Now, get the fuck out."

Nasir waited a moment, then gave a curt nod before spinning on his heel and striding down the marble hall and out of the house. He climbed into the black sedan and was on the phone before it had passed back through the gates.

"Your Majesty, I am afraid this is a matter for the Falcon," he said.

23

Violence Speaks Loudly

Philip S. W. Goldson International Airport, Belize City, Belize

The hum of the jet engines faded as Prince Omar's private jet touched down on the pitch black tarmac outside Belize City. The hatch hissed open, letting in a rush of hot, humid air. Mason, Caleb, and Benito, and the other operators stepped out onto the runway, their eyes scanning the landscape, but they weren't here for sightseeing.

A uniformed Belizean officer with dark skin and a round belly protruding over his belt and a white American with a buzz cut wearing cargo pants and a Hawaiian shirt awaited them at the foot of the boarding stairs. Karim, carrying a metal briefcase, spoke to them briefly, handed the American the manilla envelope containing their clearances and handed the Belizean the briefcase. The Belizean officer and the mysterious American looked through the papers quickly. After a brief discussion and some head nodding, the American pointed toward a van parked fifty feet away. Karim nodded, took the envelope back, and started walking to the van. The Belizean officer and the American walked away without ever opening the briefcase.

Mason adjusted the strap of the tactical bag slung over his shoulder as the team quickly moved toward the nondescript, white cargo van parked just off the airstrip. The driver, a Belizean narcotics officer assigned to the mission for legal reasons as much as anything, nodded at them wordlessly and opened the back doors.

They piled into the van with their heavy gear bags. The driver closed the doors, and the van pulled away from the tarmac and onto the road headed out of the airport. They took John Smith Road south to George Price Highway, then turned to head west. The sun was still several hours from rising.

Next to Mason, Caleb cleaned his sunglasses with the hem of his shirt.

"When the heat is on, do you think Michael will make a stand, or will he try to negotiate?" Caleb asked, breaking the silence.

"Michael's in too deep to back out now. He'd look weak in front of his father," Mason replied. "Plus, he's probably coked to the gills. He's not going to let her go without a fight."

Benito cracked his knuckles, the scars along his jaw stark in the dim light of the van. "Good. Let's make this quick and dirty then. I prefer it that way."

The highway took them deeper into the jungle, the thick canopy swallowing the sky as they veered off the main highway onto a smaller dirt track heading north through the Maya Forest Corridor. After an hour of driving, they approached a collection of buildings situated on the south bank of the Belize River near the border between the Cayo District and the Belize District.

The van rolled to a stop, and they unloaded quickly and quietly. The moon was low in the sky, and Mason could hear the calls of Yucatan Howler Monkeys and Frigatebirds from the jungle around them. There were two Land Rovers parked near one of the low buildings, and three men were gathered at the hood of one of them smoking in the darkness. Mason also noticed a long canoe with a motor tied at the river's bank. Transportation had arrived.

"Welcome to Belize," one of the men said.

"Let's get to work," Karim replied, and the man gestured for them to follow him to one of the buildings.

The door was standing open. Inside, the room was bare, utilitarian, and smelled of chemicals. There was a folding table in the center of the room where Karim rolled out the satellite maps. The floor was lined with crates of weapons, ammunition, and tactical gear.

"Gear up. Weapons are provided by His Majesty," Karim said.

Quickly, Mason, Caleb, Benito, and the six other GZD and Saudi operators set their gear bags down and began to suit up. Due to Belizean law, they were not allowed to fly in with weapons or ammo, but each had brought his preferred tactical gear including plate carriers, radios, weapons sites, and camouflage BDUs.

One of the GZD operators, a former UCS running back and Navy SEAL named Terrel Roberts, began opening the plastic weapons crates. The first contained six Heckler & Koch G36 rifles chambered in 5.56×45mm NATO. The next contained an equal number of FN SCAR-H rifles chambered in 7.62×51mm NATO.

"Nice," Roberts said.

Another crate contained a belt-fed Heckler & Koch MG4. While it also fired the smaller 5.56×45mm round, with a full-auto cyclic rate of 775 rounds-per-minute, it was a competent light machine gun.

"Oh, baby. What are we expecting to run into out there? The Predator?" Roberts joked, hefting the MG4.

Mason looked up from adjusting his plate carrier and cut a glance at Karim.

"What's the details, boss?" Mason asked.

"I will run tactical command from here," Karim replied. "The rest of you will split into two teams. Mason, you will lead Alpha Team by boat down the river. That'll be you, the boatman, and the rest of your GZD teammates, except for Caleb."

He turned to look at Caleb, who was assembling a custom-built quad copter drone he had brought with him in a specially-designed case. The arms of the drone clicked together easily, as did the motors, rotors, cameras, and a cylindrical device that hung under the drone. It resembled the cylinder of a revolver with four slots large enough to carry a variety of grenades which could be dropped from above a target. It was his latest design, and it had proven itself recently on the frontlines in Ukraine.

"Caleb," Karim continued, "you will ride in the Land Rovers with Bravo Team. Bravo Team, led by Ameer, will consist of two local drivers, Caleb, and the rest of my guys, being Khaled and Zaid."

Khaled, a tall, thin Senior NCO in the Saudi Special Security Forces, was in his late 20s and did not speak much. He walked over to a long rifle case, opened it, and retrieved an Accuracy International AXMC sniper rifle. Chambered in .300 Winchester Magnum with a suppressor and Schmidt & Bender PM II 5-25x56 scope, it was a top-of-the line precision weapon. Khaled worked the bolt smoothly.

"Khaled is one of the top snipers in the Royal Saudi forces. Under Ameer's command, along with Zaid manning the machine gun, they will establish a support by fire position overlooking the front gate. Caleb will run his drone from there, supplying video feed to Mason and myself and providing aerial support."

Samuel, one of the GZD operators, a former MARSOC Marine corpsman from Chicago, spoke up.

"Can the drone get a signal way out here?"

Caleb perked up at the question.

"Absolutely. We have a contract for encrypted high speed data transfer with Starlink. That's how we ran these in Ukraine. Works like a champ," he assured the team.

"Good," Karim continued. "Inside one of those other crates, you will find an Instalaza C90-CR 90mm RPG with an anti-bunker warhead. Mason, your team will use the rocket launcher to breach the north wall here."

"Well, that shouldn't make the news," Roberts joked as he hoisted the rocket launcher.

"Now, there are four guard towers, one at each corner of the rectangular perimeter wall," Karim pointed at the aerial photo. "We will number them clockwise starting at the northwest corner: one, two, three, and four. You will breach here, between towers one and two. Then you will assault through the breach, cross the grounds to the back of the main house where we believe the hostage is being held, breach through the back door, clear the house, and secure the hostage. Make sure to clear the house so you don't get shot in the back during exfil. Once secured, you will extract her through the front gate. Bravo Team will cover you as you make it to the Land Rovers, who will then exfil Alpha Team and Bravo Team back down this dirt road to the highway, then straight to the airport."

190

Mason stared at the aerial photo and thought for a moment.

"What about towers two and three on either side of the front gate?"

"That's Khaled's job. Using Ameer as spotter, the sniper team will take out guard towers two and three just before you breach the wall."

Mason chewed his lip.

"That still leaves tower one at the northwest corner. We won't be able to assault through the breach unless he's down."

"Tower one is on you," Karim said, grinning and slapping Mason on the back. "I trust you can handle it."

Mason chuckled, then nodded in agreement.

"It's pretty Wild West," he commented. "A little faster and louder than I'd have hoped."

"This is what we could come up with given the short window we have," Karim assured him.

"What about local cops," Benito spoke up. "How are they gonna feel about us blowing up compounds and ripping a machine gun in their nice tourist jungle?"

"Well, my friend," Karim replied, "that is always a variable we can't fully control. The briefcase I handed to the Police Commissioner at the airport in front of the DEA should buy us some freedom to operate. But Belize sits at the crossroads of major trafficking routes headed north from Colombia. Here, it is never certain who is working for whom."

"So, what you're saying is, maybe he already tipped off the target that we're coming," Benito replied.

"Relax, buddy," Khaled, the Saudi sniper said, as he popped a magazine into the AXMC sniper rifle. "Only Allah knows our fates. Our only duty is to serve."

"I don't know about you," Benito replied, "but my wife told me if I die in this jungle she's going to kill me."

The men all laughed.

The large canoe slithered down the snaking Belize River, through the dark jungle, like an anaconda. The gasoline motor hummed smoothly. At this pace, it would take about one-and-a-half hours for Alpha Team to make it the 17 clicks down the river to the point where a canal branched off. From there, the assault team would disembark and trek the remaining thirty minutes south through the jungle on foot. It was a hasty plan, but Mason and Karim agreed it was necessary to move quickly before anything leaked to the press. The Prince had called and told him that his attempt to negotiate with the Duke had failed. All that was left was to bloody the Duke's nose and let him know he wasn't the only tough guy in the game.

The rest of the GZD team were all professionals, forged in fire by US Special Operations Command and honed to a razor's edge at the GZD Training Center. Samuel was an experienced corpsman who had saved numerous lives in Afghanistan and Iraq. He was kind, but he would put a bad guy down in a flash. Mike, the third GZD operator, was a hulking former Denver SWAT officer. He would act as breacher, a job he had performed many times against ISIS in Iraq. He had blown so many holes in walls he joked that he didn't trust a door he hadn't made himself. Roberts, the former SEAL, was younger and less experienced, but he was still a lethal weapon. He had been a college athlete, and he seemed to never run out of gas.

Benito, his old friend, was now a grizzled NCO, hardened by years of violence. He glanced over and saw his old friend hunkered low in the watercraft, peering into the jungle through his rifle's ACOG site, ready for anything. After nearly dying in the Denver ambush, Benito would never let his guard down again, not for a second.

Mason had to assume Karim's team of Saudi operators were just as competent. With Caleb running his drone and Karim running the Tactical Operations Center (TOC), they had the command and control they needed to coordinate the raid. It would have to be enough.

It was time for a radio check.

"Alpha One to Falcon One, Alpha One to Falcon One. Radio check," he said into his mouthpiece.

"Hawk to Alpha One, loud and clear," Karim's voice came back clearly.

"Alpha One to Bravo One, Alpha One to Bravo One. Radio check," Mason transmitted.

"Alpha One, this is Bravo One. Loud and clear," Ameer, the Bravo Team leader, called back from his Land Rover heading south on the highway miles away. "We're about 30 mikes from Rally Point 2. I will transmit once we arrive."

"Roger that, Bravo One. Alpha One out," Mason replied.

They rode the rest of the way in the canoe in silence.

As Bravo Team approached the canal entrance, the boat operator cut the engine and let the canoe drift in silence. He used the rudder to guide the boat to the east bank, where it grounded in the mud. The team climbed out, barely making a splash, and moved effortlessly into the dense jungle. The boat man was instructed to wait 30 minutes in silence before cranking his motor and heading back up the river so as not to draw more attention. This was a remote part of the country with few inhabitants, but they had no idea if Michael had patrols out, so they maintained strict noise and light discipline.

Bravo Team needed to cover about one-and-a-half clicks through the dark jungle in about half an hour in order to arrive at the Duke's compound just before daybreak. There were numerous threats along the way, from poisonous snakes to booby traps. Even a wrong step and a twisted ankle could cause complications. Mason knew the plan was hasty, but everyone was a professional, so he moved with faith.

He took point with the rest of the team spaced out in a line behind him. He wore jungle boots, Vietnam-era tiger stripe camouflage, and the latest in light-weight ceramic body armor. He was armed with an FN SCAR-H and carried seven extra magazines on his chest. He also carried a Sig Sauer P226 9mm pistol in a drop leg holster and a Cold Steel Drop Forged Survivalist knife strapped to his plate carrier. Ever since Denver, he never went anywhere without a blade. He had a PVS14 night vision monocle, but the jungle canopy was too thick to allow much starlight through, so he proceeded as much by intuition as anything.

After about 5 minutes of slow progress through the jungle, his radio chirped.

"Falcon and Alpha One. Bravo Team has arrived at Rally Point 2. We have begun phase two of our infil. Eye in the sky is up, awaiting transmission.

Stand by."

Mason raised his hand and whistled quietly, signaling the team behind him to halt and take a knee. He unfastened the command pouch on his chest rig, tilting it down so he could view the screen of the small tablet inside. The screen lit up with a live video feed, illuminating his face. Mason was amazed at the resolution of the transmission from Caleb's drone as it soared high over the jungle, bouncing it's infrared video stream from satellites miles overhead to his screen without any apparent lag. He wished he'd had such real-time battlefield awareness during his time in the Middle East. Nevertheless, there was not much to see but treetops while the drone followed its pre-programmed flight path to the target compound.

"Alpha One, this is Bravo Two. Are you receiving the drone feed?" Caleb's voice called over the radio.

"Affirmative, Bravo Two. Clear as day," Mason sent back.

"Bravo Two to Falcon. How's your feed?" Caleb asked.

"Bravo Two, video feed is clear," Karim called back. "I have both teams' locations on GPS. Proceed to target. Both teams are behind schedule, so try to pick up the pace."

"Roger that," Mason and Ameer, Bravo team's leader, called back.

With that, Mason waved for Alpha team to resume their silent trek.

When they arrived at the Duke's jungle fortress, they stayed low and used the trees as cover, assuming the guards had night vision and dogs. Mason placed his night vision monocle to his eye and scanned the north wall. He could see the number one tower clearly right before him, about 100 feet away at the northwest corner of the fort. Then the white concrete wall of the compound, standing about 30 feet tall, ran to his left to the number 2 tower, marking the northeast corner of the compound.

"Alpha One to Falcon One and Bravo One. Alpha Team has arrived. I have eyes on the target," Mason said.

"Alpha One, this is Bravo One. Hold tight for sitrep," Ameer called back.

Then after a moment, the radio chirped again.

"Alpha One, check your video feed," Ameer called. "Falcon, are you seeing this?"

Mason ducked behind a tree and, using his hands to cup the light, checked the drone video on his chest-mounted screen. The drone was high above so as to avoid detection, but the camera was powerful. Caleb had it zoomed in to the area just in front of the main gate. It was still dark, so he was using an infrared setting, but Mason was fairly sure he knew what he was seeing. He counted one, two, three, four...

"Bravo One, I count at least six vehicles parked in front of the main gate. Four of them appear to have overhead lights. Can you confirm am I am seeing police vehicles in front of the target? Over."

"Alpha One, Bravo One. We are 5 mikes from our destination. I believe I am seeing the same thing as you but will confirm once I get eyes on. Out."

Minutes passed slowly, then the radio chirped again.

"Alpha One and Falcon One, this is Bravo One. Bravo Team is in position. Can confirm there are six—repeat, six—vehicles including four police vehicles parked in front of the target. I count twelve—repeat, twelve— guards armed with long guns at the main gate."

Mason looked over and saw Benito staring at him. He was wearing a boonie hat, and his face was smeared with black camouflage paint, but there was no mistaking the whiteness of his eyes.

"Falcon to Alpha One and Bravo One. Hold position and await further orders. Over."

Mason sighed, then keyed his mic.

"Roger that, Falcon. Bravo Team maintaining position."

He looked over to Benito and shrugged.

"I guess the briefcase wasn't enough," Mason said.

Benito shook his head, and they returned to watching the target as the eastern sky began to glow with the rising sun.

24

Clandestine Ops

The Duke's Estate, Cayo District, Belize

"Falcon to Bravo One. Bring the drone back to conserve power. Alpha and Bravo, have both your teams pull back 200 meters and lay low. Leave one man for surveillance. Await further instructions. Report on the hour. Over."

"Roger that," Mason radioed. "Alpha Team falling back."

"Back the team up 0 degrees 200 meters," Mason whispered to Benito. "Lay low and wait to hear from me. Keep your eyes open for patrols and locals. I'm going to keep an eye on things for a while."

Benito nodded, then crawled back into the brush. With hardly a sound, the rest of the team fell back into the jungle to avoid detection while they waited. Mason hunkered down under a tiger fern, using the foliage to hide his position as he watched the compound through a compact pair of binoculars.

The first two hours passed uneventfully. As the sun rose, so did the heat. As he waited, an idea formed in Mason's mind, and he decided to pursue it.

"Alpha Two, this is Alpha One," he radioed.

"Go ahead, Alpha One," Benito called back.

"I'm moving to get a view of the west side of the target. Send someone to relieve me, over" Mason said.

"Roger that," Benito replied.

With that, Mason eased back into the brush, then walked back 50 meters into the jungle to make a wide loop counterclockwise from the north side of the compound to the west side, placing him between the walled estate and the river. He waved as he saw Samuel creeping toward his hide to replace him.

Mason took his time creeping around the compound, mostly to conserve energy. Once he made it around, as he suspected, there was a shallow drainage ditch running due north from the compound to the river.

Carefully, staying out of the mud so as not to leave tracks, he stalked next to the ditch until the concrete western wall of the compound showed through the trees. From there, he belly-crawled slowly, aware that the number one and number four towers might see him.

Once he was close enough to see clearly, he crept close to the drainage ditch and peered along the depression. Sure enough, the ditch led to a concrete culvert that jutted out from under the wall. It was covered in rusted bars but appeared to be just wide enough. He slowly backed into the jungle.

Mason took a looping route to Alpha Team's position due north of the compound. When he found them, they were hunkered in a low area covered by dense jungle foliage. Mike was taking his turn resting his eyes while Roberts and Benito kept silent watch. Mason slid into their hide, removed his boonie hat, and used a bandana to wipe the grit from his forehead. Sweat had streaked his camouflage face paint, and he was sure there were insects crawling inside his trousers.

"I've got an idea," Mason said.

"Shit," Benito spat. "Me, too. It's called sit here and wait for orders."

Mason ignored him.

"Mike, what did you bring to breach with?" he asked the former Army NCO and SWAT officer.

"All I've got is a 24-inch sledge and a mini Hallagan," Mike responded. "Plus, a tomahawk and another small pry bar. No shotgun, no charges. Oh, almost forgot—and a fucking RPG."

Mason thought for a moment.

"Did one of you bring a rope? Any climbing gear?" Mason asked.

"Ah, shit, here we go," Benito spat. "What are you thinking, man?"

"Best I've got is some 550 cord and a couple carabiners," Mike said.

"That could work. Let me see," Mason instructed.

Mike removed the breaching tools and paracord from his day pack and handed them to Mason. The mini Hallagan was a short but stout bar used to pry open doors. There was plenty of paracord, but it was too flimsy by itself for Mason's intended use.

Mason keyed his radio.

"Alpha One to Falcon One," he called.

"Go ahead Alpha One," Karim called back.

"Request drone overflight for daylight recon. We could really use the clear photos," Mason called.

The radio was silent for a moment.

"Falcon One to Bravo One, Falcon One to Bravo One," Karim transmitted.

"Bravo One here, go ahead Falcon One," Ameer called back.

"Send the drone over the target and capture video and stills. Maintain maximum altitude to prevent observation. Complete single flyover then return drone to standby, over," Falcon One instructed.

"Roger that. Deploying drone for high angle single fly over. Stand by, over," Ameer called, then the radio went silent.

Mason tipped the screen on his chest rig down and waited for the transmission. After a few minutes, the screen lit up with the live feed as the drone slowly passed over the compound. After a couple more minutes, it buzzed as he received the still image files.

He sat sipping water from a canteen, chewing a protein bar, and scrolling through the high definition aerials. He used his fingers to zoom in and out while he thought. Mike and Benito kept up their watch as the jungle birds called around them and the breeze rustled the canopy above them.

After a while, Mason looked up from the screen.

"All right, here's the deal. As soon as it's dark, I'm going in there," Mason said.

Benito chuckled. "What, you're going to save the girl all by yourself, Rambo?"

"No, not for the girl," Mason replied calmly. "I want to check out this warehouse."

"Warehouse? For what?" Benito asked.

Mason chewed his protein bar for a while.

"There's something in there that I bet is not supposed to be there," Mason said.

"And? If it's not a girl named Hannah, what do you care?"

"Because right now we have nothing on the Duke or Michael except he took a surprise trip with another man's girlfriend. That's hardly a crime. But if there's more going on here, then we can make life real hard for these assholes," Mason replied.

Benito sighed and thought for a while.

"Bro," he finally said, "we're in a foreign country under bullshit diplomatic protection carrying military hardware. We're already fucked. Why worry about being proper now?"

"That's not what I'm talking about," Mason replied. "I'm used to that shit. You just described my entire military career. I'm talking about *after* this. After we get the girl. Then what? What do we have to use against the Duke?"

"Bro, I guess I don't follow. But I know you're going to do what you're going to do, so tell me what you want from me," Benito said.

"I want you to make me a rope."

Night fell over the jungle, and three GZD operators—Mason, Mike, and Roberts—crept silently through the jungle north of the Duke's walled compound using the drainage ditch as their guide. Once they were within site of the drain culvert, Mason pointed to a thick tree next to the ditch. Roberts nodded then set to work tying a loop of paracord they had twisted into a thick rope around the tree, using it it secure a strong D-ring carabiner. Then Mike laid out a long coil of the same rope that had another carabiner firmly knotted to one end.

Mason set his SCAR H rifle on the ground, attached the rope to his chest rig using the D-ring, then, after peeking at the guard towers, began to belly crawl slowly up the drainage ditch. Mike held the other end of the rope, so that it uncoiled behind Mason as he crawled. The towers had search lights, but they were not actively using them. He was able to cross the thirty or so feet to the wall and the mouth of the drain pipe without being seen, hoping the whole way that he wouldn't run into a snake. There was a few inches of water and a few more inches of stinking mud and slime in the bottom of the ditch, but Mason hardly noticed.

Soon, he was at the mouth of the drain pipe. It was covered by a grill of steel bars attached to the wall with anchor bolts. Looking around cautiously, he tugged on the grill. It didn't budge. Silently, he unclipped the D-ring from his webbing and clicked it onto the right-most bar. Then reaching to the pack of his belt, he removed the short Hallagan tool. He eased the pointed tip of the pry bar behind the right side of the grill, just above where the rope was attached, then looked over his shoulder and waved at his teammates.

With that, he felt the rope jostle as Mike and Roberts looped the rope through the D-ring attached to the tree. Using it as a pully, the two men took strong hold of the rope and pulled as hard as they could. Once Mason felt the rope tighten, he began to pry with the Hallagan. Little by little, through their combined effort, he felt a gap forming between the steel grill and the cement wall. He wiggled the pry bar deeper as he continued to pry. Soon, he felt the grill easing away from the wall as he pried around the anchor bolt, eventually working it completely out of the wall, and just like that, they had one corner of the grill pulled free.

Mason signaled for the other men to hold, and they relaxed. The rope went slack, and Mason moved the D-ring to the left side of the grill. They repeated the process of pulling and prying, and once again he was able to work the anchor bolt free. The cement wall was old, of poor quality, and had suffered in the tropical climate, so just as he'd hoped, removing the grill was simply a matter of properly applied force. Once the grill was free of the wall, he unhooked the rope and signaled to Mike and Roberts to reel the rope in. Then they retreated a few meters into the jungle to keep watch without being spotted.

Mason laid the heavy steel grill down in the mud, then peeked into the drain pipe. He estimated it was a little less than thirty inches in diameter, just enough for his shoulders to fit. He used the red light setting on his head lamp to peek inside. It was dark and covered in slime and moss, and it smelled terrible. Without another thought, Mason crawled into the pipe head first.

He inched along in the slime for about 25-feet before he came to the first drainhole above his head. Light spilled through, so he took a moment to listen and breathe the fresh air, but the hole was only about 6-inches wide, so he had to keep moving. Using his toes and elbows, he crawled forward little by little. After another 15-feet, he came to his destination: a grate about two feet square he had spotted in the aerial photos the drone had taken earlier. As he thought, it was just wide enough for him to ease through—assuming it wasn't welded down or otherwise attached.

Mason waited for a while, listening. He could hear men talking and laughing. They didn't sound close, but it was hard to tell from inside the drain pipe, so he took his time and moved silently. Once he was fairly certain the coast was clear, he poked a tiny dental mirror through the grate and slowly peaked around. There was no movement in the well-lit yard.

The grate was located well behind the main house, past the swimming pool, right next to the mysterious warehouse. He retracted the mirror and returned it to its pouch, then positioning himself in a bench-press position under the grate, used both hands to gently try and raise it. Dust and sand fell into his eyes, but he kept heaving. It didn't take much effort to lift the grate out of its resting place. It wasn't attached after all.

Mason set the grill back down and wiped the sand from his eyes with the collar of his undershirt, though it didn't help much as he was covered in muck and grime. Then he keyed his mic three times, the silent, prearranged signal that he was going forward with the plan. In his ear piece, Mike keyed back twice the OK. Taking a deep breath, Mason heaved the grate upwards then over and out of the way. He sat up quickly into the opening left by the removed grate, aiming his Sig Sauer pistol from the high compressed ready position. As his head poked through the drain hole, pistol close to his chin and aimed down range, he scanned for threats. As he had seen in the drone images, the drain hole was in a remote part of the yard, away from anywhere someone might notice. He scanned right to see the pool area which was brightly lit but unoccupied. To his left was the wall of the warehouse, and to his rear, the wall of the compound. The only likely threats were from the front, towards the main gate and the house, but he didn't spot anyone.

Like a snake, Mason slithered out of the hole. He replaced the grate quietly, then, staying as low as possible, crawled into a flowerbed filled with tropical ferns and palms. From there, he keyed his mic three times again, and Mike keyed back twice. Everything was still good.

From there, Mason crept low and slow around the back of the warehouse, using the ample, lush landscaping as cover. At the back of the concrete building, he peaked around the corner. Above, he could see the number one guard tower. A set of steel stairs ran up the wall to the tower, and he could see the back of a guard seated there. He was facing outside the compound and had his head tipped down. Mason waited for a moment, watching him. The guard was still, remaining in his hunched over position for some time, and Mason concluded he was playing on his cellphone.

Just a few feet around the corner was a back door into the warehouse. This was Mason's planned point of entry, though he had no idea what to expect inside. Ideally, he would have used some bit of technology, like a fiber optic camera, to peek inside before gaining entry, but he hadn't brought such gear. His biggest hope now was that the door was unlocked.

Cautiously, with his pistol trained on the guard's back some 60-feet away, Mason crept from the bushes towards the back door. As he was halfway there, the guard shifted in his seat, then turned his head to look to the left. Mason's breath caught and he froze, and he squeezed the slack out of the pistol's trigger, ready to fire. The guard stared for a while into the jungle beyond the wall, then turned back to his phone. Mason exhaled quietly, then continued creeping toward the door. He covered the last few feet without incident, then tried the door knob. It turned freely, so without waiting, he opened the door and slipped inside.

The warehouse was a single room 30-feet wide and 40-feet long. The walls, floor, and ceiling were painted grey, and there were thick, rectangular support columns every 10-feet. The room was lit by long fluorescent lights and filled with shelves and work tables. There was nobody inside. Mason holstered his pistol and quickly wrapped a bandana around his mouth and nose before creeping deeper into the room.

He took out his cellphone and began videoing as he carefully circled the room. There were boxes on the tables. Some were plain; others were marked with the green logo of the Santando Sugar Company. He carefully filmed everything as he went. Walking over to one of the unmarked boxes, he opened the top and filmed the contents. Inside, there was a plastic bag filled with white powder. He removed a folding pocket knife, flipped open the blade, and stabbed it into the powder . The blade came out dusted with the white substance. Looking around, he found some plastic wrap on a table. Cautiously, he wrapped the entire knife with plastic wrap, careful not to touch the blade with his bare fingers, then slipped the bundled knife into a pouch on his plate carrier. He took another minute to film the rest of the room, including the boxes from the sugar company which he saw were filled with brand new, empty packaging marked with the company logo.

Once he was done, he put the phone securely away, then made his way to the back door again. There, he drew his sidearm once again, then slowly eased the door open just enough to peek at the guard in the nearby tower. He was still glued to his phone, so Mason slipped through the door, then back into the bushes. He worked his way through the shadows back to the storm rain and into the stinky drain pipe. After lowering himself in and replacing the drain cover, he keyed his mic to let Mike and Roberts know he was on his way, then shimmied back toward the opening. Once he was out of the culvert, he propped it back against the wall and replaced the anchor bolts, which looked passable though they were not holding the grill in place anymore. From there, he low crawled down the ditch to where his teammates were waiting in the brush.

They made their way back to the hide where Benito was waiting. Mason reported to Falcon One that he was back from his recon mission. He had not informed the Saudi of his plan to enter the compound.

"Alpha One," Karim called. "Be in launch position at 0:400."

Mason checked his watch. That gave him about three hours to rest his eyes.

"Roger that, Falcon One. Out," he called back.

"Well," Benito whispered. "Did you see anything?"

"Oh yeah," Mason replied. "Wake me up at 0:300."

Then without another word, he laid on the jungle floor, covered his eyes with a bandana, and drifted off to sleep.

Inside a high-rise condo in downtown Houston, elegantly but flamboyantly decorated in white marble with pink accents, Mo sat on an overstuffed pink couch. He was wearing a champagne silk kimono and several long pearl necklaces. A man was laying shirtless on the couch with him, his head in Mo's lap. Mo traced his manicured fingers over his heavily muscled and tattooed chest, toying with his diamond chains. Jazz played softly in the background, and a gas flame burned in the fire place. A glass of white wine sat on a coffee table. The man scratched the Houston Astros tattoo on his cheek.

"Oh, daddy," Mo sighed, "what am I gonna do?"

"Do about what?" the tattooed man asked gruffly.

"Do about *what*?" Mo exclaimed. "More like, do about *who*. You know who."

"Your mom?" the man asked.

"Yes. My poor mom. I just can't stop thinking about her. The poor baby. She can't work, so they cancelled her insurance. She's stage 3, so it's still possible the cancer could be stopped, but her doctor said it'll take some kind of special radiation therapy, and Lord knows she doesn't have special radiation therapy money."

"Why not put it on a payment plan," the man asked.

"Ha!" Mo chuckled. "With that woman's credit?"

"You could help her though. You're not doing too bad."

"Oh, please," Mo said, reaching for the wine glass. "Don't let the pearls and mimosas fool you. It costs a lot to look this good."

The man stared at the ceiling.

"Yeah," he said finally, his voice a low rumble, "I guess we all could use a quick come up."

Mo continued drawing shapes on his chest with his fingertips with one hand while he swished the wine with the other. He stared into the fire for a moment before speaking again.

"Well, there is this one thing…"

25

Jungle Raid

The Duke's Estate, Cayo District, Belize

While Mason snoozed, Caleb ran two more drone flights over the Duke's jungle compound. He awoke to an assortment of photos from Caleb and text messages from Karim on his chest-mounted tablet.

Falcon One: Police presence removed. Be in position by 04:00.

Karim had gotten in touch with his police connection and had the rogue officers pulled from the front of the compound, clearing the way for a daybreak assault. The latest images and videos from the drones showed just three vehicles parked at the main gate now. Nevertheless, it was hard to estimate how many henchmen Michael had inside the walled fort.

The rest of Alpha Team was awake and sharp. Mason popped a caffeine pill, two ginseng capsules, a salt tablet, and a couple potassium pills to get his body going, then washed it all down with a protein bar and two bottles of water. He relieved himself against a tree before wiping some fresh grease paint on his face.

"Check your weapons," he whispered to Benito.

"Check your weapons," Benito passed on to Mike, Roberts, and Samuel.

Mike had the RPG with the breaching load. That was critical. Once everyone was ready, the team began moving south again, back toward the compound.

A day and two nights in the jungle had left Mason's skin raw, and he was ready to be done with the mission.

They moved silently through the darkness, careful where they stepped, using the faint light of the moon and stars to weave around the tree trunks. Night birds called from the treetops high above, and mosquitos buzzed around their exposed, sweaty necks.

They made it to the same spot from which they had watched the previous night. Mason had Mike, the breacher, stay near him. Using his night vision monocle, he scanned the perimeter and the nearest guard tower, designated tower one, being the north west of the compound.

Tonight, there were two guards in tower one.

The time was 03:41.

"Falcon One and Bravo One. Alpha Team in position," Mason whispered over the radio.

"Bravo One ready," Ameer, leader of the fire support team called.

"Roger that, Alpha One and Bravo One," Karim called back from the TOC. "Standby for mission launch, over."

Mason mounted his PVS-14 to the rail on top of his FN SCAR-H rifle, just behind the ACOG sight. Lying flat in the bushes, he peered through the rubber eyepiece of the night vision monocle, which enhanced the sight picture of the Trijicon. There was enough ambient light to see the entire northern wall clearly. He wished he'd brought a suppressor, but he hadn't had time to slip one into his kit. He felt his chest rig buzz, and he raised up enough to remove the table from its chest mount and hold it up so he could check the screen. It displayed a live feed from the drone hovering far overhead. Caleb switched the infrared camera to black hot, so heat sources appeared dark against a cool white background. There were guards milling around the front gate, and more inside the wall. He counted twelve, but that didn't count the five or more in the towers, plus some of the interior courtyard was obscured by trees, plus Michael and possibly more guards within the house.

"Alpha One to Bravo One," Mason transmitted over the radio.

"Go ahead, Alpha One," Ameer whispered back, meaning they were in position directly in front of the main gate.

"We're good to go. I count eight at the gate. Four inside. Two in tower one. Estimate minimum twenty, over," Mason radioed.

"Agreed, Alpha One," Ameer called back.

Mason went back to watching tower one. He figured the range at about 80 meters. Easy work.

Mason waved to Roberts. He also had his PVS-14 mounted to his rifle and was lying in a stable position.

"You take the right. On my go," Mason whispered.

"Roger that," Roberts whispered back, never taking his eye from the reticle.

Mason relaxed. He was comfortable, lying on the jungle floor on his stomach. He spread his feet to accept the recoil, then squeezed the rifle butt into his shoulder, making sure he had a solid cheek weld on the stock. He took slow, deep breaths, then flipped the safety off the SCAR-H. When Roberts heard the click, he followed suit.

"Mike," Mason whispered. "Get that RPG ready."

To Mason's left, Mike was kneeling against a tree, using the shadow to hide his outline. He had the C90 with the CR-BK anti-bunker warhead mounted on his shoulder and was peeking through the site.

"Ready," Mike whispered.

A minute passed slowly. The jungle noises faded. Everything went silent. Then Mason's earpiece crackled.

"Mission launch," Falcon One called. "Go!"

"Roger, Falcon One. Mission launch is go," Ameer said. "Drone drop, go!"

Mason opened his left eye to peak at the tablet propped in front of him. From the drone's downward facing camera, he watched a cylindrical object fall, then tumble downwards toward the interior of the courtyard. It was an M18 smoke grenade. It hit the ground, bounced once, then shot sparks as the trigger mechanism fired. Within a second, a plume of thick smoke began spewing out, filling the courtyard, and obscuring the drone's infrared vision.

"Smoke is good," Caleb's voice called.

The drone immediately traversed toward the number three tower, the tower left of the main gate. Here, Caleb planned to use an attack perfected on the battlefields of Ukraine.

As the drone moved over tower three, it gained a bit more altitude. Precise elevation was key to the maneuver, as elevation dictated time. The drone shook slightly as its revolving bomb mechanism rotated to the next device. Mason watched as Caleb lined up the small crosshairs in the center of the screen with the front edge of the guard tower's square roof. Then a circular object fell away. This time, it was an M67 fragmentation grenade.

Mason held his breath as the small but deadly explosive tumbled down. In the periphery of the camera's image, he could see some of the front gate guards starting to move in reaction to the smoke grenade Caleb had dropped inside. At this point, Mason knew, confusion and panic were beginning to affect them.

The tiny bomb tumbled toward the guard tower until it finally arrived right about the roofline. There was a flash on the screen, then a bang echoed from the compound to Mason's ear.

"Air burst successful," Caleb called, and Mason knew he had to be pleased with himself.

Caleb had used the altitude of the drone to time the grenade's fuse exactly right so it air-bursted directly next to the guard's face in tower three.

There's one closed casket, Mason thought.

"Roberts, on my go," Mason reiterated.

He closed his left eye and found his target: one of the guards in tower one. He lined up the reticle of the ACOG on the guard's forehead.

"Three, two, one, go."

Both men pulled their triggers at the same instant, their rifles barking loudly. Birds and monkeys screeched overhead. Both guards dropped. Mason's fell straight down like a marionette with its strings cut, while Robert's target tumbled backwards out of the tower, into the compound.

Mason quickly detached the PVS-14 from the rifle's railing as he stuffed the tablet back into the command pouch on his chest.

"Mike! Send it!"

With a loud Woosh! and a flash of orange that lit up the night, Mike fired the rocket launcher from the shadows. The bunker-busting missile crossed the short distance to the wall in a blink. There was a *Bang!* when the tip of the rocket hit the concrete wall followed instantly by a succession of rapid explosions as the tandem warhead pierced the wall then detonated from within. There was a flash, then a deafening roar followed by a shower of debris as the masonry wall was blown to pieces.

"Go! Go! Go!" Mason yelled, and the men of Alpha Team burst from the jungle and dashed toward the shattered wall.

They crossed the ground so quickly, Mason could feel sand falling on him from the blast. They crossed the open ground without incident and stacked up next to the smoking breach. Mike had aimed perfectly, blasting a gap just above ground level. The concrete was cheap and weak from the tropical humidity, so the rocket had easily blown a gaping hole.

Mason could hear full auto fire from the front gate as Bravo Team strafed the front gate guards with the MG4 machine gun. Every so often, he heard the supersonic crack of a sniper rifle as the fire team wrecked stacked bodies.

"Alpha Team, breaching now," Mason called over the radio.

"Good luck, Alpha Team," Karim radioed back.

"Alpha One, Bravo Team has you covered," Ameer sent.

Alpha Team stacked up left of the breach. Smoke from the explosion as well Caleb's grenade billowed from the hole. Mason felt his number two man tap him on the shoulder, meaning the team was ready to make entry. Without hesitation, Mason shouldered his rifle and stepped into the fray, his team right behind.

Just east of the front gate, about 100-meters out, Bravo Team was spread out in a picket line, firing rapidly on anything that moved. Caleb was kneeling behind a large tree trunk, just behind Ameer, the team leader. Ameer was working the radio, calling out orders, and running magazines through his G36 rifle with absolute professionalism. One second, he was yelling at the machine gunner, Zaid, to shift fire to the right of the vehicles. The next, he was ordering the sniper, Khaled, to eliminate a target he'd spotted inside the gate. The next moment, he was asking Caleb to reposition the drone to watch over Mason's assault team. All while keeping up steady suppressive fire himself.

Bang! Bang! Bang!

"Khaled! Shoot that guy in the left of the doorway!"

Bang! Bang! Bang! Bang!

"Zaid! Dump a belt on that Jeep in the center. There's still two guys back there!"

Bang! Bang! Bang!

"Caleb! Where is Alpha Team? Are they to the house yet?"

Bang! Bang! Bang! Bang! Bang!

His team worked like a machine. Everyone kept their cool, even as return fire cracked through the brush and whistled past their heads. Ameer knew their muzzle flashes would attract bullets, but his plan was to overwhelm and disrupt the enemy's fire so quickly and completely that they had no chance to find their targets.

With every fifth round a green tracer, the H&K light machine gun ripped the vehicles in front of the gate to shreds making sure the enemy had no strong cover. Glass and tires and sheet metal were shattered and reduced to scrap.

Khaled was an expert sniper, and the heavy rounds of the Accuracy International rifle punched right through anything in their path. If he saw movement, he stopped it dead every time.

"Where is Alpha Team?" Ameer yelled at Caleb. His rifle's barrel was starting to smoke, but seemed unbothered as he ejected an empty magazine and slammed home a new one.

"They're crossing the courtyard, about to enter the main house," Caleb yelled back, his eyes never leaving the live drone feed on his tablet. The smoke grenade had done its job by filling the courtyard with thick white smoke, concealing Alpha Team's movement, but he could still make out their dark shapes as they snaked across the yard to the rear of the main house.

He watched as they stacked up against the wall, preparing to breach the back door. One of the team moved up and began doing something to the door. There was a flash of movement, and the team seemed to collectively flinch. The man at the door fell to the ground firing. Then, a teammate from the rear of the stack jumped forward and grabbed the downed man by the drag handle at the back of his vest and pulled him back away from the door. Caleb gritted his teeth and watched closely. The lead man in the stack held his rifle out and blind fired through the doorway.

"Man down," Mason's voice called over the radio. Caleb could hear the tension in his voice. "Mike is hit."

Ameer paused as he heard the transmission. The return fire had all but stopped. A couple of stray shots cracked wildly through the trees around them.

"Zaid! Front right! Burst fire on targets of opportunity!" Ameer commanded the machine gunner.

"Khaled! Cover the main gate!" he yelled to the sniper.

"Falcon One! This is Bravo One! Prepare the evac and call the medevac," Ameer said into the radio.

"Charlie Team, proceed to Rally Point One and prepare for evac. One wounded," Falcon One called back.

"Charlie One enroute to Rally Point One," a man called back.

Charlie Team were the drivers of the SUVs who would carry them out. If they could make it on foot, Alpha and Bravo Teams would hoof it a few hundred meters down the road to a rally point and load into the SUVs. But if they were too wounded to make the trip, the trucks would pick them up from the front gate, in which case Bravo Team would cover the extraction. With one wounded already, they needed to preserve their ammo in case it came to that.

Ameer slammed a new magazine into his rifle, dropped the bolt, and scanned the front of the compound through his sight. The sunrise was about one hour away, so it was still pitch dark. He could feel his heart pounding in his chest. They had one man wounded, and they hadn't breached the main house or located the hostage yet. There was still a lot that could go wrong. It was up to Alpha Team now.

Inside the compound, Alpha Team crossed the open courtyard quickly, stepping through flower beds and trying not to trip over landscaping stones as they scanned for targets. They aimed their rifles around, watching the second floor windows of the house as well as the main gate. Luckily, the guards in the front had their hands full with Bravo Team's suppressive fire, and the guard towers had been neutralized instantly, so Mason and his men made it to the back door of the main house without taking fire, though at least two stray tracers careened past their heads from Bravo Team's fusillade at the front.

Once again, they stacked up on the back wall, this time to the right of the door. Once he received the "ready" shoulder tap, Mason tried the door handle. It was locked. He knocked his fist against his head to summon the breacher to the front of the formation. Mike came up, allowed his rifle to hang from its sling, then fished the short sledge hammer and Halligan bar from the back of his combat belt. He placed the pointed tip of the pry bar into the door jamb just above the deadbolt, then hammered it in with the sledge. He hit it once, twice, driving it home. Then, just as he prepared to rip the door open, it exploded in his face. A blast of wooden splinters burst around him like confetti and the door rocked and shook from automatic rifle fire as someone inside shot through the door.

Mike buckled and fell back as he took rounds to his body. Mason didn't hesitate. He held his rifle out front and blind fired back through the door into the house.

Samuel, the medic, dove forward, grabbed Mike by the scruff of his plate carrier, and dragged him to the back of the formation.

Mason reloaded in a blink, then dumped another magazine through the door, which was quickly turning into toothpicks. There was no return fire, so Mason reloaded again and turned to glance at Mike.

"Sam! Get Mike stabilized. Roberts, stay here and cover them. Benito! Come with me!"

"Roger that!" Benito yelled, his rifle never leaving his shoulder.

Mason peaked through the gaping bullet holes in the door. He couldn't see anything. The lights were off inside. Steadying his rifle with his right hand, he reached with his left inside one of the holes, grabbed the wood, and ripped a chunk of the door out. He reached through the resulting hole, found the deadbolt latch, and turned it.

"Get ready," he said.

"Ready," Benito replied.

Mason could see the hard resolve in his old friend's face and he remembered doing the same thing with him in Iraq all those years before. They had kicked more than a few doors together after that first time he saved him from the sniper.

"Falcon One. Alpha Team, making entry," Mason radioed, then he ripped the door open.

He crossed the threshold from right to left, clearing the left corner, then turning to clear deeper into the room. Benito followed on his heels, wrapping the doorframe on the hinge side, making sure to smash the door against the wall hard in case anyone was hiding there. Together, they flooded the room. It was a kitchen. The floors were white and yellow, and there was a table in the center of the room.

Mason and Benito moved through the kitchen quickly, their rifles glued to their shoulders, whipping their muzzles left to right as they scanned for targets. The overhead lights were mostly off, but here and there, lamps glowed. The house was two stories, and they couldn't be positive there wasn't a basement. Making matters worse, there were numerous exterior windows through which enemies could fire from outside, and they couldn't use grenades for risk of injuring the hostage.

"Alpha One to Bravo Two. I need eyes directly over the house. Call out if you see anybody moving on the outside window or doors," Mason radioed.

"Roger that, Alpha One," Caleb radioed back. "I've got eyes on the main house now. You're clear. No hostile movement in the courtyard."

They crossed the kitchen and prepared to enter the next room. Positioning themselves on either side of the open doorway, Mason cut his eyes at Benito, then signaled for him to move through but to stay low. Benito nodded, crouched low, and crossed the threshold quickly. Mason followed immediately behind him, his rifle over the top of Benito's head.

As soon as they rounded the corner, Mason caught sight of a rifle barrel poking around a corner. He put two rounds through the corner, sending plaster dust billowing into the air. A man grunted, his weapon clattering to the floor, his body tipping forward into view. Mason put two more 7.62

rounds through his skull, splattering brain matter across the rug.

From within the next room—which was a spacious living room—men shouted and automatic fire opened up. Bullets peppered the wall to Mason's left. Benito, who was two steps in front of him, side-stepped to the right and fired his rifle ahead. While still firing, he wrapped the corner and emptied his magazine into the room. Mason, wishing he could toss a grenade, instead followed his partner's lead, and fired, hoping to suppress the enemy while searching for a target. They kept moving forward, spilling into the room then splitting up, with Benito breaking right while Mason turned left. Benito quickly reloaded and recommenced firing. Mason swept the room, spotted a man in the corner who was fumbling to reload his AK-47, and shot him four times center mass. The man flopped backwards into an end table then crashed to the ground. Mason turned his muzzle just in time to see Benito drop another guard with rapid shots. They swept the room for more targets.

"Clear! " Benito said.

"Clear!" Mason confirmed. "Doorway left!"

Benito spun ninety degrees to his left, and the two men prepared to enter the next portion of the house. They proceeded like this through hallways and rooms without encountering another person. They passed a staircase, but Mason made sure to clear the first floor before moving up.

"Alpha One to Bravo Two and Falcon One. First floor is clear. Alpha One and Alpha Two moving to second floor," Mason updated the commander and drone operator.

"Roger Alpha One," Karim called back. "Bravo Two, stay on station."

"Roger, Falcon One," Caleb confirmed.

The stairs were concrete and doubled back once as they headed up. Mason led the way, his rifle pointed up and ahead as Benito watched behind so they didn't get shot in the back. The upstairs looked well lit, but he couldn't hear any voices. They topped the stairs onto a landing. There was a doorway to the left and a doorway to the right. Both were open. Mason signaled for Benito to wait while he listened. He couldn't detect anything. In this case, he decided to clear left first, so he signaled with his fingers for Benito to follow him. Benito nodded, then took up position behind him.

Mason slid through the doorway with his muzzle up and trigger finger ready to send death to anyone in his path at 2,300 feet-per-second. It was a hallway lined with doors. He and Benito moved in perfect synchrony down the hallway to the first door. Mason signaled his intent to enter the room, then with a swift kick, sent the wooden door crashing inward. Wood splinters were still flying as Mason dashed into the room searching for targets. It was an empty bedroom.

"Clear," he said.

"Clear," Benito confirmed.

They quickly returned to the hallway and prepared to enter the next room when Mason heard a female voice in distress from behind them, down the right side of the hall. Mason pointed, and Benito nodded.

They moved smoothly down the hall, Mason aiming ahead while Benito deftly trotted backwards, aiming behind them. The female voice grew louder, and within thirty steps, they came to an open doorway, the orange glow of an incandescent bulb spilling into the hallway. Mason immediately saw his target within the room.

"Found her," he said to Benito.

With his rifle up, he stepped into the room.

Michael was there, and he had a gun. He was behind Hannah, his arm around her neck, using her as a shield. She was ghost white, but Mason couldn't see any blood on her.

"Mason, no!" she said, panic in her eyes.

"Mason!" Michael yelled in surprise. "What the fuck?"

Mason pointed his muzzle right between Michael's eyes. Michael snapped out of his initial shock and, realizing the danger he was in, moved his head behind Hannah's. He pointed his pistol at her temple so Mason could see.

"Alpha One to Falcon One. I have eyes on the hostage. She's alive," Mason said into his mouthpiece.

"Roger Alpha One," Karim sent back. "Can you extract her?"

"Michael has a gun to her head."

There was a pause.

"Alpha One, prioritize the hostage," Karim sent.

"Roger," Mason replied.

Michael was slowly dragging Hannah away, inching her back as he sought to escape, but there was only a second story wall behind him.

"Michael, there's nowhere to go. Drop your gun. Let her go," Mason said calmly.

"Fuck that!" Michael yelled. He was shirtless, wearing track pants and white sneakers, and his muscles rippled in the orange glow of the lamp. His face was pouring sweat, his eyes bulging black orbs, and Mason could see white powder caked around his nostrils. "I ain't droppin' shit!"

"Michael," Mason tried again calmly, "it's over. The girl is coming with me. But you don't have to die tonight."

"Please, just go!" Hannah begged. "Michael, he'll go away. You don't have to shoot me. Please, please, don't shoot me!"

"Shut up!" Michael jerked his arm around her neck. "I'll blow her head off!"

Mason could feel Benito behind him, his rifle trained out the door protecting their six from any party crashers. Mason knew the longer they waited, the higher chance that enemy reinforcements would arrive. Then they'd have to shoot their way back out, putting the hostage in more risk. Then he remembered a trick they'd used in Iraq.

"Bravo Two," Mason said softly into his mouthpiece. "Roof knock, corner one, on my mark,"

There was a pause as Caleb processed.

"Roger that, Mason," Caleb sent back excitedly. "I mean, Alpha One... I've got you. I'm ready."

Mason took a deep breath.

"Michael," he said as soothingly as he could, "last chance, buddy. This isn't the boxing ring. You won't wake up from this knock out. Let her go. Let me take her home."

"Fuck no!" Michael yelled.

Mason sighed, then said into his mouthpiece, "Mark."

Looking confused, Michael tightened his arm around Hannah again, jerking her further toward the northwest corner of the house.

Just then, there was a heavy thump on the flat, cement roof above their heads and a sound like a metal ball rolling. Michael flinched and looked up at the ceiling.

Two seconds later, the M67 fragmentation grenade Caleb had dropped on the roof over Michael's head detonated. In the war, they had used 81mm mortars to conduct "roof knocks" during urban combat, a fact he knew Caleb was aware of, and which he had executed perfectly.

The roof was thick enough to stop the grenade's shrapnel from injuring them, but the boom was loud and the shockwave sent plaster raining onto Michael and Hannah. There was a split second where Mason lost Michael in the cloud of white dust, but only a second.

Mason's first shot hit Michael's right forearm just below the elbow, about 8 inches from Hannah's head. It blew Michael's arm apart and sent his pistol cartwheeling through the air. Michael staggered back a step and had just tilted his head in surprise to look at his destroyed arm, when, before Hannah had a chance to scream, Mason shot Michael through the Adam's apple. Michael staggered back another half step and tried to grab his destroyed throat, but his arm flopped as the shattered radius and ulna bones snapped, leaving him with a limp noodle of an arm. He started to turn away, so Mason sent the final round through his temple, blowing most of his brains against the wall behind him. A one-two-three combo, and Michael's fighting career was over forever. The young gangster slid to his knees, blood pulsing from the hole in the side of his head.

Then Hannah screamed.

"Hostage secure. We're coming out," Mason radioed.

"Roger that," Karim said. "Bravo One, prepare for extraction. Charlie One, head to extraction point now. One wounded. Alpha Team, get moving to the extraction point."

Hannah was standing still, shaking and stuttering. Mason wasted no time in grabbing her firmly by the arm.

"Are you wounded?" he asked her directly.

"No, no," she stammered. He could feel her shivering.

"Stay behind Benito here. He's going to lead you out of the house, across the yard, and through the front gate where our ride will be waiting. Just stay between us. OK?"

"Yes, yes," she agreed.

"Benito, lead us out," Mason ordered.

"Roger that," Benito agreed, and with his rifle up, he headed out of the room.

Mason grabbed Hannah by her waistband gently pushed her ahead of him as they fled the room.

"Stay right behind Benito. If I say 'down', you lay down. OK?"

"Ok," she whimpered back.

Mason knew she was going into shock by her pale complexion and the way she was shivering, but he had no time to deal with it. They made it down the hallway, then down the stairs, and were soon crossing the kitchen.

"Alpha Team, we're coming out," Mason said into the radio.

"Come on," Roberts said back.

Benito didn't hesitate as he led them through the shattered kitchen door and back out into the night. Samuel, Roberts, and Mike were where he had left them. Samuel was hunched over Mike's body, his plate carrier pulled partially off and his shirt cut open. There were blood stained trauma patches and a lot of gauze wrapped around his chest. Torn packaging, including several tampons wrappers used to stuff bullet holes, were scattered around. Roberts was on one knee, scanning for threats, keeping Samuel safe while he worked to save Mike's life. Samuel looked up as Mason approached.

"He's alive, but he needs medevac. I've plugged the leaks, but he's bleeding internally and his blood pressure is dropping. I think one lung is punctured," he said.

"We're going," Mason replied.

"Falcon One, this is Alpha One. I have the hostage. One man needs medevac immediately. We're heading to the gate," he radioed to the mission commander.

"Alpha One, evac is pulling up now. Medevac will be waiting at Rally Point Two. Get your men out of there and into the trucks now," Karim sent back.

"Roberts, help Samuel carry Mike. Benito, lead us to the gate. I'll cover our six," Mason ordered.

Samuel instructed Roberts to grab Mike's feet, while he grabbed him under the shoulders. Slinging their rifles, they picked the wounded man up and fell in behind Benito who was peaking around the corner towards the gate. Mason, still holding Hannah by the waistband of her pants, looked around one last time as they prepared to move out.

Suddenly, plaster chips shattered from the wall behind them and a rifle crack rang out from the left. Mason just had time to push Hannah behind him and yell, "Down!" when he heard Roberts groan and stagger to his knee.

"I'm hit," he groaned in pain, though he didn't drop Mike's ankles.

Mason shoved Hannah down, then lunged his body between the sound of the incoming fire and the wounded men, scanning the distance for the threat with his ACOG sight. Then he saw a muzzle flash. It was Tower 3. The guard stationed in the tower must have waited patiently for his chance to hit them as they came out, but luckily he was a bad shot. Right now, he had them silhouetted against the house's back wall. Mason took a deep breath, held it, placed the glowing red point of the sight's reticle just below the muzzle flash and pulled the trigger. The SCAR-H bucked in his hands, but he kept his aim true and he kept pulling the trigger until he saw a shadow slump in the tower.

"He's down," Mason said. "Roberts! What's your status?"

"I'm hit, but fuck it, let's go!" Roberts barked back.

"Alpha Team! Move!" Mason yelled.

As Benito ducked around the corner leading the squad toward the front gate, Mason grabbed Hannah by the back of her pants and heaved her to her feet. She scampered up, whimpering.

"Are you wounded?" Mason asked her as they ran for the gate.

"No!" she yelled back through tears.

Mason kept driving her ahead.

They crossed the courtyard in a blur past the dead bodies of several gunman sprawled across the ground, and as they approached the main gate, the fires of burning vehicles lit up the night. Here, the carnage reaped by Bravo Team was everywhere. Bodies lay scattered next to AK-47s and AR-15s; shattered cubes of safety glass glittered in the firelight; hot metal ticked and pinged as the destroyed vehicles burned; smoke and the stench of blood and burning motor oil filled the air.

Just as they passed through the main gate, two Chevrolet Tahoes skidded to a stop in a cloud of dust. Men jumped out of the passenger seats armed with rifles and wearing body armor. A man from the second Tahoe darted to the back of his vehicle and opened the tailgate.

"Here! Here!" he yelled, waving for Samuel to bring Mike's wounded body to the back.

As they got ready to load Mike's body into the vehicle, Roberts stumbled.

"We have two wounded now," Samuel yelled at the passenger, who looked surprised but waved them for them both to hurry and get in.

Benito helped Samuel load Mike inside, then he helped Roberts into the same SUV. Samuel followed them.

"Have you got them?" Mason asked.

Samuel, the medic, looked Mason in the eyes. "Yes, but we need that medevac now," he said.

"I'm on it," Mason replied. Then he slammed the tailgate closed.

Just then, Ameer, Caleb, and the rest of Bravo Team came crashing out of the jungle on the other side of the road. Ameer searched for Mason and looked relieved when he saw Hannah.

"How many wounded?" he asked, rushing toward Mason.

"Two. Not sure how serious. We need medevac," Mason replied.

Ameer rushed to the driver's side of the first Tahoe and began talking loudly to the driver in Arabic. After a brief discussion, he ran back to Mason.

"Get your men and the hostage loaded up. We're going to medevac. Yalla! Arkeb chahina!" Ameer yelled at his men.

Caleb's drone descended into the dusty road with a whir of electric motors and a cloud of dust. He grabbed it, gave Mason a quick nod, then dashed to the first Tahoe with the rest of Bravo. They yanked open the doors and dove in. Zaid lowered the tailgate and sat on it facing backwards. He had his machine gun in one hand and a half belt of ammo laid across his lap, ready to spray anyone who followed them.

"Yalla!" the passenger of the second Tahoe said after he closed the tailgate behind the wounded Alpha Team members. Mason yanked open the rear passenger door, and shoved Hannah inside. Benito came in through the other side as Mason climbed in, sandwiching Hannah between them. Both men rolled down their windows and prepared to fire on their respective flanks as the driver shifted into gear and gunned the powerful engine. He swerved around the other Tahoe, taking the lead, and headed down the dirt road rapidly as the other Tahoe fell in behind.

"We head to medevac," the passenger yelled back to Mason.

"OK!" Mason yelled back.

"Alpha One," Karim's voice came over the radio. "Medevac is enroute to Rally Point 2. Twenty mikes out. Tell your men to hang on."

"Roger that," Mason replied.

"Samuel! Medevac is enroute. Twenty minutes!" he yelled over his shoulder. "How's Roberts?"

"Roberts is OK. Leg wound. Through and through, I've got it plugged up. But Mike needs help stat!" Samuel yelled back.

"We're getting it. Keep doing what you're doing," Mason replied.

Outside, the jungle whipped past as the caravan of operators barreled toward the largest clearing nearby that could safely land a helicopter. Mason just hoped there was enough time.

Ten minutes later, they pulled into a clearing where some logging equipment sat, and seven minutes after that, a helicopter descended onto them, it's spotlight lighting up the landing zone as Mason and the rest of the unit fanned out and set up a perimeter. Samuel helped load Mike and Roberts into the chopper, then climbed in with them for the flight to Belize City. Mason had to assume Prince Omar could grease some wheels and have them treated safely without raising too much suspicion.

After the chopper took off with the wounded men, Bravo Team and the rest of Alpha Team loaded back into the Tahoes. Before they pulled off, Ameer stopped by Mason's open window to reassure him.

"No hospital," he said. "The Prince has a boat with a landing pad he uses for operations like this. It's been parked off the coast since yesterday. He has a top surgeon with all the latest medical equipment onboard. It is better and cleaner than any hospital, trust me. I've been patched up there myself. He's in good hands. Allah will protect him."

He patted Mason on the arm through the open window.

Mason nodded his thanks, and Ameer climbed into his Tahoe. This time, Zaid, the machine gunner, loaded up with him. They were in the clear now and headed to the airport for a quick flight back to Texas. It would be better for them to be out of Belize by the time the cops showed up.

They drove the down the dirt road to the highway in silence, the only sound Hannah sniffling and whimpering quietly.

26

Advancing the Position

Hotel ICON, Downtown, Houston, Texas, USA

Mason knocked on the penthouse door, and it was opened by a bearded Saudi security man in a black suit, a suppressed Sig Sauer MPX K hanging from his shoulder and an acoustic tube coiled behind his ear. He waved Mason in. Inside the luxurious three-story suite, the floors were white marble and the walls were crème-colored. The furniture was all of the finest quality, while chandeliers and recessed lighting created an atmosphere of tranquility and class. Zane was across the room wearing a sweat-stained grey jogging outfit, pacing back and forth before floor-to-ceiling windows overlooking downtown Houston.

"Mason, what's up, bro?" Zane said, dashing across the living area to clasp Mason's hand. "How's your guy, Mike?"

"He's OK," Mason assured him. "Lost two feet of intestine, so he'll have to eat a special diet for a while, but he'll pull through."

"Damn," Zane spat. "Those mother fuckers. Send me his wife's info so I can send her some stuff, OK? Has he got kids?"

"Yes," Mason replied. "But no need to go above and beyond. Mike's a pro."

"Huh?" Zane looked confused. "Bro, a million dollars wouldn't be enough. In fact, that's exactly what I'm going to send them. At least a million."

"Well, I'm sure that'll buy a lot of oatmeal and supplement shakes," Mason said. "How is she?"

Zane frowned and cast a glance at the stairs leading to the bedroom.

"Hannah's OK. She's been sleeping a lot. Prince Omar's doctor gave her some meds to help her chill," Zane said. He began pacing again. "I need to get her back to L.A. Her mom is out there. She can stay with her, go see a therapist and all that."

"That sounds like a good idea," Mason responded. "How are you?"

"Man," Zane said, his voice trailing off as he paced. "I...I...don't even know. Most of the time, I feel like it's all just a bad dream. I mean, if I could turn back time, you know? I never thought it would turn into... all this, you know?"

Mason nodded.

"Not your fault. Can't let the actions of others bring you down."

"I hear you, man, I hear you. But it kind of is though, right? My fault. I mean, I didn't have to take this fight. I didn't have to do any of this. I brought her here."

"You came here on legitimate business. You're a fighter. You were offered a fight. The most lucrative fight in history, in fact. You didn't come here to put Hannah in danger. Other men—bad men—did that. It's not on you."

"Yeah, but I just keep thinking," Zane went on, his brow furrowed, beating his fist into his palm in frustration, "that I saw shit wasn't right. I knew Michael was on some bullshit, you know? I knew everything wasn't good, but I stayed anyway. I should have sent her home weeks ago. I feel like I saw this coming but still walked right into it. Now what? She's all fucked up, your men got fucked up, and I'm here hiding from my own manager because my people killed his son. What the kind of crazy shit did I get us into?"

Mason could see the pain in Zane's face.

"All you can do is make the best decision you can given the information available at the time. The Duke lied. Michael lied. They misled you. It happens to the best of us. Do you know how often that happened to us in the tribal areas in Afghanistan? How many guides, interpreters, and warlords approached us with their hat in their hands offering to help, only to lead us into traps? You're a fighting man, Zane. Deception is part of war. But so is regrouping, learning from your mistakes, and adjusting your tactics. If you let one ambush dictate your mind frame, then you've let the enemy dictate the whole war."

Zane stopped pacing as he listened. He sighed, then walked to the windows overlooking the city. The sun blazed brightly over the concrete jungle below.

"You're right, Mason," he said after a moment. "So, what now?"

"Now, you secure Hannah back in L.A., and you get back to your training. There's only two weeks until the fight," Mason replied. "If you quit now, then everything has been for nothing, and anything you send to Mike's wife won't make it worth it."

Zane leaned his hands against the window.

"Will you take her to the airport? Make sure she gets on the plane safely?"

"You bet," Mason replied.

Mason and two of Prince Omar's men escorted Hannah to the security check at George Bush International Airport. She looked pale and hollow, with dark rings under her eyes. She held a teddy bear Zane had bought her. Mason realized that under the glamor and makeup she was still just a little girl. She threw her arms around Mason's neck and hugged him tightly before turning to show her ID and ticket to the TSA officer. Then she was gone.

Mason said goodbye to the other security men, exited the airport, crossed to the parking garage, and climbed into a black Chevy Tahoe the Prince had loaned him. The Duke's Range Rover was still under the Galleria mall. That was his problem now.

He navigated out of the sprawling airport and took Highway 59N, that familiar route, towards his childhood home in the woods. He played George Strait as he drove. He had a habit of listening to country music when he was near home.

He pulled up to his father's house just as the sun was setting. As soon as he closed the door, Bud came scurrying from the back of the house, jumping on him, and licking his face.

"Hey, boy, hey!" Mason said, tousling his ears. He noticed the dog's coat was covered in mud, but he could tell by the shine in his eyes that Bud was as happy as could be.

"We're gonna have to check you for ticks," he said with a smile.

Mason walked around to the back of the house. It was quiet in the barn. Then he heard a TV playing from inside, so he walked up the three steps to the screen door and let himself in.

"Pop!" he yelled as he walked through the kitchen, removing his sunglasses.

"Yeah!" his father's voice rang out from the living room.

Mason strolled into the room. The air was thick with cigarette smoke. The news was playing on the TV at a low volume. His father was there in the recliner, his coveralls pulled open to reveal a white undershirt, his dirty boots on the floor next to him. He had a cigarette in one hand and a glass with ice and a finger of bourbon in the other. The TV flickered in the lenses of his glasses.

"That dog's been tearing around here like a wild demon. Chased off every rabbit and squirrel for five miles. Probably got the neighbor's bitch pregnant, too. I'll have to hear about that," he said gruffly.

Mason chuckled, then sat on the couch. It was worn out, and he sank deep into the cushion. Everything smelled like smoke with a hint of diesel.

"Sounds just like you when you were young," Mason teased.

"Shit," his dad said, "I had enough sense to keep my pecker out of these bucktoothed Sallies around here."

"That's not what mom said," Mason replied.

"Ah," his father waved his hand dismissively. "Her imagination was a lot bigger than my libido. Your mom was from Diboll. Her daddy, your Grandpa Tom, was an executive with Temple, back before they were Temple-Inland, so she grew up with money. And class. She was the prettiest girl in all East Texas. But she wasn't perfect."

"Yeah? How'd she end up with a dirt poor shitkicker like you?" Mason asked.

His dad set his glass in a cupholder.

"Because I was the best looking shitkicker in East Texas, that's how," the older man said.

Mason chuckled. "You met mom before the war, right?"

"Yep. Married her as soon as I got back. She wrote me the whole time," his father said. He stopped looking at the TV and turned his eyes to some of the black-and-white photos on the wall. "She thought I was pretty hot shit, being a Green Beret, and all. Her daddy had been a paratrooper in World War 2, so he was willing to overlook my poor background as long as I conducted myself properly in the Army."

"I'm guessing that Silver Star probably didn't hurt," Mason said, and for a moment, he thought he saw his father's perpetual scowl soften. It wasn't quite a smile, but maybe a loosening of the wrinkles around his eyes.

"Yeah, your granddaddy was a Screaming Eagle, and he cut many a Nazi throat, that old bastard. But he never earned no Silver Star," he said with pride.

Mason, knowing this was the most words he'd gotten out of his father in nearly twenty years, noticed the ash on his cigarette growing preposterously long, but he dared not break the older man's train of thought.

"What about you? You're gallivanting all over the world for the C.I.A. How many metals have they given you?"

"I don't work for the C.I.A. anymore. Plus, they don't give medals like that. Not publicly, anyway."

"Huh," his father said, draining his glass of whiskey. "Damn spooks. Never knew what you saw in them. In 'Nam, we stayed far away from those fingernail pullers. You know, when they caught a V.C., they'd hand 'em over to the Montagnards—mountain savages—for torture. They'd jam slivers of bamboo under their fingernails or stake them down over termite beds. Brutal little sawed-off bastards."

Mason nodded and looked away. He happened to glance at the coffee table. There, sitting on top of a stack of Farm and Ranch Reports and Sports Illustrated magazines was an issue of Time magazine from years ago. He would never forget it since he'd signed hundreds of copies, and there were still plenty floating around the GZD Training Center. On the cover, a man in tactical gear was shown leaning on the hood of a decimated Chevrolet Suburban. He was peering intently through the scope of a sniper rifle. The photo had been taken by a civilian from an adjacent window during an armored car robbery and shootout in Denver. The headline read, "BATTLE IN DENVER." The article questioned rather the legalization of marijuana in Colorado had brought an increase in crime and violence to the city, and what that meant for the future of cannabis legalization across the country. The man peeking through the rifle scope was Mason. He had never spoken to his father about the ambush. He wasn't even sure he knew about it. But now he knew. He had never called to see if Mason was OK, or to congratulate him on a job well-done. But he knew.

"That reminds me," his father said suddenly. He pointed with his cigarette hand, the ash tumbling into his lap unnoticed. "Go in the kitchen and look in that first drawer. The one with all the tools. There's something in there I been meaning to give you."

Surprised, Mason hesitated.

"Go on," his dad encouraged. "First drawer as you walk in."

Mason knew exactly which drawer he meant. It had been the family junk drawer his whole life, and his father was not one to change habits.

Mason walked into the kitchen and pulled open the drawer. It was old and heavy, so it scraped as he pulled it out. It was filled with flathead screwdrivers, worn out pliers, and half-used rolls of white thread tape on blue spools. But on top was a leather sheath with a brown handle sticking out.

"Bring it in here," his father yelled.

Mason plucked the knife and scabbard from the drawer and walked back into the living room. His father waved for him to hand it to him. The older man took it, then drew the knife from the sheath.

"Randall Model 1 Fighting Knife," he said as he held the blade up into the light. "Grandpa Tom gave it to me before I went off to 'Nam. He carried it into Normandy. You can't hardly get one of these anymore. This one's seen a lot of Nazi *and* Commie blood."

He turned the knife around in the light, then sheathed it and offered it to Mason.

Mason leaned over and took it. He had sat back on the couch and took a moment to examine the blade. It was about eight inches long from tip to cross guard with a drop point. It was sharpened to the choil on the main edge and down about three inches on the false edge, too. The cross guard was brass, the handle made of stacked leather, and the pommel was made of stainless steel or aluminum, he couldn't tell.

"I sharpened it yesterday, so don't go picking your teeth with it. That ain't no pocket knife. That's a real-life American pigsticker," his dad said.

Mason turned the blade over and over in the dim light. The balance was superb, and the grip seemed to melt into his palm.

"Thanks, Pop. It's a fine knife," Mason said.

"Well, that's probably all you'll get from me, other than this house and land. That tractor's more warn out than I am, and the doctors are getting the rest. That Kenworth out front might bring a few dollars, but she's old and they've got fancy rigs that drive themselves nowadays, I hear."

"Hell, Pop. You'll outlive all of us."

"I'll outlive that dog of yours if he don't learn to stay away from snakes and bitches in heat," he replied.

Mason chuckled.

He tucked the knife back into its sheath, then looked around at the photos on the far wall. He remembered his mother's smile, and her eternal patience. He wondered if his father regretted all his years on the road as a long-haul trucker, or all the whiskey, or all the "bitches in heat" he'd cheated on her with over the years. His mother had been as patient as she could be, until the day she died. Then he wondered if she regretted waiting on her veteran husband, damaged from the war as he was, to be the man she always believed he could be. Then he wondered what it was like being two people, both waiting on someone to change who never did.

Then he heard a snore, and he looked over. His dad's head was tossed back against the recliner's headrest, mouth gaped open. He'd put the cigarette out, at least.

Mason looked once more around the room, wondering if he'd be back before the inevitable funeral that would come one day. Then he stood up, the heirloom knife in his hand, and walked back through the kitchen, and out the back door.

He snugged the door closed quietly, then called for Bud. The dog came leaping joyfully out of the woods, pausing to sniff here and there, before following Mason to the Tahoe, where they loaded up and headed back into the city.

That night, Lisa invited Mason to her house for dinner. She cooked steak and eggplant parmesan, a combination he'd never had before but had to admit it was pretty good. He was quiet through most of the meal, lost in his thoughts, and she noticed.

"Work's been busy, huh?" she nudged gently. She had poured herself a glass of red wine, and Mason a glass of sweet tea.

"Yeah," he replied, shaken from his thoughts. "It's gonna be pretty busy for the next couple of weeks leading into the fight."

"I understand," she said, sipping her wine. She had her hair up in a bun with chopsticks and wore dangly earrings and a low cut top, denim shorts cut high on her tanned legs, and Mason noticed a silver ring on one of her toes.

He smiled. She did that to him.

"Dinner was amazing. And you look amazing," he said.

He looked up, and she was staring into his face over the rim of her wine glass. The lights were low, but a sparkle caught in her liquid brown eyes.

"Well, then, we should stop wasting time," she said as she stood up and held out her hand.

Mason wiped his mouth with a napkin, then took her fingers. She brought her wine glass with them as she led him down the hallway to her bedroom. They kept the TV on, but just for the light. She was more beautiful with her clothes off than he could have imagined. Afterwards, laying in the warmth of her embrace, his head against her breasts, Mason slept like the dead.

27

The Duke and the Prince

The Duke's mansion, River Oaks, Houston, Texas, USA

The ashtray shattered into a thousand shards that glittered in the firelight. One henchman flinched, while Bishop, standing at attention near the study's doorway, hardly blinked, though a sheen of sweat glimmered across his forehead.

"Dead! All of them! Whoever they are! Dead! All of them!" the Duke repeated over-and-over again. He had stopped making sense earlier that day, and his voice was raspy from yelling. Most of the house was destroyed. Cabinets and tables were turned over, their contents strewn across the wood floors. Chairs were upended and bits of shattered glass crunched under their feet.

"Where the fuck is Tank?" the Duke yelled at Bishop.

The Duke's shirt was torn open, the buttons mixed with the other shattered bits and pieces on the floor, and he was bleeding from a scratch on his forehead. Bishop wasn't sure where that had come from. But that wasn't his main concern. His biggest concern was the stainless .45 1911 automatic the Duke had been flailing around all day since he learned that Michael, his favorite son, the only child he claimed, had been killed. Nobody knew who had done it or why, only that men had attacked their estate in Belize, shot everybody, including Michael, and turned the Duke's world upside down. The Duke thought it was the cartel, that Michael had pissed off somebody by running dope. As soon as he heard, he had ordered that Tank, his head of security in Belize, get on an immediate flight to Houston to answer for the tragedy.

Bishop checked his watch.

"They should be pulling up any minute, boss," Bishop assured him.

The Duke, his eyes wide, a trickle of blood from his forehead mixed with sweat running down his temple, shoved his face into Bishop's. He had been pointing the pistol at everyone, and once again he stuck it under Bishop's chin. The big man took a deep breath but didn't dare to so much as shift his weight.

"How the fuck did he let this happen? How? How?" the Duke yelled in his face.

"I don't know, boss. Like I said, he says he wasn't there that night, and that Michael had a whole gang of security with him because he had something else going on," Bishop said for at least the tenth time, but there was no calming the Duke down.

"That motha' fucka' better have some fuckin' answers..." the Duke began to say when they heard car doors slam out front. The Duke perked up, listening. Soon, the front door creaked open, and rubber soles could be heard squeaking on the marble floor toward the study. Bishop wondered why the Duke had a fire going in the fireplace, given how hot it already was. There were three other bodyguards, all big men, jammed into the study with the Duke, and all of them were dripping in sweat.

The footsteps slowed, then Tank stepped through the doorway, cautiously. He was a big man himself, heavily muscled and tattooed. He and Bishop had done a lot of work for the Duke over the years. They'd been his right-hand men all along. But Bishop knew all that could be forgotten in one moment of rage. By the look in Tank's face, he knew Tank knew it, too.

"Well, ain't it nice of you to finally join us," the Duke said sarcastically. Veins were sticking out on his forehead and arms.

"Hey, boss, man, I'm so sorry about...about Michael...about everything,"

Tank started to say.

The Duke looked mock surprised.

"Sorry?" he said, looking around at the other men. "Sorry? This motha' fucka' says he's sorry. *My son* gets killed *in Belize*, and my head of security—*in Belize*—says he's sorry."

"Like I told Bishop," Tank cut his eyes to the head bodyguard, "Michael sent me away two days before the shit happened. He told me he had something going on but it was lowkey and he didn't need me. He had off-duty police there and everything when I left. I tried to convince him to let me stay..."

"*Tried?* Tried but failed!" the Duke roared. "Tried but let my boy get *killed*, the one person on this earth you was responsible for!"

Tank started looking even more nervous.

"All I ever wanted was to keep you and him safe, b-boss," Tank stammered.

"Sh-sh-shut up, motha' fucka', and sit down," the Duke mocked him. "I'm tired of looking up at you. Sit there and shut the fuck up while I think."

He waved the shiny pistol at a wing chair near the fireplace.

As ordered, Tank sat down, but only after looking at the other men, nervously. He looked at Bishop pleadingly, his eyes begging for some indication of what was going to happen. Bishop looked away.

The Duke sighed, letting his shoulders relax, and walked over to the fire place. He leaned against the mantle, his silk shirt hanging open, the pistol in his hand flashing orange in the fire light. He rubbed his temples for a moment, collecting his thoughts. He sighed again, then he reached down to a set of fire tools and selected a steel poker. It was about three feet long and tipped with a hooked spike. Taking it by the handle, he stuck it into the flames and began poking the logs slowly. He was lost in thought, staring into the fire.

"Ok," he said calmly. "We've gotta keep our cool here. We've gotta use our heads. Figure out who did this to us. To my boy."

The bodyguards around the room stood silent, waiting.

"But I need you to tell me, Tank. What has Michael been up to down there? What'd he get involved in? Because I know there was something goin' on behind my back. And that's what got him into this shit."

Tank waited for the Duke to finish, not daring to interrupt.

"Look, I didn't want to say nothin'. But you're right. Michael was up to somethin' down there. I just didn't know if it was my place to say. I mean, I know I'm supposed to keep him safe—I mean, I *was* supposed to—but I didn't think I should be all in his business like that. He seemed like he didn't want me to know, so I stayed out of it."

The Duke nodded slowly. Turning to look at Tank.

"Yeah, see, that's good. That's what I'm talkin' about," he said. The Duke laid the poker down, leaving the spiked tip leaning on a burning log, deep in the flames. "Tell me what you knew about."

"Well, that's what I'm sayin'. I really didn't know nothin'. I just could tell, you know, that it was somethin'. These past about three months, he would show up a couple times a month and would tell me to take off. He would usually have a girl with him, or like recently he had the fighter, Zane, down there with his people. But sometimes he would come down and it would just be him, but he would have people over to meet."

"What people?" the Duke asked, his face wrinkled in concern as he listened intently.

"All types of people. Man, sometimes it would be local politicians. One time he had the Prime Minister's son over. Sometimes he would have top cops, like chief of police types. But you know how it is down there. Those motha' fucka's love to party more than anyone, so I figured he was, you know, partying with them and they didn't want to be exposed, or whatever."

"Yeah, yeah. OK. Partying. I dig it," the Duke encouraged. "What else?"

"Sometimes—a few times—he would have these Mexican cats. But not Mexican. Maybe Colombian or Venezuelan, you know? I can't always tell. But these, you know, cartel lookin' motha' fucka's."

"Hmm," the Duke said thoughtfully. "So, you're tellin' me that Michael had 'cartel lookin' motha' fucka's' over, and you thought it was a good idea for you to leave? As head of security, you left my boy alone with 'cartel lookin' motha' fucka's'?"

"Shit, Duke, it's not like I wanted to. He ordered me to go away. In fact, I only knew who came because I made sure to check the cameras and I had the maids keeping an eye out. I was using spies and shit."

"Oh, this motha' fucka' got spies, y'all," the Duke said mockingly, casting his eyes around to the other men. "Well, tell me this. What did the spies tell you was going on when these guests were around?"

"Like I said, mostly partying. I figured he was doing a little blow and didn't want me to know because he knows I tell you everything. I mean, we all know he likes to toot a little bit and that you don't like that shit, so I figured that could be it. At least at first. But after a while, I can't lie, there started to be some more shit going on, so I got more suspicious."

The Duke stood staring at Tank, his hands crossed in front of him, the pistol aimed at the floor, waiting.

"Well, damn, motha' fucka'," he finally blurted. "Don't keep us all in suspense. What the fuck else was goin' on?"

"So-so-some packages and shit, in the warehouse. Boxes and shit started to arrive a few months ago. They would come in trucks and vans and be marked like they were cases of sugar, from the new sugar plant."

"Cases of sugar? From a sugar plant?" the Duke's eyes lowered. "And you still didn't think to say nothin' to me?"

Tank looked around uneasily again.

"I mean, I don't really know what else to say..." he started.

The Duke stood looking at him, fire burning in his eyes.

Then, in one smooth step, he leaned down. picked up the fire poker that had been resting in the flames, lifted it overhead, and swung it towards Tank. The glowing red tip left a tracer through the air as it arced down.

Tank threw his arm's up to block, then screamed as the hot metal seared his skin and the heavy iron bit into his forearm. The red hot tip drew red arcs in the air as the Duke beat Tank with one hand and pointed the pistol at him with the other. Tank screamed and the room filled with the scent of burned flesh until the wing chair flipped over backwards.

"Grab this motha' fucka'!" the Duke yelled, and two henchmen dashed forward to grab Tank by the arms. "Hold him down!"

Just as the Duke prepared to shove the hot poker into Tank's eye, there was a loud thud at the front door. Bishop, the Duke, and the other bodyguards all paused and looked up quizzically.

"Who the fuck..." the Duke started to say.

Just then, there was a *boom!* from the front, and the men flinched. Tank continued flopping and trying to break free of the men's clutches as Bishop reached down to an end table and retrieved a Draco Pistol.

The Duke stood up frowning as the other bodyguards pulled pistols from their waistbands. One picked up an AR-15 leaning against the wall and racked a round into the chamber. Just then, gunshots erupted from the rear of the house.

Bishop turned to the Duke.

"Upstairs! Let's go!" he yelled, reaching for his boss's arm.

Forgetting Tank's burned and broken form on the study floor, the Duke, still clutching the hot poker and the shiny pistol, headed to the door. Bishop led the way using his body to block as the men spilled into the hallway. Immediately, Bishop spotted a man in all black, wearing a ski mask, coming down the hall toward them. The man shot Bishop in the chest, but Bishop raised the Draco and unloaded on him. A flame two feet long blazed from the muzzle of the AK pistol as 7.62 mm steel tore the man to shreds, his body jerking around. Bishop had taken a round to the body armor, and the pistol round had hardly phased the massive man.

"Stay behind me!" he yelled as he led the way towards the living room stairs. He could hear more commotion from the front entryway, and now he could see shadows flickering across the back windows overlooking the pool as men raced around the gardens, too. Then there were more gunshots and more flashes of light as his men poured from the house into the yard to engage the intruders. Men were yelling in confusion, but Bishop's priority was to get the Duke to the safe room in the back of the master closet.

The made it to the grand staircase just as another black-clad figure rounded the corner and started shooting wildly at them. The Duke raised his .45 and popped six rounds at the man who dove behind a couch and crawled away. Bishop turned, shoving the Duke behind him, as he dropped the spent magazine in his Draco and reloaded with a magazine from his jacket pocket.

He fired a few rounds into the couch as he shoved the Duke up the stairs.

"Go! Go!" he yelled.

The Duke, knowing he was out of ammo, scampered up the winding carpeted steps. Bishop tried to follow, but walking backwards up the stairs while trying to watch for the shooter in the living room was too much for the large man, and he stumbled. Falling against the steps, he shot a few more rounds wildly into the living area below, shattering a glass coffee table. Just then, he saw the man had somehow crawled across the room, and he popped up in an unexpected place behind a love seat. The masked man had just enough time to take aim and unloaded an extended magazine of 9mm hollow points on Bishop. Bullets struck all around the big man, until one hit him in the face, dislodging his jaw and blowing some of his teeth through his cheek. Another round caught him in the forehead, and Bishop went limp, sliding down the steps in his silk suit.

Meanwhile, the Duke had already climbed the steps and was running for the master bedroom. As he rounded a hallway corner, he ran headlong into another masked intruder who had taken the entryway stairs to the second floor. They collided hard, knocking the other man off balance. Before he could recover, the Duke hit him across the knee with the hot poker. The man yelled and fell back. Using it like a spear, the Duke jabbed the poker into the man's face twice. The second time, it seemed to sink in, so the Duke leaned into it. The man grabbed at the steel tool, his hands smoking as they burned, screaming, but soon went limp as the poker reached his brain.

"Motha' fucka'!" the Duke screamed into the man's face, then looking around quickly, ran towards the safety of his bedroom. He dashed through the room, into the closet, to a floor-length mirror. He pushed the mirror and with a click it popped open and swung towards him on hinges. Behind the mirror, there was a steel door with a keypad and a thumb scanner. He entered the code, touched his thumb to the reader, and the locks released. He looked behind him one last time before disappearing into the safe room, closing the door securely behind him. A moment later, the mirror automatically swung back into place.

Inside, there were numerous camera monitors showing all parts of his sprawling River Oaks estate. Men were running here and there. He could see flashes of gunfire in the darkness. On the wall, there was a rack of firearms: AR-15s, shotguns, and submachine guns. He took down a Heckler & Koch AR pistol and checked to make sure there was a round in the chamber. Then, ripping off his sweat-soaked silk shirt, he lifted a Kevlar vest over his head and secured it in place. Then he reached down for a ballistic plate and slipped it into a pouch on the front of the vest, before turning to the closed circuit tv monitors. The scars on his back from the burns he'd received in prison a lifetime ago peaked out from under the armored vest as he watched the battle playing out in and around his mansion.

"Who in the fuck?" he asked through gritted teeth.

The gunfight raged for a few more minutes, and then it seemed to die down. The Duke was glued to the screens. He could still see movement. Shadows. Men in black clothes. Masks. Moving slowly through his house. Heading to the stairs. Coming up the stairs.

The Duke gritted his teeth harder.

"Motha' fucka'," he groaned.

Then he saw them. Ghosts creeping into his bedroom. Some went to his dresser. Others started ripping pictures off his wall. They were yanking out drawers, dumping them on the ground. One said something to another. He had found something. He held it up. A chain? Was that one of his diamond chains? The man tucked the small treasure in his pocket.

A robbery? Was all this just a home invasion?

He watched one man who was passing over drawers, looking around more intently. He found the closet. Cautiously, his gun up and ready, the man crept into the master closet. He swept the room with his muzzle, crouched, ready to react. He didn't see anyone at first. He turned on a flashlight, swept it around the room. Then he crept closer. Closer to the mirrored door behind which the safe room lay hidden. Even though he knew he was secure behind several inches of steel and concrete, the Duke found himself aiming his own rifle at the safe room's door. As the man got closer, a camera just above the door caught his face. He pulled his mask down to see better.

The Duke could see a Houston Astros logo tattooed on the robber's cheek.

Who was he?

Just then, the man turned quickly. The Duke couldn't hear, but his mouth moved as if he was yelling something. Suddenly, all the men in the bedroom dashed. The Duke turned back to the monitors. He could see men running back and forth in the hallways. They seemed confused.

Then there was an even more bizarre sight. The cameras in the back garden showed trees and bushes whipping around. Then the grass laid flat and dust began to whip around as if a hurricane had blown in. Then the yard got brighter and brighter. Finally, against all expectations, he saw two ropes descend as if from the sky above, and then men slid down the ropes.

It was a helicopter. In his backyard. In River Oaks.

The men, who were wearing helmets and tactical gear and carrying rifles, unhooked themselves from the ropes and charged toward the house. In that instant, on another camera facing the front of the house, two vans skidded to a stop at his gate, and more men poured out and over his front wall. Within seconds, his house was swarming with a new wave of black clad intruders, and the flashes of gunfire resumed.

This time, the gunfight only lasted a few minutes. The new invaders worked professionally. They stacked up and flowed through the house, deploying flash bang grenades, and dropping their opponents with surgically accurate shots. Within minutes, the mansion had gone from under his control, to under the control of bandits, to under the control of mysterious saviors.

The Duke was speechless.

He stayed leaning against the desk, eyes glued to the monitor throughout as the new tactical team went body to body removing ski masks, checking the dead. The Duke thought it best to stay where he was.

A few moments later, he watched one of the men walk out the front door and into the yard. Flanked by two other men with rifles, he spoke into a radio or phone. Moments later, another man climbed over the wall like the others had, except this one was wearing a suit. The suited man walked across the yard directly to the man who had called. They spoke for a moment. The man in tactical gear waved his arms around and pointed, then seemed to shrug. They talked some more, then the Duke's stomach did a back flip. The tactical team leader was pointing directly at the closed circuit camera through which the Duke was watching.

"Who in the fuck…" the Duke whispered again.

He could hardly make out the suited man's face. He had dark hair and a dark beard. He looked Mexican, the Duke thought. The cartel? Had they come to finish him off, just as they had Michael? But who were the others, the robbers before them?

The Duke was getting dizzy from confusion when the suited man walked up to the camera. Reaching into his pocket, he pulled out a white business card and a pen. He wrote something on the card, put the pen back into his jacket, then calmly held the card up to the camera. It was out of focus at first, so the Duke found himself leaning in closer, trying to read what it said.

Then he felt his knees buckle. He couldn't believe it. His jaw hung open as he read the words on the card.

"Prince Omar sends his regards. You can come out now. It is safe."

The Duke strolled down the stairs into his destroyed living room. There was a wide streak of blood all the way down the carpeted steps wear Bishop, his loyal bodyguard, had slid down.

The Duke, still wearing body armor over his shirtless torso, carried his AR pistol loosely down by his leg as he slowly walked down the steps. There were black-clad men moving all around, and they stopped when they saw him. He spotted their tactical leader who shouted some commands in Arabic. All the men wore black balaclava masks except for the man in the suit who watched the Duke as he descended the steps, never taking his eyes off him. He looked perfectly calm, even smug, his suit and hair immaculate. The Duke finally recognized him as the Prince's emissary.

"Ah, Mr. Duke," Nasir said. "Quite a disturbance you've had here tonight. But I assure you, the Prince's Royal Guard has everything quite well in hand."

The Duke looked suspiciously at everyone as he took the final step and walked across the living room carpet toward the dapper Arab.

"You are fortunate the Prince had your house under surveillance. We spotted these, um, bandits, I suppose, watching your house two days ago. The Prince thought it would be prudent to keep a Quick Reaction Force on standby, should you need our assistance. Which you did."

The Duke didn't say a word, still too stunned and too suspicious to speak.

"Prince Omar wishes to extend his deepest condolences to you regarding your son," the diplomat said. He bowed slightly, his hand over his heart.

"What you know about that?" the Duke asked, squinting at the man. "Was that your people who killed my boy?"

"I assure you, it was not," the Arab said, bowing his head once again. "However, the Prince realizes that you have incurred tremendous loss due to the upcoming sporting event. He feels badly that this undertaking, which should have brought joy, has brought you so much pain. Therefore, to prevent you from suffering further, and to compensate you for your material loss—though the Prince understands that nothing could compensate for the loss of a son—he wishes to bestow upon you a remittance."

With that, the tactical leader shouted an order in Arabic, and another heavily armed soldier stepped forward with a black canvas bag. He unzipped it and tilted it forward. Inside, there were more bricks of shiny yellow gold than the Duke had ever imagined. The soldier set the bag at the Duke's feet, then backed away.

"This bag should help repair your beautiful home and compensate you for your trouble with the young fighter, Zane."

The Duke looked back and forth between the bag of bullion and the emissary.

"What you sayin'? My compensation for Zane comes *after* the fight," he said.

"Well," the Arab man replied, "the Quran says, 'No one but God can limit human freedom.' Zane has expressed his desire to be free of his contract with you, and Prince Omar feels it would be best for everyone if you granted him that freedom. Here. Now."

Nasir raised his eyebrows at the Duke but waited calmly. The Duke glanced around the room and realized that all the men had stopped moving. Every one of them was standing still, staring at him through the slits in their black masks. There were at least ten highly-skilled warriors with rifles in his living room staring at him. He looked at the tactical leader. His eyes were as dark as pools of Saudi oil. Then he looked down at the bag of gold.

"Well," he said, "after all, he's a Prince, and I'm just a Duke."

28

Fight Night

Toyota Center, Downtown, Houston, Texas, USA

The stadium was packed. Every one of the red and black seats, sky boxes, and VIP sections was sold out. Outside, traffic was jammed for miles around downtown Houston as everyone who could afford the costly tickets packed into the Toyota Center to see the big fight. The marketing and publicity had been handled expertly, and the crowd was a who's-who of celebrities. Grinning actors, rappers, models, athletes, politicians, and tech billionaires strutted around, clasping each other's hands and shouting greetings to their friends and followers.

Mason was in the locker room with Zane. He wore a Team InZane jacket to cover his body armor, and he had a Sig Sauer MPX K hanging vertically under his arm, ready to deploy in a flash.

"Zulu 1 to Zulu Team, five mikes until we walk. Look sharp," Mason said into his wrist-mounted microphone.

"Roger that, Zulu 1," Benito's voice, followed by numerous other GZD operators placed strategically around the stadium, radioed back.

Green Zone Defense had operators everywhere, from snipers in the rafters to plain clothes officers seated in the crowd. Mason was where he needed to be, glued to Zane's side.

Zane was on his feet working the focus mitts with his old Cockney trainer, Charlie. His hands were wrapped, his gloves on, and he wore green, black, and gold trunks in honor of his Jamaican roots.

"You've got to give 'im the Billy or the Nick. Mickie's a slippery geezer. He'll try to slip under your boat. Keep your mince. Watch for an open chin. Are you earwiggin'?" Charlie asked in his heavy accent.

Zane nodded.

He looked good, Mason thought. He'd lost weight, and every one of his muscles rippled when he swung. His punches popped the mitts sharply, and he was good about bringing his right hand back to his chin every time. He slipped and rolled smoothly, and he looked like he could go all night. But more than that, the past weeks had hardened him, the resolve showing in his eyes.

"Five minutes, champ," Mason said.

The Prince's emissary, Nasir al-Amri, was in the room, his suit, beard, and hair as sharp as ever.

"I must bid you farewell now, Master Zane," he said, "and join the Prince in his quarters. Rest assured, you have His Majesty's utmost support."

"Thank you, Nasir," Zane said. "For everything."

Nasir placed his hand to his chest and bowed, then headed for the door.

"Oh, yes, he insists you join him for dinner in Los Angeles in two weeks. I will send a formal invitation soon," the Arab said.

Then, with a regal grin, he walked to the door. He and Mason exchanged nods as he passed.

"Three minutes, and we walk," Mason said out loud.

Charlie took off the focus mitts, reached for Zane's green and gold robe with #InZane in black across the back, and helped him slip it on.

"You've got the fruit and nut on your side, so you can afford to go the distance. Don't get clucky and rush in there. Take your time and wear the old dodger down. Are you with me, bruv?"

Zane nodded again as he bounced on his toes and shook out his gloved hands to stay loose.

Mason touched his earpiece as a transmission came through.

"Zulu 1 to Zulu Team. Zulu 1 to Zulu Team. We're walking," he called into the radio.

Looking around the locker room at all the faces, he could feel the eagerness radiating from them. He turned the doorknob, and Team InZane spilled out into the hallway.

Zane walked out to Damian Marley's 2005 hit "Welcome to Jamrock", and the crowd was on fire. The lights were low as the Jumbotron displayed Zane's stats. He was an inch shorter than his opponent, Mickie Donovan, and didn't have any of the former world champion's professional record, but there was no question who had the fans. Everywhere Zane looked, he saw people on their feet, jumping and cheering for him, with more than one holding a homemade posterboard with "Go Zane!" or "#TeamInZane" blazoned across it. He tried not to let it distract him from the challenge he faced in the ring, but deep down, he felt a thrill.

Surrounded by his security team, he made it to the ring, his trainers close behind. A referee checked his gloves, then motioned for him to enter. He passed smoothly through the ropes and instantly felt the pressure of millions of eyes on him, but he was used to it. He took a lap around the ring to get the feel of it, forcing his mind to forget the fans and focus on that small square of canvas. The crowd roared, and the announcer continued his speech.

Zane barely heard the words as the man with the microphone announced his competitor. Mickie walked out to an old AC/DC rock anthem. He entered the ring wearing white trunks with green trim, and Zane realized he was smaller than he'd imagined. But then, after facing Michael and the Duke, all his challenges seemed small.

The announcer thanked the event's sponsors, and the ring girls flashed their best smiles. Zane locked eyes on Mickie. He looked confident. His ears were cauliflowered and his shoulders and abs rippled with lean muscle, but Zane stared at his chin and pictured himself hitting him so hard his head spun around like a cartoon.

Finally, the referee called them to the center and reminded them of the rules. Zane stared Mickie directly in his grey eyes, bit down on his mouthguard, and prepared for the fight of his life.

The fight lasted all ten rounds. Zane was thankful for all the training, all the running, all the jumping rope, because the match seemed endless. They had agreed on two-minute rounds, which worked out about right, because in the end, Zane was completely drained, and so was Mickie. There were a couple knockdowns, a little blood, and a lot of sweat. Zane's head rang from Mickie's incredible right cross, and he thought he felt his jaw click from a nasty uppercut, but otherwise, he had never felt so good in his life.

In the end, when the announcer called the fighters to the center of the ring to read the judges' score cards, Zane could hardly catch his breath. It was a close fight, but the former world champ ended up winning by split decision. When the referee held up the Irishman's hand, Zane realized the true victory for him was simply surviving all that he had to make it to that moment. He hugged Mickie, and they congratulated each other, though Zane could hardly hear from the ringing in his ears and the thoughts in his head.

Hannah had not attended in person, and he thought that was best.

In the locker room, a doctor examined him and said he might have a concussion. He advised Zane to rest and handed him a bottle of pain killers. Zane showered and dressed out in street clothes, then headed to the post fight conference. On a raised platform, he sat behind a microphone with Mickie and their trainers. They took turns answering questions from the press, but all Zane really wanted was to go home. When the conference was done, he shook everyone's hand, then walked back to the locker room to grab his gear. Mason, Benito, and the rest of his security team were never more than five feet from his side. He wondered if he would ever feel normal again.

As he headed down the long hallway toward the exit and his waiting Suburban, his head covered in a hoodie, gear bag over his shoulder, Zane realized that he didn't miss his old life, his old friends, or his old dreams. Through the process, he had changed, grown. He felt more like an adult—like a *man*—than he ever had, as if the training, the fighting, and the danger he had faced, all the turmoil along the way, had carved away more than just his baby fat, but also his baby ways.

He was deep in thought when the doors opened and he started to walk across the sidewalk toward the waiting motorcade that would take him to the hotel. Security was trying to hold back a crowd of eager fans, all with their cellphones and camera lights flashing.

Suddenly, there was another flash, a brighter one, just to his right, only feet away. Then a *bang* and a burning pain in his side. Then more bangs, closer. A hot shell casings fell on him, burning him. Then his whole side burned. There was shouting, screaming, then there was the cold, hard concrete. Benito dove on top of him, covering him, shielding his body. He wanted him to get off. He wanted to go home. Then he just felt tired. So damn tired.

Zane awoke at Houston Methodist Hospital with tubes in his nose and bandages around his side. Machines beeped and whirred all around him, and the lights were far too bright. He looked down to see an IV needle and a patient ID band on his wrist. He shivered with cold.

There was a man sitting in a chair, frowning, and scrolling on his phone. He looked up when Zane moved, saw his eyes open, and immediately went to the door. He opened it and leaned into the hallway.

"Excuse me!" he said firmly. "He's awake."

A moment later, three nurses in scrubs swarmed around Zane's bed, checking tubes and machines, and telling him to relax, and that a doctor would be in with him shortly.

A few minutes later, an older man wearing a white coat with an Indian accent entered. He had thick, black hair and held his arms across his stomach.

"You have been shot," the doctor said plainly. "The bullet fragmented, and we will need to take more scans. The bullet impacted your number seven rib on the right side which stopped it from doing more damage to your organs, but it did fracture the rib. You are on a lot of pain medicine, and so you will feel it much worse tomorrow."

The doctor went on to explain what they had already done, and what would still need to be done, but most importantly, that he would be confined to the hospital bed for at least another day, maybe more. Then he left, and Zane found himself alone for a while.

Finally, a nurse came in and asked if he'd like the TV on. His head was cloudy, so he wasn't quite sure what to say. Then the door opened again, and Mason entered.

"I'll help him with that," Mason said to the nurse with a smile. She smiled back, handed him the remote control, and walked out.

"Hey, champ. You thirsty? Cold?"

Zane nodded.

Mason found a blanket in a cabinet and a water bottle. He covered Zane up, twisted off the bottle cap, and helped him take a drink.

"Every time I've been shot, I always get cold and thirsty. I guess it's the blood loss. They had to give you four bags of blood. You made a mess all over the sidewalk. The doctor said the bullet didn't hit any major organs. It just left a bunch of bone fragments. He said your rib got vaporized. They think it was a small caliber, probably a .380. Still, it's a one in a million chance. You're lucky," Mason said.

"Who?" Zane croaked. Talking caused him to breathe a little deeper, and that's when he felt the pain in his side.

"The Duke's man from Belize, Tank. He was in the crowd. He got his gun up and got one shot off before Benito dropped him. Put one right here while mid dive." Mason pointed high on his own forehead. "Took the top of his cranium right off. Amazing shot. I taught him that."

Zane chuckled, realizing Mason was trying to cheer him up. The motion caused a stabbing pain in his side, and Mason must've seen the painful look on his face.

"Eh, maybe it's not the right time for an old soldier's dark humor," Mason said. "I'll let you rest. Just wanted you to know that we're still here for you. Got guys all over, including right out in the hallway. I'll be here when they move you upstairs to your own room. And don't worry about the Duke. He's got hell coming his way as we speak."

Mason turned on the TV, put it on a sports channel, then laid the remote on Zane's blanket near his hand.

"Hang in there, Champ," he said, then walked out.

29

Knock Out

The Duke's Estate, Cayo District, Belize

When the Belizean authorities, along with the DEA, raided the Duke's estate in Belize, they arrested everyone. They spent days photographing bullet holes and boxes marked as "cane sugar". They swabbed surfaces for drug residue and searched electronic devices for illicit communications. In the end, they found fourteen kilograms of fentanyl, half of which were packaged for the trip to Mexico to be eventually smuggled into the United States. The knife Mason had dipped into the white powder during his clandestine search of the warehouse had tested positive for the powerful synthetic opiate, a substance federal law enforcement was quite interested in hearing about.

Back in the U.S., The raid on The Reserve, the Duke's ranch widely known in the boxing and criminal underworlds as the "Gladiator Farm", was less interesting at first, though numerous illegal firearms were recovered, until a secret room was discovered under one of the barns. In a perfect scenario, packages marked with the green logo of the Santando Sugar Company were found, many of which contained fentanyl mixed with sugar making the connection to Belize simple to prove.

Things got much more interesting when the FBI's forensics team cordoned off Mama Heloise's farm deep in the back woods. Dozens of animals were captured and put down so the contents of their stomachs could be studied. A team in white biohazard suits was brought out to excavate the area. It took months to catalog the human remains that were recovered.

As for Mama Heloise, she was never found. Some of the agents joked about her voodoo powers of foresight and how she probably knew they were coming.

FBI Special Agent Kim Wright personally led the early-morning raid on the Duke's mansion in River Oaks. The Duke was found in bed, still drunk from the night before, still mourning the loss of his favorite son, Michael. Meanwhile, the sworn testimony of his other, less favored son, Mo Davis, had been instrumental in securing the search warrants.

The FBI tactical team tore down the front gates of the Duke's mansion with an armored car, then battered the front door in. Inside, they weaved around scaffolding and painter's drop cloths from the ongoing repairs due to the home invasion. Kim was still piecing that night together. But regardless, she was confident there was enough evidence to put the Duke back in a cage for the rest of his life.

Kim waited outside the palatial home as the tactical team secured the Duke and brought him out in handcuffs. Outside, he frowned and squinted at her.

"Mr. Davis," she said, "you are under arrest for numerous federal offenses, including drug trafficking, money laundering, extortion, and murder. In a few hours we will announce it to the world, and the city of Houston will celebrate."

The Duke sneered at her. "I *am* the city of Houston."

With that, the Duke was placed into the back of the armored car and hauled away to face a lifetime of consequences.

Mason threw the tennis ball, and Bud tore across the bright green grass after it. He snatched it up in his slobbery jaws, then looked back at Mason, his tail wagging, before running off in another direction.

"He gets the fetch part," Mason said, "but we're still working on the retrieve part."

Lisa laughed. She was wearing a sundress and cowgirl boots. Her hair was up in a clip, and in the sun he could see it was really more auburn than dark brown. Her skin was smooth and creamy, and there was something about the way her hips moved as she strolled through the park with him than made every cell in his body vibrate.

"Yeah, well, he's a boy, and boys are like that," she said as they walked. "They're good about fetching what they want, but not always so good about coming back."

Mason chuckled. "You think I won't come back?"

"Well," she measured her words, "I know you have to go back to Colorado, and I'm a big girl. I know that could mean I won't see you again."

Mason stopped, turned towards her, and took both of her hands.

"I mean, you're right. I do have to go back to Colorado. That is where my home is, where my work is. But..."

"But..." she said softly, looking down at their hands.

He rubbed her fingers gently.

"But I've got space enough for more than just me and a dog. I mean, I know there's got to be some old guys in some diner somewhere in Colorado that would love to get served an omelet by a girl as pretty as you."

She looked up at him, her eyes big and brown and soft. They darted around his face, searching.

"What are you saying?" she asked.

"I'm saying," Mason replied, "that I don't want to come back to you. I want you to come with me. Sell your house or keep it for a while, whatever you want. But I want you to come stay with me in Denver."

He felt her fingers tighten on his. He could see a smile spread across her face, and his heart swelled so he thought it might explode. She fell into his chest, almost knocking him over.

Then he kissed her, hard.

After a while, Bud came over, chewing on the tennis ball, and laid by their feet.

The End

About the Author

Rex Holloway writes crime thrillers shaped by a life that has seen both darkness and redemption.

His Mason Origins Trilogy (*The Wolf and the Lion*, *Gladiator Farm*, and *A Fire Devours*) plunges readers into a brutal world of outlaw bikers, crime syndicates, cartel violence, and elite security operators. Known for gritty realism and relentless pacing, Holloway's stories explore the thin line between justice and vengeance, loyalty and betrayal, survival and faith.

Before becoming an author and entrepreneur, Holloway lived a life far removed from the world of publishing. As a young man he became involved in gangs and the outlaw lifestyle that surrounds them. Those choices eventually led to prison, where he spent years in solitary confinement. It was during that time that he rebuilt his life through discipline, faith, and an unrelenting commitment to change.

After his release, Holloway went on to build successful businesses and begin writing the stories that had been forming in his mind for years. Today he writes stories about violence, consequence, and redemption for crime thriller readers who crave authenticity.

When he's not writing, he lifts weights, draws portraits, and spends time with his wife.

You can connect with me on:

🌐 https://rexhollowaywriter.com/home-1

Also by Rex Holloway

Thank you so much for reading this book! It is my sincere pleasure to share my thoughts with you.

I hope you will take a moment to leave this book a review on Amazon. Reviews are crucial for new authors.

Also, please visit my website rexhollowaywriter.com to keep up with my latest plans and maybe read a blog post or two.

The Wolf and the Lion: Mason Origins Book One
In a gripping tale of crime, redemption, and the search for meaning, a disillusioned war veteran named Mason, working for a cannabis security company in Colorado, and a ruthless Canadian outlaw biker gang known as the Dead Wolves MC, entangled in a deadly conspiracy led by a cunning mastermind, ultimately confront their inner demons and the consequences of their choices as they collide in a violent and fateful showdown.

A Fire Devours: Mason Origins Book Three
When coordinated cartel attacks ignite oil fields and cripple refineries across South Texas, private security operator Mason is pulled into a fast-moving war that is far more organized and personal than it appears. As the violence escalates, he uncovers a ruthless adversary who knows his past and is orchestrating the chaos to draw him in, forcing Mason to confront an enemy who is always one step ahead—or lose everything in the fire.

Executive Powerbuilding

In a world engineered for comfort and excess, modern professionals have become biologically mismatched to their environment—trading strength, resilience, and mental clarity for convenience and decline. *Executive Powerbuilding* equips readers with a top-down system to reclaim control, combining decades of real-world training insight into simple, actionable strategies for building muscle, optimizing nutrition, and operating their body like a high-performance enterprise.